Between Dreams and Darkness

DESIREE PERALTA

To my dad, the most positive and greatest warrior I have ever met. I know you would be proud of the woman I have become.

Someone is in their hospital bed right now, praying to be in your position. So do it tired. Do it sad. Do it unmotivated. Do it scared. Do it alone. But do it.

Prologue

When you turn 18, it's normal to have goals and dreams. Many people say this is when your life begins, and others say it's the best moment of your maturity because you can finally be and act like an adult, but without all the responsibilities that come with being one.

For me, it was just the opposite. At 18 years old, I have never felt more dead.

It wasn't always like that. I used to have dreams and goals like any other teenager. I used to believe I would graduate, go to college, work, have a house and a car, and maybe fall in love. My dreams weren't big, but I had them.

However, everything changed when I turned 15, and I was diagnosed with breast cancer.

Suddenly, the problems of a teenager didn't exist anymore in my life. There was no first party, first love, or even difficult tests I had to handle. The only thing I had to worry about was surviving.

Of course, my family and I were initially hopeful, mainly because it was detected early. I spent that whole year treating the disease with chemotherapy, surgery, and recovering.

I started homeschooling because I was too weak to attend classes, and I wasn't confident enough to show myself in public. I lost my hair, my weight, and my brightness, and with it, all my self-esteem.

But after that year, everything looked favorable. According to the doctors, I recovered successfully, so I tried to get my life back.

My family and I treated that year like a difficult period of our lives that made us stronger and closed those memories as much as we could.

From that moment, I tried to recuperate all the lost time.

I went back to school; my hair started to grow, I gained some weight, and I started making friends again who weren't afraid of losing me.

My life once again had a purpose beyond surviving, and I was thrilled to be able to do more than focus on medication and be better.

And it went well for two years.

I felt like everything would be normal again, so I started to plan for my future. I sent application letters to colleges, searched for jobs, and dreamed of falling in love like a normal person.

I graduated from school with my classmates, danced at my graduation party, and drank alcohol for the first time. I felt alive and happy again.

I thought I would finally have a normal life.

But then, before starting college, I began to feel weak again.

I fainted one day in the bathroom due to severe pain in my lower back, and from then on, all the memories I had blocked came back to me.

My parents tried to be as positive as possible during the first medical check-ups, but I already knew what was happening.

The cancer had returned, and this time, I knew it had come to finish me forever.

CHAPTER 1
Hopelessness

My 8:00 p.m. alarm started ringing. I opened my eyes but couldn't see anything. I took the phone from the nightstand to my right and disconnected the charger. Then I stood up and turned on the light.

When my eyes adjusted to the intense white light of my room, I put on my hat, moved to the window, and separated the heavy curtains that blocked the view.

The glass panes in this room never ceased to amaze me. They were huge enough to show a great landscape. If only there were one—I would never be apart from it. But the only thing you could see through these windows was a small park with a single tree in the middle, surrounded by parking lots. The most boring and absurd view in the world.

Gladly, there was an emergency staircase right outside, big enough to sit there, which I usually do when I'm tired of being locked up. It was the only wonderful thing in this empty and lifeless room.

I stood there with my gaze outside. It was already dark enough to see something interesting. But looking at least fifteen minutes at the small park had become a habit.

Sometimes, there would be one or two people smoking or talking on the phone there, but it was usually empty at this time.

Nurse Hellen always tells me that my room is one of the lucky ones to have a good view, and I should be grateful and use it. So part of me felt guilty if I didn't stop here for even a few minutes each day when I felt strong enough to be on my feet.

But I couldn't deny it was my least favorite part of the day. It was like hoping something interesting would happen every single day but knowing that, unfortunately, it would never happen.

Sometimes, I felt like Hellen was testing my patience. She was forcing me to do things she thought would help improve my mood, but all they did was make me hopeless.

I stood there to see if anything intriguing happened, but as always, there was simply nothing.

So. Fucking. Boring.

At this point, I would have already given up, like all the things I've removed from my life until now, but I feel that if I stop doing things from my current routine because I think they're meaningless, I'll be left with nothing and go crazy locked up here.

"Have you seen anything interesting in the park today?" a voice behind me spoke so unexpectedly that I jumped in surprise.

Hellen always enters the room quietly, so if I'm asleep, she doesn't wake me up. She's gotten so good at this that sometimes I have difficulty realizing she enters the room, even if I'm awake.

"If seeing Dr. Hunter dropping the briefcase with all his sheets and documents is interesting, then today I won a fun trophy," I joked.

Hellen smiled out of courtesy, but I was sure she was tired of my sarcasm and dark humor.

Without expecting a response, I sat on the small sofa beside the window, and she prepared the table where she usually put my food.

"Tonight, we have beans for dinner. I hope you like them. But in case you don't, here's a little pudding I stole from the kitchen." She winked at me, so I moved my lips slightly upward.

"Thanks."

I know she was allowed to bring me pudding and that her comment was to make me happy, so I didn't say anything to ruin the moment. She was the only person who still tolerated me and the only one I hadn't left out of my life by this point.

"If you need anything else, just press the button. Have a good night, Jasmine, or should I say, a good start to your day?"

"Good night, Hellen," I responded.

I waited until she was out of the room to start eating, and just as the nurse said, I prepared myself to start my day.

My routine has been practically the same since I entered the hospital again.

I wake up at 8:00 p.m. I spend my whole night working on something I have become obsessed with, sometimes reading, crocheting, playing video games, drawing, or simply watching a series. Depending on how I feel, I take a nap from 6:00 to 8:00 a.m. I then get breakfast, some checkups, and studies (by this point, I'm already too tired to be bothered by people), then finally have lunch and sleep from 1:00 to 8:00 p.m.

The principal reason for this routine is that since I discovered I have cancer again, I just want to be alone. And the best way I found to see as few people as possible is by being awake at night when no one is around.

During the day, I have a lot of people in my room. There are nurses who come to check on me or change my IV, people who clean my room and bathroom, or friends and family from outside who come during visiting hours.

So if I'm sleeping in those moments, they don't bother me because they understand I must rest, and I can ignore them easily if I have my eyes closed.

Having cancer is a free pass to sleep at any hour and not have anyone trying to wake me up because I must be in pain and I need to recover. So, I use that to my advantage to be asocial and be awake at night.

At first, many people came to see me, but my bad mood kept me from enjoying their company. Little by little, all those friends who "gave me support" drifted away, until only my parents remained.

I convince myself I'm doing this to protect the people around me. After all, soon, I won't be in anyone's life, so the best thing I can do for my "loved ones" so they don't get used to being there for me is simply to be out of their life from now on.

I also got tired of pity looks from my old friends, fake support from people I haven't seen in a while, small talk from employees who don't care about me, and lectures from my parents that I have to be more "positive because there is a big chance that everything goes well."

I don't want false hope anymore. Not when everything was supposed to go well the first time, but I'm back in this hospital with a worse condition.

When the cancer was in my left breast, things were easier to accept. It was a part of my body that could be removed without any problem, and I had the strength and energy to recover. I knew I could have a normal life once I was healthy.

Now that it's in my right kidney, it's as if life is telling me things will never be easy. A kidney is a vital organ, and although I could continue living without one, my life will never be the same. I will always have to take extreme care, have regular check-ups, and live a life that is different from everyone else's. I would never be able to be normal even if I survived.

So, I decided not to have any hopes. It is easier to go through this illness when you don't have any expectations. So, I gave up having friends, dreams, love, and happiness. If things go wrong this time, everyone will already be prepared.

And no one will miss me.

I made the mistake of having hope for the first time. I recovered and began to have plans and dreams, thinking everything would be fine, and the worst was over. But now, with metastasis in my right kidney and locked in these four walls, I have nothing more to wait for.

Today, I spent the whole night watching a miniseries that Hellen recommended, and I was very excited to watch it because of her. It was about a man who discovers that his marriage was a lie when his wife goes missing, so he is trying to find out who the person he married is while looking for her.

If it hadn't been for the sun coming through my window and Hellen bringing me breakfast, I wouldn't have realized it was already 8:00 a.m.

"I guess there would be no nap this morning," I whispered to myself and stood up from the bed.

The nurse placed my breakfast next to the sofa and checked my vital signs. "I have not-so-pleasant news for you today, kiddo. I saw your parents outside talking to your doctor, and they will be in the room in about an hour."

"What are they doing here on a random Monday morning? I thought their work was more important than coming here more than two times per week," I complained.

When my parents found out I had cancer again, and this

time in my kidney, they freaked out. They found a doctor who convinced them that the best thing for me was for me to be hospitalized while they gave me chemotherapy so they could monitor that my other kidney was perfectly healthy and be able to act quickly if any complications occurred.

Also, they needed me here in case they have to dialyze me, so my other kidney doesn't suffer much until I'm fine again. They had only done this process once when they discovered the cancer, but for some reason, they gave it more importance than ever. It was like they needed an excuse to trap me here.

Unlike the first time, when I was the center of their universe and their only priority, right now they seem busier than ever and focused on their work to "pay for my hospital-ization" rather than supporting me or being with me at this moment.

I just see them on Wednesdays and Saturdays, so having them today was out of normality.

Hellen saw me tense, so she added, "Everything is stable on your side if this is what worries you. If they are here, it has nothing to do with your current health."

"That's the minor of my problems, actually," I responded to her.

I stood up and went to have my breakfast as quickly as possible before they came because I knew their presence would make me lose my appetite.

CHAPTER 2

Disappointment

"Good morning, honey," my mom kissed me on the forehead and handed me five new books, a sketchbook, and pencils.

Gifts on a regular Monday just meant they would say something negative and wanted to make up for it with something positive. "Hello, Mom, Dad," I replied. "To what reason do I owe you the pleasure of coming today?"

They both looked at each other nervously and then looked back at me with fake smiles.

"Can't we visit our daughter without something happening?" my dad asked.

"Of course, you can, but it's not normal." I began to look through the books to give them time to come up with a good excuse for their visit.

"Well, actually..." my mom started.

I rolled my eyes. Here we go.

"We talked to your doctor, and everything is going very well with the chemo," my dad interrupted my mom before she could say anything else. "If everything continues like this, you will not need any more chemotherapy after the operation."

"Yeah, he was here earlier," I responded without showing any emotions, still focused on the books.

The information about how the cancer was responding to the treatment wasn't something new. The doctor always kept me updated to see if he could give me some hope, but I just didn't care. There was still time for many things to go wrong, so his words meant nothing to me.

"Your father and I decided we would take advantage of your good energy this week to go to Miami for a few days to rest from work. We have been working overtime lately and feel we deserve a little break."

There you go, this is interesting.

I closed the books and looked at them. "When are we leaving?"

They froze at my unexpected question. No one had to say another word for me to understand I wasn't invited. They were just letting me know I wouldn't see them for a while.

"Honey," my mom said. "You know it is unsafe for you to be out of the hospital, especially right now."

"But you just told me everything is going well, and I have good energy," I complained.

"Yes, but not for you to take a plane and leave Boston; it's too risky. What if you got an infection out there?"

"What if I got one here that I'm in a hospital surrounded by sick people?" I shouted.

"Then you would be treated here by professionals who know what they are dealing with," my father spoke firmly.

I opened my mouth to say something, but closed it again. There was no point in trying to reason with them when they had already made their decision.

They simply didn't want to deal with me. That's why I have been locked up here for two months without going anywhere else, instead of being home. Nobody wants to take care of a sick person all the time. In the end, everyone will try to make a life while I'm here trying to survive.

"When you are cancer-free and get out of here healthy, we will have a better trip than this one," my mom tried to cheer me up.

"But what if I never get out?" I asked.

There was a big silence in the room that made me regret asking that last question.

Although I had no hope, my parents were sure that I would get better. They hated the new negative personality I adopted when I was admitted here, and have been doing everything they could every time they are here to make me feel better. After all, I was their only daughter, and there was no way they would accept that eventually, I wouldn't be with them anymore, even though all the signs pointed to the contrary.

And even though I disagreed with their way of seeing life, when they were here, I tried to act as calm and happy as possible for them, even if I didn't feel that way. That's why I felt so guilty after saying my last question.

My mom got so sensitive that she had to sit on the sofa with her hands on her face while my dad looked at me, disappointed.

In my defense, I was just trying to be realistic. There's a big chance that I won't make it, so there's no point in delaying things I want to do.

But I also can't hold back people with a future and drag them into my misery. They have a life ahead of them. Not me. And the best thing they can do is to start living it from now on.

So after a whole silence and some sobs from my mother, I told them, "Don't worry."

They turned their heads to look at me, so I put on the biggest fake smile I could. "I will be fine. Have fun."

My mom smiled. "It will only be until next Monday. I promise we will come here as soon as we land."

"And when are you leaving?" I asked them, trying to sound excited for them.

"Tonight," my dad answered.

Great, I thought. *A whole week alone.*

Thankfully, my parents ensured I had my lunch before leaving because otherwise, I wouldn't have bothered.

I was so angry with myself for believing they wanted to go on a trip with me that after they left, I got out of bed and started throwing everything I had around me: my books on the shelf, my notebooks, my drawings on the wall, my socks well organized in the drawer.

When everything was a mess, I felt extremely exhausted, so I turned off the 8:00 p.m. alarm and the lights and went to sleep, hoping I wouldn't wake up today.

Journal entry 1

July 22, 2024

This is my first day back in the city where I grew up. Of course, the first thing I decided to do was start writing in my journal again. I used to do it years ago as a way to release everything going on in my mind, and right now I think I need it most. I have no one to talk to about those things, and I feel like a stranger in my own house.

When I got home, my room was intact, as if I had never left. The hole in the wall I made when I hit it with a baseball was still there, the lamp on my nightstand was still damaged, and all my things were in the same place where I left them. One day, I will thank my mom for that gesture; a little selfish, of course, but at the end of the day, we all hope our children return home. Or at least this is what I think she felt. I don't have kids, and I have been alone for a long time now, so the concept of family feels like a foreign language to me.

I never even thought I would return to this place, much less to that hospital. But there I was, in the parking lot, thinking about how I would get in and pretending everything was normal and I was just a new nurse.

Thankfully, nobody noticed me, as I expected it would happen. And I was glad for that. The job I had to do here was hard, and I needed as much focus as possible.

In the past three years, I have worked in many hospitals, assisting in surgeries, learning everything I could about basic emergencies in different types of patients, and accompanying people who were not going to make it the next day.

But becoming a psychologist of a spoiled girl? It felt like a joke. Mainly because I had never had any hope for anything. How could I possibly convince anyone to have it when I don't know what that is?

This job will be the biggest challenge I've faced yet because I have to learn from zero and believe in my own words. It will be like rejecting everything I have believed in until now and trying to be someone good for the sake of a person I didn't even know yet.

So, I spent the afternoon buried in Jasmine Russell's medical records, the patient of room 605. From the first cancer diagnosis at 15 to her return at 18, her whole life feels like a tragedy. It wasn't hard to see where her attitude came from.

I hate that I have to come to this place. I hate that it's to help someone be happy again. And I hate feeling like I won't be able to do it.

But it was clear that if I wanted to get out of here, I had to do this job. So I'll have to be the best thing that happens to this girl if necessary.

Anything to get out of here soon and have the peace I so desire.

CHAPTER 3

Embarrassment

I DON'T KNOW how long I'd fallen asleep, but when I got up, the light was on, and someone was in the room making a lot of noise. I grabbed my hat as quickly as I could and put it on; I hate when people see my almost hairless head.

When my eyes were fully opened, I settled on the bed to focus on what the person was doing.

It was a guy I'd never seen before.

He had nurse's clothes on, so I assumed he was someone new, but he was too young to be a professional, so I guessed he was an intern.

The young man was cleaning up the mess I'd made earlier, and I felt a little embarrassed by it. It was my problem, not his, but apparently, he had to fix it because I wasn't in a condition to do it myself. Maybe one of the nurses had come into the room at some point in the afternoon and saw the mess, so they sent him to clean it up.

One thing I was sure of was that I needed him to stop what he was doing because it wasn't his problem to fix. It was mine.

"What the hell are you doing? Stop touching my things." I

tried to make him stop with my grumpiness, but he seemed immune to it. The guy ignored me and continued cleaning—like he didn't hear me at all.

My dinner was on the table next to the sofa, so probably Hellen had come earlier and left it there.

I took my phone to see what time it was: 11:48 p.m. I'd slept a lot, but not enough to change my mood. I was still sad from the conversation with my parents, and all I wanted to do was be alone.

But now I had to deal with this guy.

I turned my gaze back to him. He wasn't very tall, but he was definitely taller than me. He looked like he came from a wealthy family because he was too young to be professional, but from his messy dark hair, dirty sneakers, and the tattoos on his arms, it seemed like he'd decided to be a little rebellious in the process.

I wonder if he was forced to study medicine, and his dream was to be a guitarist in a band. That would suit him more than being a nurse.

I hadn't seen anyone new in so long that I didn't realize I was mesmerized watching him.

I looked away toward the window for a few seconds out of embarrassment at the thought of him noticing it, but then I turned to him again to continue my bad attitude. I didn't want him here, so I had to do something to make him leave quickly. He'd already picked up most of the things I'd thrown on the floor.

Even though what he was doing was a kind act, I couldn't be more uncomfortable with the situation. The mess in my room showed I'd thrown a tantrum, and I didn't want him to think I was an immature child.

I couldn't remember the last time I felt this exposed.

Being surrounded by doctors and nurses constantly

checking my body had made me immune to feeling vulnerable, but this was different.

Watching him pick up my personal things one by one was like exposing my soul.

But why did it bother me that he thought something of me?

He was just a random stranger who had to do a job. And I was just a sick girl who wanted to be alone. This was what I had to focus on.

"Hello? Are you deaf?" I started moving my hands so he could focus on me. "Where's Hellen? No one is supposed to enter here after 6:00 p.m., only her."

He stopped what he was doing and looked at me. "I'm not deaf, and I don't think you're the type of person who should be insulting others with an illness."

Ouch. That was rude.

But he was also right. I shouldn't have said that, but his indifference was making me impatient.

I tried not to put any emotions on my face, or he would win this fight and not leave. "Then answer me."

"Hellen's not here tonight, and I'm cleaning this place." He kept organizing my stuff again, like the conversation was over.

"I don't want you to clean my mess. It's like that for a reason," I replied, determined not to give up until he was out of my room.

He looked at me again with an expression I couldn't decipher. "I don't care what you want. This isn't your home. This isn't your personal room. And I'm not your private employee. I like this place clean, so I'm going to clean it," he said, then bent down to continue picking up things, this time my pencils.

I was so indignant by his attitude that I was speechless.

Who does this boy think he is?

I realized he wouldn't leave even if I continued arguing, so

I stood up from the bed and bent in front of him to pick up things, too. The faster we finished cleaning, the faster he would leave.

However, before I could grab anything, he grabbed my wrist.

Surprised by his action, I looked forward and found his face quite close to mine. He was serious, like I'd done something wrong, but my nervousness didn't stop me from admiring it up close. At this distance, I could notice his little freckles around his cheeks and his big black eyes with an empty look.

This boy was as broken as I was.

"Holy shit," I managed to reply. "What's wrong with you? I thought you wanted this place clean."

He began to stand slowly with my wrist still in his hand, which forced me to stand as well, neither of us looking away from the other. It felt like whichever of us looked away would be the weaker one, and I wouldn't be the first to fall.

When we were fully up, I was forced to lift my chin to keep looking at his face. He wasn't very tall, but definitely taller than me. And his attitude made me feel tiny and powerless.

"I wanted it clean, so I would be the one cleaning it," he whispered. There was no need to speak any louder at the distance we were at. "Eat your dinner, Jasmine. It won't take me long."

Oh. So he knew my name.

He released my hand, and for some reason, I obeyed him. It was like my mind didn't want to listen to it, but my body did anyway.

I sat on the sofa and started eating while watching him finish cleaning silently. When he was done, he went to where I was and took my empty plate. "Good girl."

My skin got goosebumps from his last words. I didn't like

17

this boy and how he was making me feel. But I felt too tired to complain. It was like I was the one who'd cleaned this whole place.

Maybe I shouldn't have made that mess.

The anonymous guy turned back and started walking to the door. I felt the need to ask him his name, but I didn't want him to feel I cared about him. Hopefully, I'd never see him again, and he was just there to cover Hellen's absence.

I stayed on the sofa after he left, unable to move for a while, but with my mind thinking about a million things.

What the hell had just happened?

CHAPTER 4

Inspiration

THE NIGHT PASSED EXTREMELY SLOWLY. I didn't know if it was because I didn't feel like doing anything at all or because my mind wasn't leaving me alone.

By this point, my parents were probably asleep in some luxurious hotel, and I was locked in the same four walls where I didn't even have Hellen to talk about the series she'd recommended to me.

I opened the window and sat on the floor of the emergency staircase. This was the only place here where I felt a little free.

The wind was hitting my face, so I closed my eyes to imagine for a moment what it would feel like to be on a beach right now, at night, breathing the sea air and listening to the waves as they hit my feet.

I opened my eyes slowly to discover that there was someone in the park.

It was the nurse from earlier.

First, he ruined my sleep, then my dinner, and now my night with his presence. Today was definitely not my lucky day to search for peace.

Despite that, I didn't look away from him.

A perfect silence surrounded him, and I felt I was intruding by watching him from there. I couldn't help but think why he was there alone.

He was looking at the sky with an agonized expression as if God himself were speaking directly to him. He had one hand in his pocket and the other holding a cigarette.

I laughed at the irony.

I was here thinking about how I would love to be able to be free anywhere in the world, and there he was, with the power to do it, but also locked up in a hospital with cancer patients and a cigarette in his hand.

I almost thought he was making fun of us with that action.

"What an asshole," I said. We were too far away from each other for him to hear me, yet he moved his gaze toward me when I said that phrase.

We both looked at each other with serious expressions. Once again, I began to feel the sensation of being exposed, as if he'd just discovered I sat here to escape from my reality or the fact that I was spying on him.

After five minutes of looking at each other in silence, he threw the cigarette and walked away slowly without doing anything else.

Suddenly, all my overthinking disappeared, and I felt like doing just one thing.

I entered my room, took one of my sketch notebooks and pencils, and then went back to the window and started drawing.

I spent the night drawing until I was satisfied with the results of my art.

It was a landscape of a beach at night—there were many stars, and the moon was new. The sea was calm, and it was almost empty, except for one person. Just like in my thoughts, there was someone on the shore feeling the breeze and the waves on their feet.

But instead of drawing me, for some reason, I drew the new mystery nurse. He was dressed casually—a shirt with buttons on his chest, regular jeans, and was barefoot, feeling the waves of the sea. His expression was focused on the sea, and just like I'd seen him in the park, he had a gloomy look, as if something was bothering him.

I would have liked to picture myself at the beach, but he had more chances than I did to make that dream happen, so I chose to be realistic.

I couldn't get that scene of him looking at the sky out of my head. At least that stupid guy inspired me to do something.

Hopefully, it's the only thing he'll be good for.

CHAPTER 5

Boldness

"Good morning, my favorite night girl."

Contrary to the nights, Hellen always comes in in the morning, making as much noise as possible. She knows I'm usually up at this hour; if I'm not, she wakes me up to have breakfast and a little social interaction. If it weren't for her, I'd probably spend days without talking to anyone.

That's why I think I felt more stressed than necessary the night before. Without her, I'll probably have to deal with that hellish nurse who was here yesterday.

I began to observe her going from one place to another, almost dancing, putting breakfast on the table, cleaning the place a little, and looking for the instruments she needed to check on me.

"Looks like someone had a good night," I teased her.

Today, she looked more joyful than ever, as if she'd spent an incredible night away from here. And I don't blame her; anyone would spend a good time outside this hospital, even if it's watching television locked in a random room.

"I had, actually. How do you know?" She tried to play

innocent, but we both knew she wasn't at the hospital last night for a reason.

"I don't know. Maybe because you left me here alone to my fate to be happy in the real world, don't you care that you probably wouldn't have found me this morning?" I tried to sound super dramatic. She was the only person I knew who could handle my dark humor, and I always took advantage of it to be miserable without hearing a lecture.

"I'm not so lucky." She smiled. "The day I don't have to see you every day, I'll ask for a week's vacation to celebrate more than just one day."

I rolled my eyes. "Ha-ha."

Hellen came to me and started checking my vital signs. "How do you feel today?"

"Better. Last night, I felt so tired that I almost believed I cleaned the whole hospital."

"It's normal, especially with the chemo. The day of the next one is approaching. Your mind and body are probably preparing. Anything else happened in my absence?"

I hesitated to talk about it for a while, but then I decided to do it anyway. "Yes, who was the nurse who took care of my dinner last night?"

She looked at me, confused by my question. "I don't know. Why is that relevant?"

I'm usually never interested in anyone at all. Hundreds of doctors have treated me, and they're like blurry faces to me.

I try not to pay too much attention to them so as not to make them feel guilty they meeting me. Hellen has been the only one with whom I've formed a relationship because she's tried to let me know she'll be okay when I'm gone, so I've gotten used to her.

"I just want to know who he is," I responded without looking at her. If I glanced at her, I knew she'd realize my embarrassment.

"Was he hot or something?" she asked, smiling.

Memories of the moment he took my arm and looked into my eyes flashed through my head again, making me blush a little. He was cute, but that wasn't why I was asking about him.

"No. I don't know. I didn't pay attention to him that way," I hesitated.

Thinking about it better, I didn't even know why I was asking. This whole conversation was nonsense.

Hellen seemed to read my thoughts because she next asked me, "So why do you want to know about him?"

I didn't want her to feel like I was making too much of this whole event, so I replied, "He ruined my peace. I just want to know who he is so I know with whom I'm dealing."

"Jasmine Russell is feeling something. I'll definitely find out who he is so we can switch patients." She looked at me over her glasses with a mischievous smile.

"You know what? I don't want to know anything anymore. This conversation is over."

I got out of bed before Hellen could say another word and went to the bathroom to wash my hands so she could leave me alone. I heard her laughing from here, and I regretted even the simple fact that I made her believe I cared about something.

Because I didn't—he was just another person that would not leave any mark on my short life, and I shouldn't be thinking about it anymore. For the little peace I had left before surgery, the best thing I could do was to forget him.

Hellen was back, and that's all that mattered.

Contrary to the night before, the morning passed quite fast. I was busy most of the day doing some routine exams, and then I sat in a small room that the hospital has with a TV and some magazines; I was alone, but I entertained myself by watching the people walking in the aisle through the window.

This wasn't something I used to do often, first because I didn't like people staring at me, and second, and more importantly, for the sake of my health and the complications that catching the flu from other patients could bring. Still, I felt exhausted from being locked up today, so I convinced the nurses to let me stay a little outside my room with a mask, and they agreed.

After lunch, I realized it was later than usual, so I turned off the 8:00 p.m. alarm to ensure I got enough sleep and left a note for Hellen on the table so she wouldn't wake me up.

And finally, I tried to sleep.

Happiness didn't last as long as I expected because, at one point early in the night, I began to hear a noise inside my room, and even with my eyes closed, I felt a light.

That's weird, I thought. Hellen is always so quiet when she enters at night that it doesn't even seem like she's the one in my room.

Unless it definitely wasn't her.

I opened my eyes abruptly and started to look around, everything seemed to be intact and in its place. But then, I saw him. The mystery nurse from yesterday was seated on my sofa with my sketchbook in one hand and his phone with the flash on in the other.

"The hell are you doing?" I shouted at him while grabbing the hat from the nightstand as quickly as I could and putting it on my head.

He looked at me and smiled. "You're quite talented, although I would have drawn myself a little taller."

I started to feel my cheeks hot from embarrassment. He was looking at the drawing I'd made of him on the beach.

I stood up and snatched my notebook from his hands.

"You shouldn't be touching my things," I protested,

sounding as mad as possible so he'd realize he had made a mistake. However, he didn't look bothered at all by my words. To the contrary, he looked amused.

"I was wondering why you were spying on me last night. I'm glad to know I'm your muse and not that you were looking for a witness to throw yourself out the window so that at least someone would know what happened."

"And why would I do that?" I started to walk to the other side of the room to get as far away from him as possible, but he stood up from the couch and started walking behind me.

"It's no secret that you're the most depressed and miserable person in this hospital. We never know what you guys are capable of doing." I heard him from my back.

I felt very offended by his words. Obviously, I felt dead already, but I would never do anything to end my own life by myself, especially since cancer was doing it for me already.

"We who? And who are you anyway?" I turned abruptly to face him, but I didn't expect him to be so close to me, so I took two steps back in shock when I saw him.

"I'm Liam. Nice to meet you." He extended his hand for me to shake it, but I stayed in the same defensive position with my hands crossed. When he realized I wouldn't shake his hand back, he took two steps forward. We were now so close that I could touch him without even extending my hand.

This guy needs to learn what personal space is.

"Aren't you going to tell me yours?" He broke the silence again.

"You already know it." He'd called me by my name last night, so pretending he didn't know who I was was pointless.

Without taking my eyes off him, I took two steps back.

"I want to hear you saying it." He took the same two steps forward.

I don't know if he was doing that to see me better because the room was very dark or because he wanted to make me feel

27

nervous; either way, I didn't like this game. I tried to take two more steps back, but we'd reached the door.

Damn it. I was cornered.

I kept looking into his eyes to figure out what he wanted, but he didn't seem to have any expression on his face.

"Jasmine," I finally responded.

"Jas. Mine, Jas. Mine," he repeated twice. "Can I call you Mine?"

I started to feel chills from the tips of my feet to my head. I was speechless. It was like his only purpose was to make me nervous.

His mood was different from the other day; he felt less gloomy and calmer. I didn't like either of his personalities. They were both too impertinent for my taste.

"Of course not," I finally managed to say after a minute. Then I pushed him hard enough for him to move to the side and started walking towards the window. "This whole situation is completely inappropriate. What do you want from me?"

"I want to keep giving you a purpose to draw and dream," he said, like it was the most normal thing to say to a stranger.

He was too shameless. I didn't need a purpose. I needed peace, I needed to be alone, and I needed to get out of here.

This was nonsense.

"You should leave this room before I report you, and don't come back if you don't want to lose your job," I said without looking back. I didn't want him to have a reason to come to me again, and apparently, my uncomfortable face wasn't enough to keep him away.

"Well, then, good night, Jas-mine," he emphasized the word mine.

I didn't say anything back.

Seconds later, I heard the door opening and closing.

When he left, I took a deep breath.

He was very unprofessional and made me feel very nervous. My heart was beating too fast for everything that just happened. Part of me thought he would never leave. And if he didn't, I'd be in trouble.

Because after three months of being here, I was feeling something. I felt that I hated him, felt uncomfortable, and that my peace was ruined. Although they were negative emotions, all these things were feelings. Something that I tried to keep locked from the moment I got here.

But he was right about one thing.

I felt inspired to draw again.

Journal entry 2

July 23, 2024

If I thought the job was going to be difficult long before I started it, I was totally wrong. This is worse than hell. A new level of hard.

When I entered Jasmine's room for the first time, everything was a complete mess.

All her things were on the floor, some broken. It was as if all the rage she had inside had materialized into ruining the entire room—like a physical manifestation of the storm brewing inside her.

But then I saw her. Her eyes. They were empty, filled with a kind of pain that reflected something deep inside me. It was a flash of recognition, a shard of broken glass that reflected my own fractured past. At that moment, I felt a strong urge to protect her, hug her, and let her know everything would be okay.

But I also knew she wouldn't let me in that easily. I've watched her all day, and she won't let anyone near her. She's locked in her own circle of misery, and I had to find a way to break it.

After our first encounter, I went back to my old habit of smoking. I knew it was wrong, but I needed it. I don't know how I'd be able to save her because I don't know how to save myself.

And I see my old self in Jasmine. Someone I still haven't been able to save.

CHAPTER 6
Empathy

THE FIRST RAY of sun came through the window, and with it, some yawns from a long night of work. The entire floor of the room was covered with sheets full of different sketches and portraits. Some of them were random landscapes, others of faces or doodles.

In my hands were the two drawings I was most proud of. One of them was the representation of Liam and me looking into each other's eyes while lying down next to the door, just as we were the night before, and the other was Liam on the sofa in my room. He was seated like a king, with his arms resting on the sofa's handles and one leg crossed over the other.

I stayed looking at them for a few minutes until the door burst open, and I jumped a little in surprise.

"What does this mess mean?" Hellen said, almost hysterical but amused by my smile.

"Come here; let me show you something," I said, ignoring her question.

She began to walk towards me, careful not to step on anything while holding the breakfast and her medical kit with both hands. When she was almost in front of me, I took one of the portraits from the floor and showed it to her.

"Look, he's the nurse I told you about. Do you know him?"

She put the materials she had in her hands on the table and took the drawing. "You're very good at it. It's like I'm seeing a picture." She started analyzing the piece of paper with a doubtful expression, and then she said, "The person in the paper looks familiar. I feel like I've seen him, but I don't know who he is."

"He came back last night, saw one of my drawings, and told me to keep doing it. I guess he inspired me to keep myself busy."

I still didn't like Liam, but the guy was helping me keep my mind occupied, and I should take advantage of these spikes of inspiration while they lasted. It wasn't every day that I felt joyful.

Normally, the nights are long and heavy. I keep changing from activity to activity to pass the time, and there are days when I can't stand myself. Sometimes, everything seems boring, and all I want to do is run away.

However, I've been creative for two consecutive nights, where the only thing I want to do is draw and create.

That nurse could be a pain, but I had to take the positive from this situation.

"I'll definitely look for him to thank him for keeping your mind thinking about something other than your miserable life," Hellen said, taking me out of my thoughts.

I rolled my eyes with a smile on my face. "Jesus, Hellen, stop being so dark."

"Oh, so am I the dark person now? Who are you, and what did you do with Jasmine?"

We both laughed and started organizing the papers so we could go back to our daily routine.

I put all the drawings in a folder and hid them under my bed before starting my morning. This time, I didn't want him to see them and believe I'm thinking about him every day.

Before Hellen left, she gave me one last look. "Seriously, Jasmine, I'm glad you're looking for a reason to smile."

The last thing Hellen told me left me too pensive. I couldn't concentrate on practically anything else after her visit.

I had no significant medical study today, so most of my morning was dedicated to my thoughts.

I'm glad you're looking for a reason to smile.

I wasn't doing that. Feeling hopeful and dreamy was the last thing I wanted. One thing was feeling inspired to draw to pass the time, and another, completely different one was feeling happy about something.

Or someone, in this case.

Liam was ruining all the strength and determination I'd built up until now to be a lonely person. And I began to fear this feeling of inspiration would turn into something more.

He was just a reason to draw at night and nothing more. Hellen was exaggerating when she said he was a reason to smile.

The last thing I needed right now was to have someone new in my life. The surgery was in three months, and we still didn't even know if the chemotherapy was going to keep me alive by that date.

I looked at the clock on my phone; it was time to sleep, and I hadn't even touched my lunch.

Liam was ruining not only my moods but also my routine. It was clear what I had to do: get rid of him as soon as possible if I didn't want to change my way of being until now. It was the most correct thing to avoid disappointment. This was the

35

way he could be safe from getting used to being with a temporary person. No one should get attached to someone who's like a time bomb.

I sat down on the sofa to eat so I could finally sleep. My thoughts were clear, and I had a new purpose. I needed to make this nurse want to be as far away from me as possible.

As I took my first bite, I realized the food was cold. Sighing, I pushed the plate away, and my appetite started decreasing.

Perhaps a snack from the vending machine on the top floor would be more appealing.

It was a risky venture, considering it was 2:00 p.m., and there would be a lot of people around. The last thing I wanted to do today was meet someone who wanted to chat. I wasn't in the mood for Hellen, much less any stranger.

But I decided to take the risk anyway because the alternatives were either nothing to eat or cold hospital food. So I grabbed my wallet, pulled out a twenty-dollar bill, and snuck out of the room.

Instead of taking the elevator, which was usually packed with people, I took the stairs. I was determined to do whatever it took to avoid seeing anyone, and it was a perfect way to look around before stepping onto the new floor.

When I finally reached the seventh floor, I heard a familiar voice. I tried to look cautiously from behind the wall, and there he was. Liam was there, standing near the food machine. He wasn't alone. There was a child with him, looking visibly distressed.

I hesitated for some minutes, debating whether to go back to my room or not. They were so busy talking that they hadn't seen me yet, so I could easily go back without being noticed. However, curiosity got the better of me, and I found myself hiding behind a nearby pillar, observing them discreetly.

From here, I could hear their conversation perfectly.

"But you're not a doctor. How do you know the surgery is something simple?"

"I'm not a doctor, but I have participated in thousands of surgeries. Believe me, getting that little ball out of your head is easier than trying to get candy out of this machine without coins."

The little boy laughed, and my heart softened at the scenario. Liam was definitely lying about being in many surgery rooms, but his words and reassuring smile seemed to have a calming effect on the child, who gradually relaxed in his presence.

My body began to fill with guilt. Here was Liam, offering comfort and support to someone in need while I'd been plotting to push him away. Maybe there was more to him than just an interruption to my routine and a pain in the ass.

I decided to walk back down the stairs as quietly as possible so they wouldn't notice I was there, and once in my room, I took a deep breath.

So this is what he does. Go to every patient and offer words of encouragement so they keep looking for a reason to fight and to be at peace.

Perhaps I shouldn't be so worried that he was trying to get close to me only to lose me. Maybe his intentions were completely professional like Hellen's, and I've been locked up here for so long that I mistook his approach.

However, no matter his reasons, there was still how he made me feel. And I didn't want to change who I am because someone wants it that way. But one thing I was sure of now, he wasn't the one who needed to protect his heart; it was me.

CHAPTER 7

Delusion

I SPENT the next few nights trying to ignore Liam the best I could. Every time he entered the room, I made a conscious effort to be as busy as possible to avoid any unnecessary interaction.

I pretended I was listening to loud music with my headphones, being super entertained watching a series on my iPad that I didn't even bother looking away from, or reading a book I'd read probably thousands of times.

Whether he was there to clean the room, check my vital signs, or administer medication, I kept my gaze averted, refusing to meet his eyes or acknowledge his presence in any way.

Resisting the urge to speak or even look in his direction was challenging, especially when he did things that didn't make sense—like entering to clean the bathroom at midnight when there was clearly no schedule for it before.

I wished I could say I didn't care that he was in my room, but that would have been a lie. Things felt different every time he was around.

There were moments when his proximity was almost suffocating.

Liam's presence was a constant reminder of the tangled mess of emotions swirling inside me. But I didn't say anything about it, determined to keep my distance and protect myself from the turmoil he was causing.

Every time he entered and left the room, I remained silent, my eyes fixed on anything but him as if daring him to break the unspoken barrier I'd placed between us. But he didn't do it, and I was relieved about it. It was easier that way.

And I was sure he'd get tired of coming, or maybe I would ignore him enough that I wouldn't care about his presence anymore.

Today was one of those days when I couldn't stay locked up between these four walls for another minute. Nothing around me seemed to calm me down. I felt like I was drowning.

At least my parents' visit made my days a little different. I'd been on bad terms with them for the past few weeks, but at least I could pretend everything was okay for a few hours.

I decided to take a walk through the hospital corridors. At night, almost no one was here anyway, and I thought maybe I'd find something interesting to break the monotony of my days. The dim lights and the quiet halls felt a little eerie, but in a way, it was soothing.

I wandered aimlessly for a while, climbing staircases, reading signs, glancing into empty rooms, hoping for some-thing—anything—to catch my attention. I wasn't sure what I was looking for, but at least it was better than feeling trapped in my room.

As I turned down another corridor, I spotted Liam. He was sitting in a small waiting room, alone this time, staring at a snack he'd apparently bought from the vending machine but wasn't eating. His posture was tense, his eyes distant.

I stood there for a few minutes, just watching him. Something about him pulled me in, the way he seemed so lost yet calm. I wasn't sure why I felt drawn to him, but I couldn't help it. There was something different about him. Something I couldn't explain.

I decided to leave before he noticed me.

I turned quietly, tiptoeing back towards the corner, hoping to slip away unnoticed. But just as I was almost out of his sight, I felt a firm grip on my hand.

I gasped, startled by how quickly he'd caught up to me. My heart raced as I turned to face him.

How had he moved so fast? I hadn't even heard him get up.

His eyes locked onto mine, and there was a slight smirk on his lips. "Do you think you can spy on me so deliberately and without consequences?" he said, his voice low but teasing.

I felt my pulse quicken, both from the surprise of being caught and the intensity in his gaze. I felt my cheeks flush with embarrassment, but I wasn't about to let him see that. I pulled myself together and raised my chin, trying to stay cool. "I wasn't spying on you. I was looking for someone," I said, my voice steady, though I could feel my heart pounding.

"Who?" he asked. There was an expression of amusement on his face, as if he knew I was lying. "Maybe I can help you find him."

"None of your business."

I tried to yank my wrist free, but his grip tightened.

"Mine, Mine, Mine," he murmured, his voice teasing. "You're such a pretty liar."

The way he said *Mine* made my heart race. I knew it was a shortcut for Jasmine, but it still didn't stop my mind from thinking that he said it for another reason.

I shot him a glare, refusing to back down. "You've got a

41

big ego, you know that? You should really leave me alone. And my name is Jasmine, Jas-Mine."

"You're the one looking for me when I'm not around," he replied, his smirk widening.

Before I could say anything, we both heard footsteps and voices approaching from the other side of the hallway. Without warning, Liam opened the door to a small supply closet behind us and pushed me inside. The only light this narrow place had came from the sliver of the corridor seeping through the crack in the door. When my eyes adjusted to the darkness, I could see him staring at me, making a shiver run through my body.

"Are you out of your mind?" I hissed, trying to keep my voice down, though I was on edge.

He leaned in close, his breath warm against my ear. "Did you really think I'd let you get away with talking to me like that?"

"Of course, you have to," I shot back, glaring at him in the dark. "I'm not your pet."

His grip on my wrist loosened—I hadn't even realized until that moment that he still had my arm. Instead of letting go completely, his fingers lightly traced up my arm, brushing along my skin until they reached my neck. His other hand settled gently on my waist. His touch was slow and deliberate, but what unnerved me most was how I couldn't move. Not because he was forcing me—but because, somehow, I didn't want to.

"Tell me you're not affected by this," he whispered, his fingers lingering just at the base of my throat. His eyes focused on my mouth. "This connection between us."

"You're delusional, darling," I replied, trying to sound unaffected, but my voice betrayed me.

"Now I'm your darling?" he teased, leaning in just a little

closer. "Looks like you're the one who wants to keep me delirious on purpose."

His words gave me all kinds of feelings, and I hated that he knew exactly how to get under my skin.

I pushed him lightly to the other side of the closet, and he slumped against the wall, laughing.

"I hate you," I said, leaving the closet as quickly as possible before he tried to keep me there somehow, and I finally gave up to his desires.

Later that night, I took a shower, tried to watch countless series, and walked around the room over and over again, but nothing could erase the feeling of his skin on mine. Or the way his eyes looked at my lips, like he wanted to do something.

What was happening to me? Why couldn't I stop thinking about him?

Maybe Liam's plan was to keep me angry because anger was better than feeling nothing.

CHAPTER 8

Fear

SOMETHING WAS INVADING ME. It started with a strange tingling in my feet, but it quickly grew, and soon I couldn't move. My body felt heavy as if something invisible was holding me down.

Panic set in as I struggled to break free, but no matter how hard I tried, I stayed frozen, trapped by this strange force. No matter how hard I fought, I could not move, helpless against the approaching darkness.

Then, I saw it—a huge, swirling black hole, growing larger and larger, coming straight for me. It was like it was trying to pull me in, and I couldn't do anything to stop it. I tried to breathe, but it felt like the air was being sucked right out of my lungs.

I was terrified, feeling myself slipping away, almost swallowed by the darkness.

But just when I thought I couldn't take it anymore, I jolted awake, gasping for breath, my heart racing. Sweat covered my forehead, and it took a few moments to realize it was just a dream.

As the terror of the dream began to dissipate, I grasped the reality of my surroundings, grateful that it had only been a nightmare. But even as I lay there, trembling and shaking, I couldn't remove the sense of anxiety that remained in the air, a reminder of the nightmare that had just haunted me.

That night, I woke up before my usual 8:00 p.m. alarm because of a bad dream. I didn't want to sleep anymore, so I put on my hat, brushed my teeth, and then opened the curtains, as usual, to wait for Hellen.

No one was in the park today, so I went to the bathroom to shower and put on new pajamas.

When I came out of the room, Liam was leaning against the window, looking at the sky, with one foot dangling inside the room and the other on the emergency staircase.

His profile resembled a perfect portrait. If I'd been brave enough and my goal wasn't to keep him away from me, I would have found a way to draw him right there. Today, his hair was messy, his short curls fell across his forehead carelessly, but as if they knew exactly where to fall so that it looked perfect.

He looked beautiful.

But he also appeared to be in pain.

Thankfully, I always take my clothes to the bathroom in case a nurse comes into the room while I'm showering. It's not like most of them haven't seen me already, but if I can avoid it when it's not necessary, I will do so to keep my modesty.

In this particular case, I was grateful that I continued this habit.

"Has no one taught you to knock on the door before entering?" I knew I should have ignored him like every other night, but I was tired of him not understanding that my

45

silence meant I didn't want to have any interaction with him anymore.

"I'm a nurse, Mine. And this isn't a five-star hotel. I'm supposed to enter here unannounced." His voice was sadder than expected, as if he were suffering from something; his gaze remained on the sky.

He looked completely different from the person I saw the other afternoon with that child, as if he'd lost all hope he had in giving it to the kid. He also looked different from the person in the closet, with his hands around my waist, confident that he was making me shudder.

Stop, Jasmine, focus on the present.

I didn't care if he was sad or mad. I needed to tell him that he couldn't come and turn my life upside down whenever he pleased. It didn't matter that he was making me feel inspired and motivated; these nonsense visits needed to stop before he changed my attitude for good.

I wanted to keep being the dark, miserable soul I was before he appeared, and I wasn't going to let him alter that.

I walked to the window firmly, ready to make him leave. When I was close enough, I started speaking, "How many times do I have to tell you that I don't want you in here so you understand that I don't want to see you?"

He looked at me with a dark expression, intimidating my confidence. I almost regretted getting so close to making my point, because it worked against me.

"As many times as it takes before you realize you can't escape from me," he whispered, then turned his gaze to the outside again.

In the silence that followed, I could sense my heart racing and my palms growing clammy.

I felt a mix of conflicting emotions inside me. Anger at Liam's intrusion, but nervousness at being so close to him.

I moved back to lie on one of the walls at the other end of the window and sighed. I didn't know what to do with him, but I didn't know how to push him away either.

His presence was overwhelming, clouding my attempts to set boundaries like I wanted. Despite my best efforts to appear composed, I couldn't shake off the feeling of vulnerability in his presence. It was as if his mere existence had the power to unravel the carefully constructed walls I'd made.

I shot him a quick glance, only to find his gaze fixed on the distant horizon again, oblivious to the confusion I had inside of me.

I also tried to look through the window to distract my thoughts, focusing my gaze on the distant lights and the sky.

But even forcing myself to think about something else, I was unable to ignore his presence at that moment. Part of me couldn't deny my curiosity about Liam, a feeling that defied logic and reason.

Lost in my thoughts, I barely noticed when Liam finally spoke, his words pulling me back to the present moment.

"Come, sit with me." He opened the window more and accommodated himself so I could fit in front of him.

I hesitated for some seconds, but without saying a word, I sat down and started looking at his face.

He looked like he'd had a shitty day. Part of me wanted to comfort him, but that would mean letting my guard down on the decision I'd already made.

I couldn't let this boy let me feel. I had to be strong.

"Don't you get tired of being so defensive all the time?" he asked. Our knees began to rub, and I couldn't help but watch as he moved them from side to side.

"Sometimes," I admitted. "But I've done it for so long that it's become a part of me."

I didn't know why I was being honest with him, but part

of me felt like I needed to tell him the truth. Sometimes, I felt like I needed to let out my feelings. Being on the defensive all the time was difficult.

Maybe if he understood my reasons, he'd leave me alone. I'd already realized that being rude or ignoring him wasn't working, so maybe asking him nicely and explaining why I was like that clearly might have some effect on him.

"And why keep doing it? Wouldn't it be easier to be at peace? More chill?"

I looked at his face again and realized he was already staring at me. Our gazes connected briefly, but then I sighed and looked outside. "Loneliness is my peace."

"I think that's what you want to make yourself believe, but we both know it's not the truth."

"And what is the truth?" I said with a sarcastic smile. I hate it when people want to talk like they know what I'm going through, especially if they don't know me.

Everyone always wants to try to put themselves in your shoes to give you encouragement and hope, but no one really knows what it means to be in a life-or-death situation where you don't know if you're going to wake up the next day or if the medication is going to work.

"The reality is that you feel sad and devastated, and you have no choice but to try to act like that so that others don't feel sorry for you. You think that by acting that way, you'll make it hurt less." I opened my eyes, incredulous at what I'd just heard. I was completely offended, but I didn't know if it was because of his impudence or because, deep down, he was right.

He said those words with such certainty that I began to doubt my own convictions. But I wasn't going to let him know that I agreed with him.

"I think that you're full of bullshit. There's no point in

telling me all this. And you know what?" I said, taking on a defensive attitude again.

"Of course, there is a point." He interrupted me before I could say anything else. "I consider your position to be quite bad already. But I think your attitude in this situation is more miserable than the cancer itself."

He left me speechless, incapable of arguing back. I stayed in silence for a second, finding the correct words to say, but the only thing I managed to ask was, "And how should I feel and behave, Liam? Happy and optimistic?"

"I think you should stop wasting time feeling miserable and start doing things that really have meaning to you. If you really don't have that much time left, the worst thing you can do is not make the most of it."

I shouldn't have let my guard down. I thought that I would make him feel good with my earlier words, but it was all a trap to believe that he could deliberately insult me. However, now I was intrigued about what he was saying.

"And what's the point of doing meaningful things? I'm dying."

"We're all dying, Jasmine. But you think you're special because you have a slight idea of when you're going to leave this world." He grabbed my chin and gently moved it so I could look him in the eyes, then, without taking his hands off me, he continued, "The reality is that we all have the same chances of dying as you. The only difference is that we're taking advantage of the time we have left."

I couldn't say anything to contradict him. His arguments were completely valid. Thousands of people die every day, and I'm still here. "But I can't do anything worthwhile locked up here."

"Then keep drawing until you realize there's something more than just being locked up."

"Why are you telling me all this?" I asked without leaving my eyes on his face.

"Because maybe I also need this same advice. Maybe I'm trying to save myself by saving you."

His words left me stunned. I couldn't understand why Liam would need hope. He seemed so free that I had a hard time believing that his gray moments were so heavy. What burdens did he carry under that facade of indifference? And why did he feel the need to share his feelings with me, a stranger trapped in this room who couldn't offer him any comfort?

However, despite the confusion I felt inside me, I couldn't look away from him. Our eyes met silently, each searching in the other for answers that we both refused to acknowledge.

But before I could delve deeper into Liam's enigma, we heard the food cart approaching the room down the hall, snapping us back to reality. With a weary sigh, I broke our silence and turned my gaze once more to the world beyond the window.

"I think you're right about something. Everyone is dying. It may be a waste of time to focus on things that don't make you happy," I replied. I don't know if I said that to comfort Liam or me, but something inside me believed these words I'd just said.

When the door next to my room opened and closed, Liam stood on the emergency stairs and said, "I think my time here is over for now. Good night, Mine."

"Do me a favor, Liam," I responded. "Don't come back."

We both laughed, principally because we knew he'd be back. But it was a way to make him understand that I still wasn't willing to be his friend, even if he'd somehow managed to get us to have a halfway decent conversation.

I kept seated there, watching him escape to the first floor

with the stairs and enter the hospital again, like he was supposed to be elsewhere and not here with me.

As I was there, a thought came to my mind. If he left before Hellen could enter, that only meant one thing: He wasn't allowed to be in this room with me after all.

He was doing it because he wanted to see me.

Journal entry 3

July 26, 2024

This week has been a nightmare. I haven't made the slightest progress with Jasmine. She doesn't fall for my charms, she doesn't soften about all the things I've done for her with my nurse skills, she doesn't care when I compliment her drawings, and even at my most vulnerable moment, the last thing she made sure to tell me was that she didn't want to see me again.

I don't know what I can do to gain her trust. It's as if she enjoys being miserable, as if her only goal in life is to suffer and draw, and she's very good at both.

Also, I made the mistake of being seen twice. The first was a nurse who chased me as

I was leaving Jasmine's room one night—luckily, I was able to escape before she reached me. The other was a child who was crying on one of the upper floors when I was on my way to the rooftop. He looked at me with tears in his eyes, and I knew I couldn't just leave him alone there, so I tried to cheer him up.

From now on, I should exclusively use the window to see Jasmine, but I need a good excuse when she asks me about it. Until now, I've been acting like I was her designated nurse at night, entering like I owned the place and deserved to be there, but it's all bullshit, and I hope she doesn't realize that.

The only good thing about all this is that she's been drawing me. It makes me think even if she doesn't like me, at least she thinks about me. And it makes me feel special—like at least I'm serving as her inspiration.

From now on, I must think of a better strategy to access her heart. But first, this weekend, I have to de-stress. My well-being is directly tied to hers, and if I don't get myself together, I won't be able to help her. Time is running out, and I'm a complete mess.

Why doesn't she like me, and how can I change that situation?

CHAPTER 9

Curiosity

"WHAT HAPPENS when a nurse is found in the room of a patient that he or she should not be officially caring for?" I asked the young man who was drawing my blood with a needle. It was the first time I'd talked to him beyond *yes, no, and okay*, so he was being as cooperative and interested in the conversation as possible.

I discovered that his name was Frank, and he'd been working at this hospital for a while, mostly in the mornings. He continued studying in the afternoons and one day wanted to specialize in surgery. If I'd never spoken to him, I would've thought he was a boring, grumpy guy, but after pestering him with questions, I discovered that he was simply shy.

It was amazing how much you could find out about another person through casual small talk. But my main intention was not to get to know him better—I was simply looking for a way to get information out of him.

"Normally, we do not question the reasons why a person would be in a patient's room. We have so many things to do daily that we're not attentive to our colleagues' schedules."

That made sense.

"But what would happen if a nurse were constantly found in a specific room? Could he or she have a problem?"

The nurse was visibly nervous, like I'd found him doing something wrong, and now I would talk if he didn't answer all my questions.

"Well, clearly. We have our codes, but it all depends on his or her reasons to be there. We have nurses with family here, so most of the time, it's normal."

The guy wasn't giving me the answers I needed, and I was losing my patience, so I kept pushing him. "And what would happen if you found an outside visitor in a patient's room during a non-visiting time?"

He stopped what he was doing and stared at me. "Are you thinking about sneaking your boyfriend here or something?"

My jaw dropped. "What makes you think that a person in my condition could have a boyfriend?"

He opened his eyes like he knew he'd messed up. "Well, you're a young, beautiful lady. I couldn't see why not." He cleared his throat, realizing he was making it worse. "But I didn't mean to offend you, miss. I was just curious. My apologies."

I decided not to continue pressuring the poor nurse because he already seemed a little intimidated by my very personal questions.

But I needed to know why Liam didn't want to be seen by Hellen, so I could threaten him and make him not come back. I was sure that Hellen wouldn't be bothered or say anything about his presence. She'd even be happy if I were talking to people other than her. But he didn't have to know that.

After lunch, I went to bed as quickly as possible so I wouldn't lose any extra minutes of sleep. I needed to be awake when Liam arrived so I would be the one to ambush him with uncomfortable questions he couldn't answer, as he did to me last night.

Despite having decided to keep him as far as possible from my life, a part of me had been looking forward to seeing him again.

I don't know if it's because I've been bored or if my parents' absence made me need to fight with someone, but I've been starting to despise Liam a little less each day.

Seeing him for a few minutes each night made me look for a reason to keep my mind occupied for the rest of the night and even part of the morning, so I should be grateful for that.

It took me a while to find some sleep, but I finally managed to calm my mind and relax.

Although my last thought was undoubtedly Liam.

As usual, my alarm rang at the same time as always.

Rubbing the sleep from my eyes, I sat up in bed and glanced around the dimly lit room. There was no one here yet, so I stood up as quickly as I could, put on my hat, and brushed my teeth.

When Hellen came to the room with my dinner, I started eating it immediately.

"Looks like someone woke up really hungry today. That's great."

It was the first time in a while I'd waited for her on the sofa, and I began eating as soon as she handled the food. I wasn't particularly hungry, but I also didn't want Liam to find me eating.

"I want to finish a drawing idea that I have in mind, and I don't want to lose inspiration," I lied, taking another bite of the food.

"I'd love to see what you're going to draw now. You're getting better at it." She replied.

"Thanks, as soon as I'm satisfied with one of the pieces, I'll let you know."

"I hope so, Jasmine," she answered while gathering everything and preparing to leave.

When Hellen left, I grabbed a book and settled down again to wait for Liam, but no matter how long I waited, he never showed up. I checked my phone repeatedly, thinking maybe he was just busier than ever today or finally working instead of bothering me. After all, if my suspicions were correct, he had no official reason to be here.

I began to imagine all the tasks they could give to an intern here. It shouldn't be anything like diagnosing or dealing with an emergency; maybe it's things like injecting patients or checking vital signs.

He told the little boy that he'd been in many surgeries. Maybe he's not as inexperienced as I think, and he's doing some specialty.

I checked my phone again, this time it was 11:00 p.m. The book was still closed on my lap, but my mind kept wandering to the reasons why Liam hadn't shown up yet.

Maybe he decided to listen to me once and for all and would leave me alone.

Incredibly, this last thought didn't please me at all. This is what I thought I wanted for the last nights he'd been bothering my patience, but now that I finally thought I had gotten it, it didn't seem like a positive thing.

I want to keep giving you a purpose to draw and dream.

Liam's words came to my mind as if he had whispered in my ears, so I decided I couldn't wait for him any longer. I gathered my drawing tools and settled in to work on a new piece. My pencil danced across the white page, sketching out the image of Liam in a big library; his expression was contemplative as he gazed up at the shelves of books, lost in thought.

He was wearing a white shirt and black pants. His hair was slicked back, but some of his waves looked unruly.

I started to wonder what books Liam might like, with his arrogant attitude, probably some self-improvement or thriller.

As I added the finishing touches to the drawing, I realized I missed reading books, the feeling of discovering a new story, and losing myself in another world entirely. It had been too long since I'd allowed myself to read for pleasure.

With a sigh, I set aside my drawing and reached for the book again. But as I opened it and tried to focus on the words, my mind kept thinking about where Liam could be now or if he'd gotten bored with me.

Unable to bear the uncertainty any longer, I put on shoes and left the room with the book in my hands. I started walking until I reached the nurse station, where Ronnie, the nurse on duty, was using her phone without noticing that I was there.

"Excuse me," I said, my voice barely above a whisper. I was a little bit nervous because I barely spoke with others in this hospital, but this week, my life was upside down, and I felt like a different person.

She put her phone on the table and raised her gaze to me. "Hi Jasmine, how can I help you?"

"A nurse agreed to bring me a pill because my head hurt, but he never came back. Can you see if he left or something?"

"Of course. What's his name?" the nurse asked, typing on her computer.

"Liam," I replied confidently.

But she looked back at me with a disappointed face. "I need his full name."

Oh.

"I don't know," I admitted. Liam could be a psychopath, and I didn't know it. This made me realize I should start investigating more about him instead of being here, missing his presence.

"Well, young lady, there are three people called Liam in this hospital; two of them are not working right now."

Maybe he was one of them. Maybe the reason he didn't come to my room tonight was that he was free. Relief flooded through me, and my mind began to calm down again.

He wasn't tired of me. He was just not here.

I smiled at Ronnie and thanked her, but before I could turn back and go back to my room, she said, "If you want, I can check you and see what I could give you for the pain."

I laughed nervously. I had forgotten about my little lie. "Walking here made me forget the pain. I think I'll be fine."

"Maybe you shouldn't go back to your room now," she responded. "This book you have in your hands is very good; why don't you find a place outside your room and read it for a little bit?"

I looked at the book for a few seconds, and then my attention focused on her again. "You know what? You're right," I told her, knowing exactly where I wanted to be.

I sat on one of the park benches that I see every night from my window and closed my eyes for a moment just to breathe. I'd never been here before, and from this angle, the place felt much bigger than it did from my room.

The breeze wasn't cold enough to need a coat or be inside, so it was the perfect spot to have a good time without worrying about anything.

For a moment, I allowed myself to forget about the worries, people, and uncertainties of my regular life and decided to lose myself in the pages of the book that I had brought with me.

As the hours passed, I realized that the nurse was right. It was an excellent book, filled with fantasy, plot twists, and a story that kept me intrigued all night until I finished it.

I didn't even realize what time it was until I looked up at the sky and realized it was about to dawn.

I'd never thought I would have the concentration to focus on just that for the whole night. I felt a peace I hadn't had for a long time. Normally, my mind is constantly changing tasks because my mind doesn't let me concentrate on any of them for a long time. But away from that room, everything seemed to be forgotten.

Maybe what I really need is to be away from this hospital.

I closed the book and leaned back on the bench, feeling satisfied. The sun began to rise, and I looked back at the building I lived in. I wasn't ready to return to my room, so I stayed there, just looking around.

From here, I noted that the stairs in my room led to a terrace on the roof. I imagined how good the sunrise must look from there, and I imagined myself up there just contemplating the city.

"I'm going there tonight," I said to myself. "It's a plan."

I almost didn't believe the words that came out of my mouth. Jasmine Russell was making plans. She was looking forward to seeing a new day. She was making sure to do things that made sense to her.

"Oh my God, my poor baby, what are you doing here?" I heard a woman screaming.

I looked forward and saw my parents in front of me, with the biggest worried faces they could make.

"Hey," I replied, trying to ignore their question. "I didn't expect to have you here so early."

"We came here as soon as the plane landed. You barely responded to our texts, so we were worried," my dad said. "You could have caught a cold here. Can you explain to us why you're not in your room?"

"I just wanted to feel the morning sun," I lied. But they were not happy with the response. If they knew I actually spent the whole night here, I think they would be horrified.

"If you needed vitamin D, you could talk to one of the doctors about including it in your daily pills. It couldn't be possible that they pay so little attention to their patients that you went out without anyone noticing," my dad replied, taking me by my arm to bring me inside.

"I think you're making a big deal about something simple."

"It's not something simple, Jasmine," my mom argued. "Anything could have happened to you out there. We're not willing to accept these types of mistakes."

I stayed silent the rest of the way to my room. Arguing with them was useless. It didn't matter if I told them I felt perfectly fine; they always reminded me how sick I was.

Back in my room, my parents called Hellen and demanded a full check-up to ensure I didn't get anything while I was outside.

Noticing my discomfort, Hellen told them to get out and that she would take care of it. They both relaxed and kissed me on the forehead.

"I know you're a warrior, honey. We admire your strength, but you need to understand that you must rest," my mom told me before leaving the room.

I laughed sarcastically at the irony of how they didn't care enough to take care of me, but were completely upset that I could be doing anything here while they were gone.

When we were alone, Hellen started organizing my breakfast as if she didn't have to ask me a hundred questions and a thousand check-ups.

"Aren't you going to fight with me, too, and tell me all the reasons why it's not good for me to be out at night?" I broke the silence.

Because of me, she had to listen to my parents scream, and they were probably going to complain in the lobby, too. So, I expected her to be mad at me and tell me how irresponsible I was.

"Why would I do that?" she asked, as if nothing had happened.

"Because I'm sick," I responded. "And because I did something irresponsible."

"You look perfectly fine to me," she corrected me calmly. "But I do have a question. What were you doing there alone in the park?"

"I was being happy, Hellen. I was escaping the depression that these four walls were giving me."

She stopped what she was doing and looked me in the eyes, shocked. "Then screw them," she finally said. "It's time to start doing everything that makes you happy if you feel fine to do it."

CHAPTER 10
Vulnerability

LATER THAT NIGHT, I began to prepare a bag with everything I'd take to the roof: my sketchbook, a new book, headphones, and some snacks. Breaking free from the monotony of my daily routine excites me in an indescribable way, and I couldn't wait another minute to be away from this room.

With my bag slung over my shoulder, I went to the window. Just as I was about to climb out to the stair floor, I saw Liam coming up, his expression a mix of surprise and concern when he saw me.

"Are you escaping?" he asked, approaching my window as fast as he could.

"It's not what you think," I hesitated, caught off guard by his sudden appearance. We both stood in silence, watching each other like we didn't know what to do.

"I'm going on an adventure," I finally replied, trying to sound casual despite the butterflies fluttering in my stomach.

"An adventure? Where to?" He moved his body to block me from the window, eliminating the space between us. I didn't know if it was an attempt to keep me trapped here until

I forgot the idea of leaving, or because he wanted to be close to me, but it made me take a step back.

"Up." I limited myself to saying. I didn't want to go into details because I didn't want him to stop me from leaving. After seeing my parents' reaction this morning, the last thing I wanted was more drama.

A smile began to form on his lips, making me relax my defensive position.

"That sounds perfect. Let's go then." Before I could react, he started climbing the stairs.

I ran to the window and looked at him.

"You coming or what?" he said when he saw that I still wasn't following him.

"You're not invited. Do you think you can leave for days and then come back, and we'd be friends? That's not how this relationship works." Despite my harsh words, I felt relieved he was back. Part of me had gotten the idea that he came to see me because he wanted to, not because he had to, and his absence had made me doubt whether I'd been too cruel to him in the last few days, and he got tired.

Liam smiled. "I missed you, too, Mine. Let's go. I'll tell you where I was. You'll love to hear about it."

I doubted for a few minutes. While the idea of spending the night on the terrace alone excited me, being there with Liam made me feel nervous.

I should hate him. Hate how he interfered in my things without being called, how he didn't know what personal space meant, how he was ruining my peace. I should be hating him, and yet, I just couldn't.

I stood at the window for a few minutes, but then, I finally gave up. My curiosity about what he was going to tell me won, and I knew that no matter what I said, he wouldn't leave.

So, I started climbing after him, and we both ascended to the top.

~

I was right.

The view from here was spectacular, nothing to compare to my window room. I could see the lights of the city illuminating the sky, some significant buildings from afar, and the street full of busy people with lives and goals.

I stood on the edge of the terrace in silence for a few minutes, only admiring the beauty of everything. From here, there was a peace and serenity that I couldn't describe; everything seemed so small and insignificant, yet at the same time, full of opportunities.

I turned to see Liam, who was beside me at that moment but keeping a good distance between us, watching me quietly with his hands in his pockets. "Have you ever been here before?" I asked him, turning my gaze to the city again.

"A couple of times. I come here to think because I know I won't be bothered, but I use the principal door like normal people."

I listened to his steps approaching until he stood next to me, resting his hands on the wall in front of us. "If you look at the sky from here, you forget that you're even in a hospital."

I did exactly as he suggested, realizing how beautiful the sky was tonight without a single cloud, and I couldn't help but put a big smile on my face.

When I looked back at him, Liam was looking at me in amazement, with a beautiful smile, like he was witnessing someone seeing for the first time. "Look how beautiful you look when you're not in the mood to fight and hate everything around you," he whispered.

I laughed.

"Don't be a liar. I've had enough with my parents today."

"I'm telling you the truth."

"I feel the complete opposite," I confessed. "Like I'm already dead inside."

Without taking his eyes off mine, he took my right hand and placed it on my heart. "Do you feel that? Your heart's still beating. This means you're still alive."

I turned my gaze again to the city to hide how red my cheeks turned. But I couldn't hide the happiness that his words gave me. It had been so long since anyone had taken the time to look at me, compliment me, and say a few words beyond "you're strong and brave, and you can do anything" that what he said touched my soul. I didn't care if he just said that out of politeness; for the first time in a while, I decided just to accept the compliment.

"I'm sorry, my parents just put me in the worst mood ever when they came. It's like their mission is to destroy all the spirit I gain during the week."

He got serious, putting his hands on the wall again. "I heard they found you in the park this morning. Tell me more about it."

"They always tell me how strong and admirable I am, but if I try to do something that goes against being locked up, they get stressed. Do you know their last words before they left today, after dragging me back into the room? 'You're a warrior.' But I'm not a warrior. I'm not a hero. I hate when people talk about me like I'm a soldier. Because this isn't how I feel, and if I had to choose, I'd prefer not to be one."

He listened to me patiently as I spoke, then sighed and said, "Nobody wants to be in a war, Jasmine. What makes them special is the attitude they take towards what they're battling."

"But a sickness isn't a real battle," I complained. I hated the way people said that those battling cancer could be compared to soldiers going to war. One of them was strong and brave, the other just had bad luck in life.

67

"You are wrong. Cancer is the worst of all battles. People fight each other for ridiculous reasons, sacrificing healthy lives for a destiny that sometimes makes no sense. When you battle with a sickness, you battle for your life against something that doesn't care about anything; its only purpose is to kill you."

I sighed. "But I see soldiers as strong people capable of achieving anything. I, on the other hand, am weak and incapable."

"You're wrong in that part, too. These people spend years training and go to war in their best condition." He pointed at me with his finger and continued, "However, you're in one of the worst conditions anyone can be in. That makes you stronger than a lot of them because your body is constantly trying to keep you alive while you're dealing with cancer. You're the only one who knows the pain and all the things that you're going through to not give up. You may be grumpy and depressed all the time, but I know your body's trying its best to be alive."

I smiled. That was a better way to see myself. I never wanted to be a warrior, but now, being strong and combating this illness was the only thing that made sense.

"So, where were you?" I asked, trying to change the subject. It was enough to talk about myself, my problems, and my insecurities. I'd come up here to clear my mind, and the last thing I wanted was to spend the whole night talking about my illness.

"Come, let's sit first," he said, taking my hand and walking.

I looked around us. The roof was empty. "Where? This place doesn't have any chairs."

"You'll see."

We got to where the main door was, and he climbed to the top of that space. Then he gave me both of his hands to help me climb as well.

I hesitated for a moment, glancing at the structure he'd just climbed. It was a small, square block attached to the roof, maybe about eight feet high. The metal door at the base led back into the building, but up here, it looked like a quiet little escape. The walls of the structure were plain and weathered, the kind of dull gray that seemed to blend into the concrete floor beneath it.

I finally took his hand and jumped. The top was flat, just big enough for the two of us to sit comfortably, like a hidden space overlooking the rest of the rooftop.

"Welcome to the highest place of the hospital." He removed his coat, placed it on the floor, and lay down.

"This looks uncomfortable," I said, sitting next to him and placing my bag on my back for support.

"Get used to it, Mine; life isn't comfy."

"Close your eyes and give me your hands," Liam said, putting one hand in his pocket.

"I'm not going to. I'm scared." I put my hands behind my body as a joke, making Liam burst out laughing.

It felt good to be able to joke around with someone. Right now, I felt like Liam and I were just two people getting to know each other and joking around, not a nurse making sure his patient was okay on a roof.

"Scared of what? I'm not a monster, Jasmine; close them." Liam put his free hand on his heart, pretending to be hurt, and now I was the one who started laughing loudly.

When we were both calm, I got completely serious, so he knew I wasn't playing.

"Okay," I said, "but if you pull out a spider or something creepy, I'm going to push you off this roof. Got it?"

His smile widened, and he promised, "I swear you'll like it."

I closed my eyes and gave him my hands, my heart full of anxiety. Trusting someone was hard for me; my parents were constantly lying, my friends left me when I came to this hospital, and even Hellen tried to be my friend because it was her job. But for some reason, I decided just to follow my heart for a moment.

I felt something small and cold settle into my palm. A moment later, I opened my eyes.

I gasped softly as I looked at what was resting in my hands. It was a tiny bottle filled with sand, glittering under the dim light of the night.

My heart swelled with emotion. It wasn't just a gift—it was a piece of the outside world, a world I hadn't seen in so long. It meant that Liam had taken my drawings and actually gone somewhere I dreamed of.

"I didn't have any plans this weekend," he said casually, as if it was nothing, "so I decided to do something different and went to the beach at night, just like the drawing you made. This is a little bit of sand I brought back for you."

I couldn't stop the torrent of emotions inside me. Liam had done that. He'd gone to the place I'd drawn just to bring me a piece of that place. This thing in my hands was more than just sand. It was proof that freedom still existed beyond the hospital walls, that maybe, just maybe, I could experience it someday too.

"It's perfect," I whispered. "I love it."

He smiled. "I did exactly what you pictured. I took off my shoes, walked to the shore, and let the water relax me while I watched the sky."

I closed my eyes, trying to imagine it—the ocean waves, the cool sand underfoot, the stars overhead. The idea of Liam being there, soaking in that peacefulness because of something I drew, made my pulse quicken.

"And how was it?" I asked, my voice soft.

"Totally recommended," he said with a grin. "I felt relaxed. It was just what I needed after a long week."

But his short answer wasn't enough for me. "That's it?" I raised an eyebrow, not convinced. "I need the details, Liam. Did you go alone? Was the water cold? Could you see the sea, or was it too dark? Come on, I want to live through your experience!"

He chuckled, shaking his head. "I'm not telling you everything. I don't want to ruin your experience when you finally go."

I frowned, crossing my arms in mock frustration. "I don't know if I'd be able to do it, and you'll be responsible for me never knowing what it really feels like."

Liam's eyes softened. "You have the same chances of living as you do of dying, Jasmine. I think it's easier if you believe you'll live. It makes each day less heavy."

His words hit me harder than I expected. He was right. My doctors were optimistic. I should be, too. But that lingering fear of hope had already ruined me once.

"My only problem with being positive is... I was positive the first time," I murmured, my voice trembling. "And I still ended up here again. This is my second fight with cancer. I can't let myself get too excited about the future just to be trapped here again."

He was quiet for a moment, then said, "Life isn't about a single problem that you solve and then everything's fine, Jasmine. That only happens in movies. Life is one challenge after another, and if we let each one of those problems depress us, we'll never find joy in between."

I tried to focus on his words, but my mind was spinning. He made it sound so simple, so matter-of-fact. But life wasn't always like that, especially in my condition. "My problems are ten times worse than most people's," I muttered.

"And some people's problems are ten times worse than yours." His voice was calm but firm. "If you compare yourself to others, you'll always find people better and worse off than you. Some don't have access to treatments, and some don't even have meals. Compared to them, this hospital is a palace."

His words made me pause. I started to think about what would happen to me if I were in another family, and the thought terrified me. I never thought I'd be lucky to have my parents, especially after our tough morning. At least they were working hard to keep me alive.

"That's why comparison doesn't help," he said, pulling me from my thoughts. "Every life is different. You'll always find someone better or worse off than you."

I nodded slowly, absorbing his words. He was right. It wasn't about comparing. It was about my own path, my own journey. "Okay," I said quietly, "I'll go to the beach once I leave here. But I still want to know your whole experience, so when it's my turn, I can live through your stories."

"With one condition." He realigned himself, his eyes suddenly intent upon mine. "You need to keep drawing them, and you need to tell me what excites you about that place before I go so I can experience them through your eyes, too."

I smiled. That was a fair deal. After all, if I wanted to experience the places I dreamed of through his eyes, it was only right to continue capturing them through my drawings. "Sounds like a good plan."

"It's a deal, Jasmine Russell," he replied. "I can live for both until you're strong enough to live for yourself."

~

Liam told me the details of his trip to the beach, from why he decided to go there on Saturday to when he decided it was time to go home.

Last week in the hospital was highly exhausting for him, and even if he tried to rest on his free day, he couldn't concentrate on sleeping or just chill. It was like his body was telling him he needed to keep working even if he was free, so he decided to do something out of the ordinary to help his mind realize he was out of the hospital.

He'd started out just driving around aimlessly, but then he remembered the drawing and how he'd never had the chance to go to the beach at night, so he headed to the closest one he found on the map.

He told me how amazing he felt because he liked the peace his body found there, and he was finally able to rest. He actually went home when he started seeing the sunrise.

I listened with rapt attention, imagining every word as he described it from start to finish. I felt like that story was better than all the series Hellen had recommended to me because it was something I created, and contrary to a series, it was something I could do one day if I got better.

No.

When I get better.

With each word Liam said, I could feel the excitement building inside me. I could almost picture the endless expanse of sand stretching out before him, the gentle lapping of the waves against the shore, and the soft glow of the moon casting its ethereal light over the landscape.

But more than that, I could sense the peace and tranquility that Liam had found there. It was as if, for a brief moment, he'd been able to escape the confines of the hospital walls and truly embrace the freedom that comes with being alive.

One day, I wanted to feel that same peace.

What I liked the most about the whole story was how he found a happy ending after a tough week. It reminded me that even if everything goes wrong for a long period of time, there's always a possibility of finding happiness.

In that instant, I wondered if I could find the same happiness locked inside here.

I reached for my backpack and pulled out my drawing folder. I carefully removed my last sketch of Liam at the library, taking care not to let out any other page.

"Here I have your new adventure," I said, passing him the page.

He took it and analyzed it in silence. Part of me was nervous about what he might think about the fact that I'd drawn it again before our deal. But he didn't seem to care about that part. "That's a cute illustration, and I think I know exactly where I'll go," he started, "but I have to ask first, what excites you about going to a library?"

"I've always liked to read. I have a good imagination, so when I do it, it's like I got teleported to another world. Libraries are a magical place. There's the sense of possibility that comes with being surrounded by so many stories waiting to be discovered. It's like every book holds the promise of a new adventure, just waiting to be opened."

I realized that my voice had risen from the excitement of talking about books, so I paused to look at him and found his gaze directly on mine, amused.

"Please continue," he said. "Have you ever been to one?"

"Surprisingly not. I've been to small bookstores or the book section of shopping stores, but not a real library. I think I'd feel a little overwhelmed not knowing what to choose."

"I don't believe so. I think you'd know exactly where to go and what to pick when you go to one."

I thought of it for a minute, but then I shook my head. "I

74

have no idea. How would I know which one is the best among so many options? I think I'd be paralyzed."

"Let's make it simple for you. You have a favorite genre. Correct?"

"Yes. Fantasy," I replied without hesitation.

"See? You're very sure about exactly what you like."

"But surely there'll be hundreds of fantasy books. I still wouldn't know which one to choose."

"That's the best part about books and many other things in life, Mine," he replied. "You don't have to choose just one thing you like. You can pick a random one based on what you think you'd enjoy, read it, and then move to the next one. Life isn't about choosing just one thing forever; it's about many different decisions based on what you're feeling at the moment."

I opened my mouth to speak, but I couldn't say anything. As much as I wanted to be a negative soul, Liam did his best to make all my arguments pointless.

Before I could think of a good answer, a sound came from Liam's pocket. "What's that alarm for?" I asked.

"For two important things." He stood up, picked up his jacket, and stretched slightly.

At that moment, I was seated, hugging my legs to my chest, watching him. He looked calm and rested, and a peace came out of him that I couldn't explain. Contrary to the last time I saw him, this time, he looked utterly improved, as if he'd dedicated the weekend to taking care of himself.

Part of me felt pleased to be an inspiration for the things he did to change his mood.

Had he thought of me when he was on the beach?

He didn't say anything about me, but I wonder if it was one of the things that was explicit among all the things he had told me.

When he finished breathing and stretching, he turned to

me and bent to his knees, lowering his body so our faces could be at the same level.

There was Liam, once again crossing my personal space without warning or permission, and yet this time, I didn't care that he did it.

"This alarm is set to 12:00 a.m. It means that I must start working."

Our faces were so close that I could feel his breathing when he said those words. Our gazes were connected as if he was waiting for me to have some reaction, but I simply didn't do anything.

He always looked for a way to make me feel shy and unable to take any action.

"And the second important thing?" I whispered, trying to break the silence between us.

"That you managed to make it to another new day alive, congratulations, Jasmine."

Journal entry 4

July 30, 2024

I finally feel like the world is in my favor. After a dark week, I'm already seeing the light.

It all started on the weekend when I decided to take the day to think and rest. Honestly, I didn't know where to go. It was as if I no longer knew this city. And I was alone here. It felt weird, like I was a stranger in my own life, lost in the familiar streets of a city that used to feel like home. But then, I thought about the drawing Jasmine made of me at the beach, and it was the perfect plan I could think of.

I went at night just like the picture she made and did exactly what she wanted me to do: breathe and feel the waves on my feet. My mind thought about a million things at that moment, but the most important thing was what I really had to do.

All these days, I'd wanted Jasmine to get out of her bubble and be another person, but maybe the best way to reach her was to enter her world. I'd never tried to hear what she really had to say, and that's why my methods failed over and over again. I'd been so focused on changing her, molding her into what I thought she should be, that I never considered just trying to know her.

How had I been so blind?

When I came to her room on Monday, she was already at the window with a backpack on her shoulders, ready to escape. I was glad I arrived on time because, thanks to it, I was able to be with her for the next four hours on the rooftop of the hospital building.

And we connected in a way we never had before.

Now I understand her a little bit better. She's been locked up all this time without people who really listen to her, without living, without doing anything worthwhile, and the only thing left for her was to be the strong and impenetrable person she is now.

However, this time was different. Up there, she had an inexplicable glow, the feeling of freedom. Even though we were on a simple roof, she looked at the city and the sky as if they were the most wonderful things in the world, while I looked at her the same way. Her eyes were so beautiful; the way she smiled made me forget why I was even there.

It was incredible how, for some people, happiness could be something as simple as breathing in a new environment.

We talked about everything and nothing. I told her about my beach adventure, and she told me about another place she wanted to go. I promised her I would go to every place she wanted me to go as long as she was willing to keep drawing and dreaming.

If I'm honest, I wasn't interested in going anywhere, but seeing the excitement on her face made me want to go to hell and back if it was going to make her happy.

I finally felt like I was getting closer to her. The answer had always been there. I just had to listen to her.

The problem was that the more time I spent with her last night, the more I wanted to know about her. I wanted her to tell me everything. What she wanted to be when she grew up, what she liked to do. What was her least favorite food.

I need to find a way to keep my feelings from interfering with my work because if I fail, I could risk everything I've built so far. And I need both of us to be completely okay if I want to succeed.

But at the same time, I haven't stopped thinking: how inappropriate would it be to kiss her?

CHAPTER 11

Determination

I SPENT the rest of the night alone on the roof, thinking about all the things I wanted Liam to do. I didn't know how long he'd like to keep doing them, so I wanted the places to be special and full of memories.

He told me that he was going to the library on Thursday morning and wanted to do something else on Saturday, so I had to make a drawing by then. I took out a pencil and paper from my bag and started analyzing all the possibilities.

But as expected, the sun started to make its appearance, and I had zero ideas.

I'd spent so many months blocking out the outside world that I didn't know what things I found fun anymore. Even the last series I'd watched was boring. They were about police cases, thrillers, science, or historical events.

As the sun was beginning to rise, I packed up everything to go to my room before anyone entered and noted my absence.

When I arrived, I scanned the place to see if anyone had come while I was gone. Everything was in its place. This place was still the same white and dull space, and a big silence embraced all my thoughts.

Last night was explosive and messy, full of colors from the sky, the city, and his eyes. Liam's point of view about my situation made me reconsider everything I've believed so far, and I no longer want to be locked in these four walls, doing nothing and waiting for my time to come; I need every minute of my life to have meaning.

But how?

Although yesterday was an escape from the same old routine, I was still locked up here, and the empty list in my hands was proof that Liam was the only extraordinary thing that had happened in my life in the past months.

I put the backpack on the floor and the notebook with the page titled "To Dream List" on the nightstand to go to the bathroom. When I came out of the bathroom, I found Hellen writing something on the paper.

"What are you writing?" I got closer to take a better look at what she was doing, and I read, *"I want to go to a nightclub full of people, take a shot, and dance in the middle of the room."*

"I saw the list practically empty and thought you needed some help from people who are actually having fun out there," she said proudly, passing me the notebook.

And there, I realized. I didn't have to do the list alone. I was surrounded by people who were living day to day. I just had to tell them that I needed help.

As I sat on the couch, I asked Hellen, "So, what do you like about nightclubs?"

"For starters, there's the music, and if you find a place where they put your favorite songs, you'd never want to leave. The pulsing beat of the bass, the catchy melodies that get stuck in your head for days. It's impossible not to feel alive when you're surrounded by such energy."

She paused for a moment as if considering her next words.

I saw her face light up with the thoughts that came to her. "And then there's the dancing," she continued with a grin. "There's something liberating about losing yourself in the rhythm, letting go of all your worries, and just moving to the music. It's like a form of therapy if you ask me."

Hellen's enthusiasm was contagious, and I found myself nodding along in agreement with her words. "I can see how that would be fun," I said, a smile tugging at my lips. "Thanks for sharing, Hellen."

She left the room, and I ate my food as fast as possible. Today, I had a mission, and I didn't want to lose any minute of the day.

In the morning, I asked each person who came into my room which places they frequent and which ones they recommend.

The cleaning lady, Donna, loves a coffee shop close to her house called "Cookies Paradise" and recommended some desserts from the menu.

Frank, the guy who did my blood tests the other day, told me that he loves to go bowling with his friends every month. Ronnie loves camping. Dr. Butler loves to use his yacht (something that I probably wouldn't do because I don't have one, but I loved hearing his fishing stories).

When the night came, I went to the nurse station to keep asking people about new places, and they were thrilled to talk about it.

The nurses there didn't let me go back to my room before hearing hundreds of different stories and places.

Even a guy who was visiting a patient and was there hearing the conversation gave me some options.

Anna, Ronnie, and more nurses that I didn't even know the names of told me stories about dates that went wrong at a place, but they still went back there because they liked it, how they discovered their new favorite place, and what things they hate to do after a bad experience.

I discovered there was a lake outside the city where people go and make bonfires. Some people prefer to go to museums and movie theaters, and others like to go to food festivals to try new recipes.

I didn't realize how talkative everyone around me was until today. Little by little, the blurry faces began to have a name, voice, and personality, and I realized that the barrier I'd put around myself to keep me away from everyone was now completely broken.

By the end of the day, I went to my room with the list full of options. Many of them were interesting, and others didn't catch my attention at all.

But the most important thing I got today wasn't ideas for my new drawing but new experiences and stories I can keep in mind.

The next day, Dr. Butler brought me photos of his yacht so I could have a clearer view of the things he'd told me the day before, and Donna brought me some cookies from the coffee shop (not before asking Hellen several times if it was safe for me to eat them).

I hadn't even acknowledged that today was the day my parents visited me until they opened the door.

Because I didn't feel alone anymore.

I didn't crave attention.

To dream list

- I want to go to the beach at night
- I want to go to a crowded club, have a drink, and dance in the middle of the room
- I want to go to a bookstore and pick out books at random.
- I want to eat cookies at Cookie Heaven
- I want to go bowling with friends
- I want to go on a yacht and watch the sunset at sea
- I want to go to a lake and have a bonfire
- I want to go to the art museum
- I want to see a movie with friends
- I want to go to a food festival
- I want to go to an amusement park
- I want to play go-karts

CHAPTER 12
Confusion

"THE DOCTORS TOLD us that you've been in an excellent mood lately. I'm happy for it."

I looked at my dad, who was seated on the sofa, and nodded.

My mom was in bed, sitting with me, giving me a massage while I showed her some drawings I'd made. I skipped the ones with Liam to avoid unnecessary questions I didn't want to answer.

We'd been talking about everything since they arrived. They told me how Miami went, and I asked them about some places, too, for my list. I gave them the books I'd already read so they could put them in the home library, and my father promised to bring me more on the next visit.

Even though I was angry with them for the way they treated me when they found me in the park, something inside me felt that it was no longer worth being in a bad mood, so I simply tried to take advantage of the fact that they were here.

"I see you've been quite inspired lately, too," my mom said, looking at the drawings. "I need to know what happened while we were out of the city so we can keep making you do it every day."

I stayed silent for a few seconds, trying to formulate the correct words in my mind. "I'm just seeing life from another perspective. I think the old me doesn't make sense anymore."

My mom put a big smile on her face like she was waiting for me to say those words forever.

"I'm glad to hear that," my dad responded. "Looks like it's a good time to start planning college applications then."

I looked up, confused.

College was something important to me before I was diagnosed with cancer the second time. I'd started to fill out some forms and look for options to be a lawyer like them, but everything was interrupted after my diagnosis, and I haven't had the strength to try to continue something that made no sense if I was going to die.

"Dear..." My mom tried to calm the situation. "I don't think she's quite ready yet for the pressure and responsibilities of college applications."

"But if she doesn't start now, she may lose a year. She can start her first semester online, and then when she gets better, start taking some classes on campus to see how it goes."

"I don't even know what to study anymore," I admitted. "I think we're rushing things unnecessarily; what about one step at a time? I don't mind losing a semester. There are a lot of things I want to do when I go out of here before—"

I didn't finish what I was trying to say because my dad interrupted.

"I thought we agreed that you'd be a lawyer. What made you change your opinion? What things do you want to do that are more important than your education?"

His tone wasn't like someone who wanted to argue; it was more like someone disappointed and confused. I was acting differently; I was more talkative, and many people around the hospital told me I was planning many things to do.

Maybe they thought that talking about college would make me focus on the near future, but that wasn't what I wanted anymore, not for now, at least.

"Living," I responded without hesitation. "Being in a good mood now doesn't mean I want to keep my life like nothing is happening."

There was a big silence.

They both looked at each other with guilt. Like they knew they had ruined the moment.

And I knew the conversation was over.

CHAPTER 13

Passion

"How DID you know you wanted to be a doctor?" The question slipped out before I even realized it.

After my parents left, I wandered aimlessly through the hallways, unsure of what to do before lunch. The stillness of my room felt suffocating, so I ended up at the nurses' station in the lobby.

Anna was there, her bright smile as welcoming as ever. She's one of the oldest nurses at the hospital, and many new employees come to her when they need help. She always seems to have all the answers. So I thought it would be a good idea to ask her this question.

She was organizing a pile of patient charts, her movements efficient but unhurried. Watching her work was comforting. It was like she always knew what her next move was going to be. But I was tired of being in silence.

Anna looked up, surprised but intrigued by my question. "A doctor? Oh, Jasmine, I'm not a doctor—I'm a nurse. Big difference, you know."

I shrugged, suddenly feeling awkward. "Well, you're still in the medical field. You help people every day. Maybe you always knew this was what you wanted."

She leaned on the counter, her smile softening. "That's an interesting question. And no, I didn't always know. In fact, I almost didn't end up here at all."

I tilted my head, curious. "What do you mean?"

Anna chuckled, gesturing for me to follow her. She led me to a small seating area just off the lobby, where we could talk without interruption. As we sat down, she smoothed her scrubs and began to speak.

"When I was younger, my parents had this big plan for me. They wanted me to be a surgeon. To them, it was the ultimate dream—prestige, money, stability. They were so proud when I got into medical school. I thought, 'Well, if it makes them happy, it'll make me happy too.'"

"But it didn't?" I guessed.

She shook her head, her expression bittersweet. "Not even close. Every day felt like a battle. I hated the environment, the seriousness and concentration I needed for everything, and the constant competition. I started to dread waking up in the morning. It wasn't until my third year that I finally admitted to myself: I was miserable."

I frowned. "So, you just... gave up?"

Anna laughed softly. "I wouldn't call it giving up. I'd call it finding myself. You see, while I was in school, I volunteered at a free clinic on weekends, helping with paperwork and translating for patients. I didn't realize it at the time, but those Saturdays were the only time I felt alive. I loved being there, seeing the impact we had on people's lives. That's when it clicked—I wasn't meant to be in a surgeon's room, with all the concentration and quietness. I was meant to care for people, to be there when they needed someone the most."

I leaned forward, captivated. "But weren't your parents upset?"

"Oh, they were furious," Anna admitted, her eyes twinkling with amusement. "They thought I was throwing my life away. And honestly, it was hard at first. Being a nurse doesn't feel as prestigious as being a top doctor in the surgical field. I felt like I was disappointing them. But as I went through nursing school, I realized something important: You can't live your life trying to make other people happy. If you do, you'll wake up one day and realize you're the one who's miserable."

Her words hung in the air, heavy with truth.

"So, what happened? Are they still upset?"

Anna smiled, a hint of pride in her expression. "Not anymore. They came around eventually. Once they saw how much I loved what I was doing and how fulfilled I was, they started to understand. And now? They tell everyone their daughter's a nurse, like it was their idea all along."

I laughed, but her story left a deep impression on me.

Anna leaned closer, her tone gentle but firm. "Jasmine, whatever path you choose in life, make sure it's yours. Not your parents', not society's, not anyone else's. Some careers might give you money or fame, but none of that matters if you hate what you do. Passion is what keeps you going on the hard days. Without it, even the best paycheck won't make you happy."

Her words struck a chord I didn't even know existed. For so long, I'd been focused on what my parents wanted for me, on being the daughter they could be proud of. But now, I wondered: What did I want?

Anna must have seen the look on my face because she patted my hand reassuringly. "You don't have to have all the answers right now. Just promise me one thing: When the time comes, listen to your heart, not the noise around you."

As Anna stood to return to her duties, I stayed behind, replaying our conversation in my mind. For the first time, I felt a flicker of hope, not just for the future my parents wanted, but for a future that felt truly mine.

I had felt guilty about the way I had spoken to my parents in the morning, but now I knew it had been the right thing to do.

CHAPTER 14

Overwhelm

THE KNOCK on the window made me jump, sending a jolt through my entire body. I didn't even need to look to know it was Liam. He always had his own way of doing things—like using the window instead of the door.

I set my book down and hurried to let him in, my heart secretly racing because deep down I'd been waiting for him.

When he walked in, his presence filled the room. Only he could make a nurse's uniform look good. The soft light of the evening caressed his face, making his features look even more perfect. Today, he had messy hair with some strands falling over his face, making me want to move them away so I could see him better.

"You're staring too much," I muttered under my breath, trying to force my eyes away.

Stop looking at him like that.

But before I could do something, he caught me. It was like he could sense everything I was thinking. Our eyes locked, and a knowing smile tugged at the corners of his lips.

We stayed like that for a moment that felt eternal. Despite

my best efforts, something about him always pulled me in, making it harder and harder to resist.

"Guess where I was today," he finally said, putting his backpack on the floor and bending down to open it.

"The library, of course," I replied with a playful smile, my eyes focused on what he was doing.

I'd been waiting for Thursday to come for hours. I knew he would come and tell me about his experience with the new place I recommended, and I was anxious to know if he liked it.

He pulled something out of his bag and held it out toward me. It was a beautifully crafted bookmark adorned with intricate designs and vibrant colors.

"For you," he said softly, his voice carrying a warmth that made my heart skip a beat.

I took the bookmark in my hands, unable to hide my excitement. It was a thoughtful and unexpected gift, but it was a way to show me he cared.

"You didn't have to bring me anything," I said softly, without taking my eyes off the bookmark. I felt a little guilty thinking that he felt he would have to bring me something from every place I recommended, but at the same time, I was happy he took his time to think about me.

"I know," he whispered. "But I want you to have a memory of every place you dream of, to make you feel everything it is real, and that at some point you'll be the one who will see those things."

There was nothing more to add. At that very moment, my night felt complete.

∾

"So, tell me everything, and don't avoid any details like the last time," I demanded. We both sat at the window facing each other. This time, I made a deliberate effort to sit with my legs crossed, creating more distance between us. I knew that whenever I got closer to him, something inside me stirred with a feeling I couldn't quite define. And I didn't want to keep feeding it.

"I chose the public library because it was the biggest one I could find in the city, and I'm glad I did it; it was beautiful," he started. "You were right about something; it was a little overwhelming at first. But then I spent hours looking at every shelf," he admitted.

As he spoke, I found myself fascinated by the passion and enthusiasm in his voice.

"Also, I picked three random books," he explained. "I didn't even bother to read the summaries. I just went with the book cover and vibes."

I laughed hard. "Wasn't it difficult not knowing what the books were about?"

He shook his head. "Sometimes, it's more about the experience than knowing what to expect. Besides, I wanted to prove a point that it doesn't matter what you pick if you like the genre."

I found these last words difficult to believe. I hated surprises and uncertainty, especially because I feared the unknown. I began to wonder if this feeling was thanks to the cancer or if it had always been like this.

I don't remember much of my childhood. I felt it was pretty average. Maybe being an only child meant that I never fully developed independence and initiative like other people. My parents had always been overprotective and made almost all the decisions for me, which made it easier for me to just go with the flow.

"What about you?" Liam asked, taking me out of my thoughts. "How was your week? Did you draw me the next place?"

"It was a good week," I replied, thinking about all the new

things I'd learned from the people I started talking to around the hospital. How different individuals from various worlds have distinctive points of view about what a good place means.

I stood up and went to my folder of drawings, taking the one I made for today. I also took the list of places I'd collected from the employees and people I met during those few days, as well as one of the cookies Donna brought me that I'd saved for Liam.

"Here," I said, handing him the drawing. "I also have a lot of places I collected from many people. You won't believe all the stories the employees told me."

Liam took the sketch and started analyzing it. The new drawing showed him sitting at a bar counter; bottles of alcohol were in the background, and he was scanning the place.

I'd never been to a nightclub before, so I was afraid my drawing wouldn't be accurate. But based on what I'd seen in movies and the way Hellen described it, I felt like I did a good job.

"Do you want me to go to… a bar?" Liam asked, confused when he saw the paper.

I sat next to him and nodded. "Hellen and some nurses told me good stories about those places. I thought it would be a fun spot."

I looked at him and realized his expression was doubtful as he looked at the drawing. "What's wrong?"

"You don't look like the type of person who would enjoy those places," he admitted.

"Are you telling me I'm a boring type of girl?"

He stayed in silence for a while, as if he were thinking of the correct words to say how he felt. "I just don't picture you there. I've never been to one before, either," he finally added.

I looked at his tattoos and looked at him with a raised eyebrow, incredulous.

He understood my expression and said, "Are you being prejudiced, Mine?"

I smiled. "Don't blame me. You started. I could be a pretty bad girl trapped in this place. There are a lot of things I haven't done that I wish I had."

He got serious and looked at me with an expression that made my stomach feel tickled. "What things? Can you give me an example?"

My nerves kicked into overdrive, and I struggled to form a coherent response. "I... I don't know," I stammered, avoiding his probing gaze. Maybe it was a mistake to say those words. Maybe it was better if he thought I was a shy, simple girl with nothing to offer because the alternative was having to prove something that I wasn't yet capable of.

He let out a sarcastic laugh, clearly sensing my nerves. His eyes bore into mine as if daring me to meet his gaze, but I refused to look at him.

"Here," I offered, passing him the cookie in an attempt to shift the conversation. "Donna, the cleaning lady, bought me these cookies. I left one for you."

As he took the cookie from my hand, his fingers brushed against mine. It was as if he were deliberately testing my boundaries. I looked at him, and he was already glancing back at me.

"Thank you," he whispered softly.

Slowly, he opened the plastic package and broke a piece of cookie. Then, he brought it to his lips, his eyes never leaving mine. "You're right. They are delicious."

I knew he was talking about the cookie, but my heart started racing uncontrollably. I began to feel like my breathing was becoming more difficult to manage. Yet I stayed there, looking into Liam's eyes. Unable to take any other action.

"Jasmine?" Someone's knock on the door startled me,

causing me to jump in my seat. From her voice, I assumed it was Anna.

I tore my gaze away from Liam, feeling a flush of embarrassment creeping up my cheeks. "What's up, Anna?" I called out, my voice betraying a hint of nervousness.

"The door is locked. Can you open it, please?"

"Yeah, give me a minute." I started walking, but Liam grabbed me by the left wrist and pulled me toward him. I instinctively placed my free hand on his chest, creating a physical barrier between us.

He drew me closer, his touch firm yet gentle as he cupped my chin, forcing me to meet his gaze. "Thanks for everything, Mine," he murmured softly. "See you on Monday."

"Don't leave. Everything will be okay," I whispered, my voice barely audible above the pounding of my heart.

"It's my time to go. Congratulations again, you made it to another day," he replied.

I looked at the clock. It was 11:55 p.m. He said this phrase again because I survived another day. He made me feel that every day counted. Like every extra minute I spent breathing was worth it.

Life had never felt like this to me. I used to waste so much time just lamenting myself. Now it felt like every minute I'm not doing anything meaningful is a sin.

When did I start thinking differently?

Reluctantly, he released me from his grasp and made his way toward the window. I watched in silence as he disappeared into the night, and when I couldn't see him from where I was, I rushed to the door to let the nurse in, trying to recover my breath in the process.

"Why was the door locked?" she inquired as she entered the room, her eyes scanning the space for any signs of distress.

"I'm not sure. Perhaps Hellen accidentally locked it when

she left after dinner," I replied, attempting to compose myself. "Why are you here, anyway?"

In all the months I'd been locked up here, I could count on my hands the number of times someone had come after Hellen gave me dinner. It was a surprise to see someone here.

"The monitor on your right hand notified us that your heart rate was accelerated. I wanted to make sure everything was okay. Your cheeks are a little reddened. Let me check if you have a fever."

I looked down at the bracelet that I always have on my right hand and smiled.

"Don't worry. I'm better than ever."

CHAPTER 15

Anxiety

AFTER ANNA LEFT, I found myself lost for what to do next. My mind was in a thousand places at once, making it difficult to focus on anything productive, so I opted to watch a series.

But that didn't work. My thoughts raced in different directions. I was thinking about Liam's touch on my wrist, his presence still palpable even though he was no longer there. His big eyes. His words. Despite my efforts to maintain a distance between us, it seemed like he had a way of drawing me closer with each passing moment.

Could it be possible that he also has feelings for me? Even a little portion of it?

Part of me felt it. But there was no way it could be true. I was uglier than ever. I didn't have hair. My nails were purple. I was very thin.

I'd heard stories of people who saw past physical appearances and valued inner beauty above all else. But I struggled to believe that such a thing could happen to me.

I didn't even have a good personality.

Even if Liam felt something for me, what could I offer him in return?

I looked at my iPad. I didn't understand what was happening in that episode of the series I was watching because I wasn't paying much attention. I didn't have the concentration to watch a series either.

I stopped the video, stood up from the sofa, and started pacing the room, as if I could outrun my thoughts. But it was pointless. No matter how fast or far I walked, I couldn't escape the storm inside me.

Maybe what I truly needed was to see him again, outside this room, where he couldn't hide his true personality.

How would he react if we were around a lot of people?

Maybe I felt special because I didn't know what he was like in the real world. He was probably like that with everyone, and I was here making a movie in my head.

I might have been projecting my own desires onto him, mistaking his kindness for something more than it truly was. I'd seen how tender he was with the kid. Maybe his frequent visits were merely his way of trying to lift my spirits, nothing more.

Without fully realizing what I was doing, I found myself at the door, my hand poised to open it, ready to find him wherever he was.

I opened the door carefully and started wandering. I didn't even know where his workstation was, but I was determined to track him down.

After walking aimlessly for a while, I arrived at the lobby, where Ronnie was using her cell phone. She turned her gaze up to where I was standing, doing nothing. "Hello, Miss. Will you need the pill tonight?"

"No, actually, I want to thank Liam for taking care of me when I had a headache the other day. Could you tell me exactly where he has to work tonight?"

This was the second time I'd asked Ronnie for Liam. Hopefully, this wouldn't cause any problems.

"You still don't know his last name?"

I shook my head. "No, sorry."

She looked at me, worried. "And are you sure you don't want to wait until he goes to your room again?"

"It's not like I have anything better to do," I responded, making her stop all the questions and start searching on the computer out of guilt.

She wrote down on a sheet of paper three possible places where each Liam in the hospital worked. "One of them is in a building outside this zone. I don't recommend you go there tonight; it could be dangerous for your health. I wrote it just in case, but I don't want you to go there, okay?"

"Okay," I agreed, taking the list from her and making my way to the door.

But before I could leave, Ronnie stopped me. "Jasmine, before you go, I wanted to ask you a question."

I turned around a little nervously, thinking she'd already figured out my plans. "Sure, what's up?" I tried to say casually.

"Did you finish the book from the other night?"

The question took me by surprise. I remembered that she'd told me it was a good book and suggested I read it in the park, but I didn't know she was actually paying enough attention to me to do a follow-up.

Was she really genuinely interested in being my friend, or was she just being nice?

"I did, it was good, thanks."

She smiled. "I'm glad you liked it; you should read the last book the author released; it's just as good as the one you read. Let me know if you want me to lend it to you. I've already finished it."

"Thank you very much, I'd like that," I responded. "I should probably go before it gets late, but it was nice talking to you."

"Of course, good night, Jasmine. I'm here if you want to talk more about books."

As I walked to the lab, I kept thinking that maybe the people in this hospital were nicer than I'd imagined, and I was just blocking everyone out because of my own fears. Perhaps the only person worried about leaving this world or hurting someone with my absence was myself.

~

The first location on the list led me to the hospital laboratory, where two young men were busy organizing bottles. None of them was Liam.

"Excuse me," I said, my voice weak from the nerves of talking to unknown people. "Is Liam here right now?"

The two guys looked at each other like I'd made a joke, and then one of them spoke up, "I'm Liam; what can I do for you?"

My expression turned sad, filled with disappointment. "Oh, I'm sorry. The nurse must have mistaken the person I was looking for."

I turned and started walking before they could speak again, ready to go to the next location, the Diagnostic Imaging zone. I'd never been there at night, so there was a possibility that Liam was there, especially considering interns were often assigned to this department.

When I arrived, I took a deep breath, already exhausted from the cardio session. I sat in an empty chair to recover my breath with my head down when someone stood up in front of me.

"Jasmine? What are you doing here?"

I looked up and saw Dr. Lynn, one of the ultrasound technicians, standing in front of me.

"Oh, hi, I'm looking for someone," I said casually, trying

to sound as chill as possible. "His name is Liam. Do you know if he's here?"

Dr. Lynn nodded in acknowledgment, gesturing toward a group of interns gathered behind the reception counter. "He's over there, the one behind the computer. You shouldn't be here at this time of night; let me arrange for someone to escort you back to your room once you're finished."

Thanking her, I approached the counter, where a young man I didn't recognize was busy working on the computer. He looked up and greeted me with a friendly smile. "Hi, what can I do for you?" he asked politely.

He wasn't who I was looking for either, and although I tried not to show a disappointed face again, my frustration was palpable.

"Oh, uhm, yeah, I want to know when my next sonogram is scheduled?" I lied.

Dr. Lynn was still close to where I was, and it would have been weird not to ask him anything after I was supposed to be looking for him.

"Sure. What's your name?"

"Jasmine Russell."

He started typing on the computer in front of him, and after some seconds, he said, "Next Wednesday. Just before the chemotherapy."

His words gave me chills all over my body. I'd been so distracted these days that I hadn't realized that the next chemo was close.

Chemo days were the worst part of my life. It was like feeling pain and death close to me over and over again. The anticipation was almost worse than the treatment itself. A slow, suffocating dread crept into my bones, making every breath feel heavy with exhaustion and uncertainty.

Each session was a brutal assault on my body, where toxic chemicals would flood my veins, simultaneously fighting the cancer and destroying everything in their path. My muscles would ache, my skin would feel like it was burning from the inside, and waves of nausea would roll through me like relentless tides. Sometimes, I felt like there was no point in putting me through all this, but the only person who never had any hope was me, so I had to suffer through each treatment until my body couldn't take it anymore. Each chemo day was a battlefield, fighting a war inside my own skin with no guarantee of victory.

"Thanks," I managed to say with a forced smile.

I turned around and started walking towards my room before Lynn could find someone to accompany me, feeling like I'd failed this mission.

Where are you when you're not in my room, Liam? And why does no one seem to know who you are?

CHAPTER 16

Trust

THE NEXT DAY, Ronnie showed up in my room with the book she'd promised. I'd just finished my breakfast and had nothing to do until lunch, so I told her to stay so we could talk more about other books.

"Did you really read that thriller in one night?" Ronnie said, laughing.

"I couldn't stop!" I admitted, holding up my hands in mock surrender. "I had to know who the killer was!"

She laughed, shaking her head. "You're amazing. Honestly, I'd have done the same if I had more free time."

We chatted for a bit about the twists in books and how neither of us saw some endings coming. But as the conversation lulled, I found myself staring at the book in my lap, my thoughts drifting elsewhere.

"Ronnie?" I said hesitantly.

"Yeah?"

"What would you do if you had a friend who you felt was hiding something from you?"

She raised an eyebrow, tilting her head curiously. "Are we still talking about books?"

"Uh, yeah, sure," I lied quickly, trying to sound casual. "I read this book where a guy was constantly lying to the protagonist. But, like, he was doing it for good reasons. Do you think lies are ever justified?"

Ronnie leaned against the wall, crossing her arms as she considered my question. "That's a tricky one," she admitted. "But first, let's get something straight—hiding something isn't always the same as lying."

I looked at her, puzzled. "What do you mean?"

"Well," she began, leaning forward, "sometimes people keep things from us because they're trying to protect us. It's not about deception or betrayal—it's about love. They're not lying; they're shielding us from something they think will hurt us."

"But isn't that still wrong?" I countered. "Shouldn't we always know the truth?"

Ronnie sighed, her expression softening. "In an ideal world, maybe. But life isn't black and white, Jasmine. Sometimes, the people who love us have to make hard decisions. They might not tell us everything because they think it's what's best for us. It doesn't mean they don't trust us—it means they care so much that they're willing to carry the burden themselves."

Her words sank in, but I couldn't shake the unease in my chest. "But doesn't that make it harder to trust them?"

Ronnie nodded slowly. "It can, especially if we don't understand their reasons. But that's where communication and trust come in. You have to ask yourself: Has this person ever given me a reason to doubt their actions? Do they have my best interests at heart? If the answer is yes, then maybe it's worth giving them the benefit of the doubt."

I glanced down at the book in my hands, running my fingers along its spine. "So, you're saying it's okay for someone to hide things if they're doing it for the right reasons?"

She smiled gently. "I'm saying that love isn't always easy or straightforward. The people who care about us will sometimes make choices we don't understand. It doesn't mean they're trying to hurt us—it means they're human. And trusting someone you love means accepting that they might not always tell you everything but believing they have your best interests at heart."

Although I didn't want to admit it, I felt that part of what she was saying made sense. I thought about Liam and the moments when I'd felt he was holding something back. Was it possible that he wasn't lying to me but trying to protect me in ways I couldn't see?

Ronnie reached out and placed a hand on mine, her eyes warm and kind. "Trust isn't about knowing everything. It's about believing in someone's intentions, even when things don't make sense."

I nodded slowly, letting her words sink in. "Thanks, Ronnie. Your words helped me a lot."

"Anytime," she said with a smile. Then, with a teasing glint in her eye, she added, "Now, if we're done being philosophical, how about we talk about that new book of yours? I want to hear all your theories before you spoil the ending for me."

I laughed, grateful for her change of topic. I didn't feel like explaining to her why I was asking those questions. And she seemed to have realized it.

CHAPTER 17

Lonliness

OVER THE PAST FOUR DAYS, my life has become a spiral of new activities during the night hours.

After Dr. Butler showed me the photos he'd taken on his yacht and after the conversation I'd had with Anna the other day, I became interested in photography as a career. So, every night after dinner, I'd been researching photography courses, studying different types of cameras and lenses, and determining what preparation I needed to take good photos.

So far, I've found two good courses on it.

I mentioned it to my parents on Sunday, and they were positive that I'd found a new hobby, so they agreed to buy me one of these courses by the end of the month. My father apologized to me for our conversation about college the other day. He said he was worried that I didn't want to think about a future, which was why he was pushing me toward a career. But seeing me talk about photography gave them hope that I had something to focus on.

So they were totally supportive of whatever I wanted to do.

My nights weren't only filled with study sessions and

camera diagrams. A significant part of them was also dedicated to conversations. I started spending at least an hour every day interacting with everyone around me.

As word spread that I was becoming more extroverted, the nurses, staff, and even the doctors began to engage in small talk every time they popped into my room. Our discussions evolved from just places to explore to music, series, and even books.

Thanks to their talks, my entertainment options expanded, and I no longer had only Hellen's limited catalog of recommendations.

Every person offered a unique perspective and preference in things to do, so I'd found myself with a wide variety of options, from listening to soap operas to watching cartoons and horror movies.

I learned that Ronnie always had something to say about books, that Frank was a shy person but very eager to socialize with others, that if Donna comes to clean my room and I talk to her about her children, she probably won't leave until Hellen comes with lunch, and that Anna is a very focused but kind-hearted person.

Even Dr. Butler, who seemed serious and intimidating, told me that he cries at the end of Korean series that he watches with his wife.

Seeing how everyone was actively collaborating to make me feel human again filled my heart with joy. Not because of the small gossip, the feeling of being included, or the polite smiles; it was the realization of being genuinely cared for, of being seen not as a case number but as a person with dreams, fears, and desires.

Every conversation I had, every shared interest, and every moment of understanding made me realize that people were willing to make connections with me despite my condition.

I was never truly alone.

For that reason, now I knew I had to make every minute count like I couldn't waste another second anymore.

However, there was one problem I couldn't get out of my head this week: Wednesday's chemotherapy.

"Happy start to the week, Jasmine!" Hellen entered the room, screaming so loud it almost got me out of bed.

"There will be no happy week; chemo is on Wednesday," I replied, more discouraged than ever.

She began to organize the table to put my breakfast there, and without moving her gaze toward me, she began to speak. "Of course it's going to be a happy week. It's one less process you have to go through, one less week to be here, one less week to wonder if you'll survive. There are a lot of good things about chemo week."

"I could mention a couple of bad things, too."

I got out of bed and sat on the couch. She looked at me directly and handed me the napkin and fork. "Well, if you want negative things, you'll find them. Everything in life has its positive and negative side to it."

She was right, and the last thing I needed this week was to start a pointless argument with her.

"I need a favor from you," I said, changing the conversation.

"There you go, I like this; give me some missions for today, honey," she said, more excited than I would have liked.

I rolled my eyes at her enthusiasm. "On the paper on the nightstand, there's a place I want you to go. Apparently, Liam works in that area; I just want you to go and confirm that it is indeed him."

She crossed her arms and raised an eyebrow, making me blush at what I'd asked her to do. "Why don't you go by yourself?"

"It's too far, and I don't want Liam to think I'm following

him. I already had too much embarrassment with the last two guys who work here."

"What did you do? I need to hear that story."

I started stuffing food into my mouth. "No thanks, what you really need is to go to work and stop bothering me."

She laughed. "You'll never change, right?"

"It's not in my plans for today." I smiled.

Three hours later, my mind went back to Liam.

Did he follow my request and go to a bar this weekend? Is he coming to my room tonight? Will I be able to confront him about who he really is?

Every moment, my curiosity intensified, pushing me to the edge of my comfort zone. Why did I distrust him so much? Why couldn't I just accept that he was a nurse who was changing my life, as Ronnie explained to me? Did I really always look for the negative side of things?

Hellen was right. I should have gone by myself; seeing him working with my own eyes was the only way I could calm down.

For better or worse, answers were what I needed. And it was about time that I got them.

It was almost ten-thirty when Liam appeared at my window.

"Let's go upstairs, I have to show you something." He extended his hand for me to go out the window, and I took it without thinking much.

The truth was that even though I'd been consumed by thoughts of him all weekend, now that I was face-to-face with him, I was scared. Being in front of him paralyzed my ability to confront him. His presence made me feel different, like I could no longer behave like a little girl anymore.

His mere existence made me want to forget everything I'd

been thinking to tell him and just focus on us, on the moment. Deep down, I knew his presence was going to be brief, and I wanted to take advantage of every second he would allow me to be by his side.

I don't know if I was feeling all these emotions because he just had this effect on me or because he looked better than ever today. His hair was neat; it seemed like he had a new haircut. Plus, he was smiling. A smile that made me question if every bad thought I'd had of him in the past four days was worth it.

His face and demeanor made me think that he had a really good weekend.

Had he met someone at the bar and wanted to talk to me about her?

I felt a churn in my stomach, and my cheeks flushed at the thought, so I tried to banish it from my mind before he noticed. I didn't want Liam to make me feel all those emotions, but it was like I couldn't control them anymore.

When we reached the top, I stopped for a moment to contemplate the entire surroundings. In the middle of the floor, there was a tablecloth and some pillows, a speaker, his backpack, and a bouquet of jasmine. He'd made us a picnic.

"Are all of these for me?" I asked, feeling my face starting to brighten with the whole scene.

"Of course they are," he replied. "There was nothing I could bring you from the bar that wouldn't do you harm, so I had to improvise."

Everything was perfect, just like him.

My lips curved upward, and I punched him lightly in the arm. I didn't know how to act around him, especially now that my walls were completely destroyed. I'd never had a friend this close. I'd always had schoolmates, but not anyone to share moments like these with, so I didn't know what it was like to act normal. So, I walked to the spot he'd prepared, sat on one of the pillows, and picked the bouquet to admire it closer.

Liam sat next to me and fixed his gaze on me. I knew I had to face him, but I couldn't take my eyes off the flowers. And I wasn't prepared to say anything yet.

It was the first time that someone who wasn't part of my family gave me flowers, and even if it was a cliché, the fact that he brought me jasmines felt like a special thought. It was magical, even surreal in a way, because I knew I didn't deserve it. I hadn't done anything but be rude to him all this time.

"So, how was the bar?" I asked, breaking the awkward silence between us.

He changed position so that we were facing each other, close enough so that our knees touched each time he moved them, like he wanted to see my face all the time he was going to speak.

"I'm going to be completely honest with you, but I don't want you to feel bad because it wasn't your fault." He paused to observe my expression, so I tried to remain completely neutral so he wouldn't change his opinion.

"I hated it."

"What?" I shouted, finally moving my gaze to his face. "I need a logical explanation; all the nurses told me it was one of the most entertaining places you can go with your friends to have fun. What did you do wrong?"

"Why do you think that if it didn't work, it's because I did something wrong?"

Caught off guard by his unexpected question, I tried to ease the tension with a weak attempt at humor. "I don't know. Maybe you don't know how to have fun."

To my relief, Liam played along. He pretended to be in pain and then stated, "I know how to have fun. Bars are just not what you imagine." His playful way of answering brought a smile to my face.

"So, tell me, what did you do there?" I was a little curious to know the whole story, but what I wanted most was to be able to hear him speak as long as possible. It was a perfect excuse to be able to admire him up close without being awkward.

Will anyone ever be able to look at me the way I was looking at him right now?

"I chose a random place that was busy enough to carry out our experiment and looked around. Everyone was busy at their tables with their drinks or trying to impress the person they had in front of them; some people were simply using their phones. I was alone, so I sat at the bar and ordered a shot. Then I stared at the people dancing and realized that this was definitely not my place."

He remained silent, looking at me, and that's when I realized that the story was over.

"And that's it?" I said, feeling a pang of disappointment. It wasn't the grand adventure I was hoping to hear.

Many of the girls at the nurse station told how they met different people there, danced with strangers, and even made new friends to hang out with later. Maybe he wasn't telling me everything so as not to make me feel bad. Maybe he'd met someone and didn't want to tell me that part.

"What were you expecting?" he asked as if he genuinely didn't understand what he should have done.

"I don't know, maybe I thought that you would meet someone and dance all night."

"Did you want me to meet someone?"

I looked at him with a serious expression. Obviously, I didn't want to. The last thing I wanted was for Liam to find love thanks to me. It wasn't like I believed he would fall for me, but hearing him talk about someone else would feel strange. So I lied. "Sure, that was the whole point."

"Maybe I'm not that cute to be approachable," he whispered, like it was hard for him to tell this lie.

Because we both knew he wasn't telling the truth. He was

beautiful, and any woman would be lucky to just admire him. I couldn't imagine how someone would see him and not want to talk to him right away. But of course, I would never say that to him. I didn't even know why I was suddenly thinking about him differently.

What changed?

I looked at him again and realized that he was still waiting for me to answer, so I switched the conversation a little bit. "What a disappointment. You almost took away my desire to go to one. Now I'm 100% sure it was your fault. You probably had an unfriendly face the whole time there."

Ignoring my last words, he took the speaker that was on the side of the blanket. "That's why I brought this with me. I wanted you to feel the bar experience tonight. Maybe when you go to a real one later, you won't be disappointed like I was."

I watched as he set up the speaker on top of a pillow, a small smile playing on his lips.

Then, he reached into his bag and pulled out a bottle and two shot glasses. "And I even brought a little something to drink. Don't worry, it's apple juice," he chuckled, and I let out a laugh.

"See? That's why I think you're not funny at all," I replied, nudging him playfully, to which he feigned a hurt expression. But a moment later, we both burst into laughter.

Liam turned on the speaker, filling the air with music that I didn't recognize. He opened the bottle and filled the glasses in front of him. "So, do you come here often?"

"What?" His question took me by surprise. He knew this was the second time I was on the roof. But I realized he wasn't being literal; he was playing a role, keeping up the "bar" pretense. The game was ridiculous—and yet, somehow, I loved it.

"You have to pretend we just met. That's how it works," he explained.

"You're impossible, Liam."

"This is my first time here, actually," he kept ignoring me. "What do you recommend I drink?"

I took one of the glasses and handed it to him. "It's a little strong, but you'll get used to it with the second glass. The first one's on me."

He took the glass and smiled. "I knew I should go straight to you from the moment I saw you walk through that door."

I raised an eyebrow. "Are you always so intense?"

"Just when someone looks interesting enough."

I rolled my eyes, but inside, I made a mental note of his pickup lines. I felt that I would probably use them somewhere one day.

We played along for a while, exchanging small talk as we pretended to be just two people meeting in a bar. Talking to him was easy in a way I wasn't familiar with, maybe because of all the time I'd spent here avoiding everyone or because we simply shared a strong connection.

And then, out of nothing, he stood up, extending his hand toward me. "May I have this dance?" he asked.

I froze for a moment, unsure of what to do. I wasn't sure if I was ready for that kind of closeness. But then again, wasn't that why I was here with him in the first place? To escape from my room as far as possible, even if it was with my imagination? So, I took his hand and stood in front of him. "I don't know how to dance," I confessed, adjusting my hat because of the nerves.

"Me neither," he whispered, his mouth against my ear. "But don't worry; we're not in a real bar; nobody is actually watching us."

He took my hands, guiding them to rest around his neck. The touch was gentle, almost hesitant, like he didn't want to scare me off. Then, with a confident yet gentle touch, he placed his hands on my waist, pulling me closer as we swayed to the rhythm of the music.

I wasn't sure if what we were doing could even be called dancing. We were simply moving in circles, shifting from one spot to another, our movements slow and deliberate. But as we twirled in this quiet, intimate dance, our eyes remained locked on each other's faces.

There was something so casual, yet so thoughtful, in the way he did things—like he genuinely wanted me to feel some joy. I hadn't realized how much I needed to be distracted until now, standing on the hospital roof with him, pretending we were somewhere far away.

Being with Liam felt effortless, like we were in our own little world, far away from where we really were, and everything that came with it.

This was different from anything I'd ever experienced before. I almost felt sad about how meaningless my life had been. At that precise moment, I realized that I no longer cared who he was. He could be the devil himself, and I was happy that he was guiding me to hell.

Journal entry 5

August 5, 2024

My relationship with Jasmine has been improving little by little. She has been smiling more, is being more communicative, and is even nicer to everyone around her.

I've been watching her from afar during the day, and I've seen how she's been talking to everyone who approaches her. I'm glad to know that I've been such a positive influence in her life.

I now know why it never worked with anyone else. Jasmine needed someone like me, who could understand her in the best way possible. And I needed someone like her, too.

She's been helping me understand a lot about my life: how hope was never part of it, but it was necessary, how negativity only clouds your vision of what is really worth it. And how sometimes we worry about the wrong situations when there are better things in life where we can focus our energies, even in the most diffi-cult moments.

For that reason, I decided to do something positive for her before her next chemo to clear her mind a bit, and it turned out better than I expected.

I bought her flowers, which was a very basic move on my part, but seeing her light up when I gave them to her was worth every penny.

We danced under the moonlight, and it felt like everything was normal for a moment. I saw her with happiness that I'm sure she hadn't experienced in a long time.

The whole time we were up there, I wondered what things would have been like if we'd met under another circumstance. I know she won't forgive me when she knows the truth, so I decided to be selfish for a moment and just let things flow. I chose to be happy, too, while it lasted, because I knew it wouldn't be for long.

But here's the thing. A part of me feels like a jerk. Sneaking around, showing up at her window, all this secret stuff—it doesn't feel right. Jasmine deserves better than some mystery guy. She deserves someone who's honest with her, someone who's there for her, not just watching from the sidelines.

The problem is, I'm scared. Scared of what she'll say if I tell her the truth. I'm scared she'll lock herself away again because of me. Scared of ruining the good thing we have going, even if it is built on a foundation of sand. I don't know what to do. Maybe I should just keep quiet and hope for the best. But that guilt keeps gnawing at me.

I've never had a job where my identity was an issue, but now it's weighing on me more than ever. She's starting to trust me, and I feel like I'm going to betray her when she finds out who I really am.

CHAPTER 18

Comfort

MY MOM WAS SITTING NEXT to me, using her phone with one hand and holding my hand with the other. In my free arm was the IV, with the chemo going inside my body slowly. Every drop that came down felt like it was draining my energy.

We were in a special room where nurses were monitoring my vital signs every fifteen minutes to make sure everything was going well. My family and doctors made sure I was as comfortable as possible. But I'd only been here an hour and already wanted to run as far as possible.

Dr. Butler scheduled the chemo for as early as possible today so that it wouldn't affect my sleeping routine and I could go to sleep after lunch. But I'd been here long enough to know that today wasn't going to be a typical day.

This medication was going to turn at least the next five days of my life upside down. I was already feeling nauseous. My veins were itching, and my head felt like it would explode at any time.

"Do you need a bag?" my mom asked.

I turned to see her and found her scanning me, worried; it seemed like my facial expressions were hard to hide.

"Not yet, don't worry. I think my mind is making this process feel worse than what it actually is," I lied.

This was one of the worst sensations I'd ever felt. No matter how many chemo treatments I've had or how many I have left, I'll never get used to them. But it was pointless to worry anybody. This was the only way to have a chance of survival, and I didn't have any other options.

This was my third chemo for this cancer (plus the other eight from my previous one), and my dad had never been present for any of them. He made sure to come enough times the days before so that his presence would be "unnecessary" on these days.

His excuses are always "that it's better for one person to stay while the other works, just in case," and that "it's better to divide the workload and my mother is better at taking care of me in a delicate state," but deep down, I knew that he couldn't stand it, see me like this. His only daughter, weaker than ever, was on the verge of not being able to make it.

I didn't blame him. I understand his position and why he does it. I wouldn't want to see a loved one in this state, either. However, part of me has always wanted to have him close. I would like someone other than a nurse to be able to help and support me in this process, especially at night, when my mom was so tired that she preferred to go home.

This happened in the last two chemos. She left me alone in the room, with nothing but an emergency button and no one to hold me when I was in pain with the excuse that I wouldn't need anyone while I was sleeping.

By the time it was over, it was time for lunch. However, I could barely stand by myself, not because I was feeling pain already, but because I was too tired. Hellen took me in a wheelchair to my room, and finally, I was able to close my eyes.

I didn't want food or people around. The only thing I wanted was to sleep.

I don't know how long I'd fallen asleep, but when I woke up, Hellen was sitting on a chair waiting for me.

As soon as she saw that I was waking up, she stood up to check my vitals. "Hi, how are you feeling?"

The chemo doesn't start to take effect until after twelve hours, so all the symptoms I was going to feel after the medication were going to be from now on.

"My head is a little dizzy, and I have chills all over my body, but I'm okay. Where's mom?"

She looked at me tenderly, as if she felt sorry for me, so I knew instantly that my mom wasn't here anymore. "She had to go. It's 10:00 p.m. already, and she works tomorrow. She wanted you to know that she was with you all afternoon. And that she'll come after work tomorrow."

I knew my mom wouldn't be here when I woke up, so there was no surprise in her words. I didn't say anything to Hellen; the scene alone was depressing enough. I nodded slowly, letting her finish the usual checkup.

When she finished, she helped me sit on the couch. "Everything seems to be going well. I wanted to ensure you ate before I left, so take your time, but finish the whole plate. Remember that your defenses will drop considerably, so eating well is crucial."

I tried to eat as much as possible and then said goodbye to Hellen. When I was alone, I attempted to distract myself by watching a TV show on my iPad. But as the minutes stretched into hours, I felt weaker and weaker.

Around 1:00 a.m., the fatigue hit me like a ton of bricks.

With every ounce of energy drained from my body, I tried to reach my bed, and when I was finally there, I closed my eyes.

In the quiet darkness, my mind came alive, drifting through memories and emotions I had long ago buried. My illness wasn't just about the physical pain—it was a heavy weight of hidden feelings, thoughts, and regrets.

I couldn't help but think of all the things that I still wanted to do and how, for all those months, I had done nothing but push everyone away.

I felt this was finally my end, and there wasn't even going to be anyone close to me who could help me in my last moments.

I began to feel discomfort throughout my body. My head was spinning, and even with my eyes closed, I couldn't get rid of that feeling.

And then, I passed out.

～

I felt fingers massaging my cheek.

I tried to open my eyes, but they felt so heavy that I just couldn't do it. The fever had worsened, and despite the cold I felt on the outside, my blood felt like it was boiling, as if it were burning inside. I felt a weight on my head and back, like someone was behind me. Or below me. But it was impossible. Nobody was ever with me at this time. I must have been hallucinating.

Even though I still felt out of energy and the pain was increasing, the way the person was touching my face relaxed me. I didn't know where these hands came from, but they felt like a little piece of heaven in this hell.

Maybe it was my mom who realized that she should be here, so she came back to take care of me and asked for another day at her job. Or dad, who finally let go of his fear of seeing me so fragile and came to make up for his mistake.

"I think I'm dying," I whispered. I wanted whoever was holding me to know I wouldn't last much longer, so they could do something about it.

"Don't be dramatic. You will not die tonight."

That voice. It couldn't be.

Liam?

Suddenly, all my senses were activated. A wave of shock washed over me as my mind struggled to piece together the situation that I was in.

What was he doing here tonight? And why did it feel like my head was in his legs?

"You know why," he answered, sounding like he'd just heard my thoughts. "You wanted me to be here, so I came. You know I wasn't going to leave you alone."

Had I said my questions out loud, or was he reading my mind?

This was all very confusing. I tried to make sense of his words and what they could mean. I'd never told him I wanted him here. This was my most vulnerable state, and all I wanted to do was throw up and suffer in silence.

It was definitely not a situation I wanted him to see me in.

Also, all of this was wrong.

He wasn't supposed to be on my bed. This is the time he's supposed to be working. And if someone entered and found him here, he would be in trouble.

I started thinking about all the reasons why he shouldn't be here right now, but my mind suddenly went blank. He started touching my face again.

If all this was so bad, why did it feel so good? How could he feel like home, feel so safe, and at the same time, so dangerous and problematic?

After a long moment of silence, I decided that I was just going to let myself enjoy the moment. At the end of the day, I was going to die.

A little bit of pleasure wasn't going to hurt anybody. And in his arms, I found the peace I needed to be able to sleep again.

It scared me how much I wanted this—how much I wanted him. But I was also tired of being scared.

For once in my life, I just wanted to feel what made me happy and gave me peace.

CHAPTER 19
Gratitude

OVER THE NEXT THREE DAYS, my mother and Hellen took turns caring for me during the day. Hellen spent the entire morning and afternoon with me, and after 6:00 p.m., my mom would come and help me with whatever I needed until 10:00 p.m.

Thursday and Friday were my worst days. I didn't even have the strength to stand up to go to the bathroom without help.

My sleeping schedule was practically ruined, since all I wanted to do was sleep. And my mental energy didn't let me do anything else either. I was tired, frustrated, and feeling really sick all the time.

However, there was a ray of light among so much shadow and darkness.

I didn't know how, but Liam managed to spend every night with me. He was worried something would happen to me when my mom or Hellen wasn't here, so he ensured I didn't have to be alone during the nights when I felt most vulnerable.

Part of me didn't want him to be there, helping me every

time I had to go to the bathroom to vomit or change my sheets because the ones I had were very sweaty due to the fever. I felt so ugly and weak that I was embarrassed that he was looking at me in that state. If I had to decide, I would tell him to come next week, like my father.

But he didn't give me a choice. He was there because he wanted to take care of me, and he was very good at helping me with all my needs. It was as if he had the exact experience to know what was happening to me at all times, and he always had a way to control every symptom.

I knew he would be an exceptional doctor one day. The way he handled everything I was going through was very professional. He had a passion and talent that only a few nurses had, especially at his age.

~

Tonight was Saturday, Liam's day off.

I wasn't expecting to see him here, but when I opened my eyes at 2:00 a.m., he was there, sitting in a chair beside my bed, his head resting on my bed, and his hand holding mine like he needed to make sure I was there.

I tried not to move or make any noise so he could rest, but that didn't stop me from admiring him. He seemed so peaceful yet so tired.

With my free hand, I moved the hair on his face to see him better, but as my fingers made contact with his skin, I found myself moving my hand all over his face. I wanted to memorize each of his features with my strokes so I could draw this moment later.

He opened his eyes slowly, and our gazes met.

A shy smile graced his lips, mixed with a hint of embarrassment. "Sorry, I didn't mean to fall asleep," he murmured softly.

He didn't move, and our hands didn't stop touching. It was as if he was as comfortable as I was being so close to each other. "You look tired. Why are you here? It's your day off."

"You need me. I couldn't simply go to my home knowing you would be here alone."

"But why?" I asked again. I knew I was sick and needed someone, but sacrificing a day off for me without being mandatory wasn't something someone does for just anyone.

"I've been nothing but rude to you all this time, but you don't seem to give up on me."

"Because I need to save you, Jasmine. I need to make sure you'll be fine." There was urgency in his words, as if he were capable of altering the course of my illness.

Save me?

How could he save me if my sickness was something out of his control? Out of anyone's control?

"But I don't want to be saved," I confessed quietly, my voice barely above a whisper. I didn't want him to feel like he had to protect me. There was nothing anyone could do for me.

I felt different from the person I was weeks ago. I had more energy and began to set goals and plans again. But I still didn't have hope. This was something no one could make me change.

He began to lift his head, so I instinctively sat up to watch him more directly. Our eyes locked, so he got closer until we could feel our breath. My pulse started rising.

"And that's why I'm here," he whispered, his words hanging in the air with a weight that sent a shiver down my spine. "To do everything in my power to make you change your mind. To make you want to live. At least for me."

For him?

I felt like my breath was cut off, but not because of the sickness. Right now, his words were more powerful than any symptoms the chemo could give me.

"Would you do that for me, Mine?" he asked, looking at my lips.

I didn't know what he was referring to; my mind was focused on his eyes, lips, and hands. One of them was still holding mine, and he didn't seem like he was going to let it go any time soon.

"Do... what?" I hesitated, with millions of thoughts running through my brain.

His free hand went up to my cheek as if he was afraid I would escape, and that was his way of keeping me still. He didn't know that there was no other place in the world I would rather be than here, alone in his arms.

"Live," he finally responded. His expression was serious, and the way he said his words sounded like a command. "Live for me."

"I don't know if I could do it; I feel so weak right now. There is still much to heal and—"

"And yet, your heart is beating so fast," he interrupted me, lowering his gaze to my chest and then going to my eyes again. "You want this. I can feel it. So promise me you'll live."

And he was right. At that moment, even with all the complications I'd had in the last three days, I'd never felt more alive. Liam made me feel powerful, like I could be capable of everything. Even to beat a cancer that was killing me inside.

But I just couldn't bring myself to say those words. "I can't promise something that is out of my control."

I was terrified. I didn't want to disappoint him with lies. That's why I had distanced myself from everyone, so I wouldn't have to look them in the eye and tell them that I was going to make it, knowing that I didn't mean it. I got tired of giving false hope to my loved ones while I was dying inside.

"You can, and you will," he responded firmly as if he could make his words come true if I agreed.

And part of me wanted to believe it. Even if I had no hope,

there was something more inside of me growing to the point that having hope didn't matter anymore, and they were all my dreams—all the things that I have been imagining I could do and have been drawing, all the things that other people make me want to try, all the things that I still haven't done and wanted.

Maybe it wasn't hope that I needed but trust.

"Liam."

"Jasmine." He got up and put one knee on my bed, removing more and more space between our bodies.

"I will live."

And just like that, without giving me any warning or asking me if it was the right thing to do, he hugged me with all he had.

And I felt guilty because that hug made me feel like he believed that my words would change everything that was happening to me.

A tear began to fall slowly down my cheek. I could not believe that someone had so much faith in me, even if no one else had it, not even me. Maybe I had been too hard on myself all this time. Maybe a little bit of confidence could help me go through this less painfully.

"Thank you, Liam."

He stopped hugging me and looked at my face. "Why?"

"For being my angel."

A corner of his mouth rose, but there wasn't a drop of happiness in that smile.

Journal entry 6

August 11, 2024

I cannot express in words my feeling of impotence over everything that has happened in these last few days.

Jasmine had her third chemotherapy, and her father wasn't present on any of the days she was sick. Not only that, but she was also left alone every night. As if she didn't have a family.

If only they knew the feeling of regret they would have if something happened to her, they would spend every possible moment of their lives with her. They would never have left her in this hospital in the first place.

I've seen similar situations countless times in the other hospitals I've been to. However, this time, it affected me more than I wanted. I know the story behind it, and I know that she doesn't deserve to be alone.

On several occasions, doctors and nurses try to console themselves by saying that perhaps a patient was alone because they'd been mean to their loved ones, and no one wanted to be with them. But now I know that's not always the case because Jasmine was a good girl full of broken dreams.

I hadn't met anyone who wanted to connect with another person like her. Someone so shy, but at the same time, so eager to express herself.

Luckily, she had me there. I knew exactly what to do and how to support her with every symptom. I haven't left her side for a single night. Seeing her in that state broke my heart; I wanted to be able to transfer all her pain to me if it was going to make her feel better.

So, I crossed a line.

I went to her bed and held her in my arms to make her feel safe. One night, she woke up, and I made her promise to fight, to cling to life, even if it was for me. When she whispered that she agreed, I held her tighter, as if those words themselves could mend the broken pieces inside her.

I know I shouldn't have done any of this. Every second I spent next to Jasmine, I knew it was wrong. But I couldn't do anything else.

Because even if I am the most selfish being, she is the only thing I have. We are connected in a way that no one will ever understand. I knew I risked ruining the mission entirely, but I didn't care. I wanted to hold her and let her know she was safe.

I am desperate to save her, not for myself anymore, but for her.

Because she deserves to live.

CHAPTER 20
Optimism

THAT NIGHT, I slept better than ever, dreaming of a beautiful garden full of colorful flowers that I was collecting in a basket. I was wearing a summer dress, and my hair was long again. It felt so serene and peaceful, as if everything would be okay and that the only thing I should worry about was the next flower I wanted to pick.

When I woke up, I felt different. I had more energy, and for the first time in days, I could get up and walk to the bathroom without feeling completely drained. It was like the effects of the chemotherapy were starting to wear off, and I could finally begin to be myself again.

I stood in front of the mirror in the bathroom and really looked at myself for the first time in a while. Since I'd lost my hair, I'd been avoiding looking at myself too closely. But today, it was like I was glancing beyond my face. And my eyes had a shine that I hadn't seen for a long time.

"You're alive, Jasmine, and you'll stay that way," I whispered.

I had been too hard on myself throughout this entire

process, but not anymore. I wanted to make an effort, not only for myself but for the people who wanted me to be here.

A few hours later, my parents arrived and found me seated at the window, drawing.

"It seems you are already recovering your spirits," my mom said, hugging me.

"I brought you a surprise." My dad handed me a wrapped gift and sat next to me to watch me open it.

Another guilt gift for not being present. He's been doing that since my first cancer. He disappears when I need him the most, and then, when everything is fine, he comes back with gifts to show me that he thought about me all this time and that he misses me. I wonder if my father would change if someone showed him everything he was doing wrong, like Liam had been doing to me, or maybe some people don't change, no matter how wrong they are.

Part of me wanted to yell at him that I didn't want any gifts, that what mattered most to me was his presence, especially if I had little time left, but I didn't want to fight or have a bad time when I was newly feeling well, so I focused on the present. I took the box with my two hands and opened it carefully. When I saw what it was, I couldn't believe my eyes.

"It can't be possible," I exclaimed, looking at my parents with the biggest smile I could put on my face.

It was a professional camera. I held it in my hands as if touching it could make me acknowledge it was real.

I was going to be able to practice right here, in this room, even before I left the hospital. I felt a wave of happiness that I hadn't felt in a while. It was like the moment I decided that everything would be fine, the world started conspiring in my favor.

"I don't know what to say; thank you so much." I stood and hugged them. I knew the sacrifices they'd made to keep me here and ensure that I had everything I needed, but the feeling of abandonment had clouded my ability to be grateful for a long time.

My dad cleared his throat, pulling me out of my reverie. "Remember that this isn't just a toy. You told us that you wanted to see how good you could consider photography as a career, so I hope you practice with a professional approach," he started lecturing.

"Of course," I promised, barely able to contain my excitement, "and I want a favor the next time you come."

"Sure, honey. What else do you want?" my mom asked, with an amusing tone in her voice. She was happy that I was finally excited about something, and I knew she would agree to whatever I asked.

"I want real clothes, like a summer dress," I replied.

They looked at each other like I was asking for a war tank. My pajamas had become all I'd worn these past few months, so wearing different clothes was extremely out of the ordinary. But if, at some point, I wanted to take a photo of myself, I didn't want to look so ugly.

"Really?" my mom asked.

"Yes, why not?" I asked.

My mom laughed. "You're right, why not?"

Later that afternoon, Frank came by my room for a routine blood test. His presence was always calming, though it was clear he didn't realize how much. Frank wasn't like Hellen or Ronnie—his confidence wasn't loud or commanding. Instead, it was soft, like the kind of strength that didn't need to announce itself.

As he prepared his equipment, I watched him in silence

for a moment, gathering the courage to ask the question that had been swirling in my mind.

"Frank?" I finally said.

He looked at me, his eyebrows raised in curiosity. "Yeah?"

"How do you know if someone has... different intentions with you?"

Frank froze mid-motion, the cotton swab in his hand hovering above my arm. His cheeks turned an unmistakable shade of pink, and I couldn't help but smile. For someone who could handle needles and blood without so much as a blink, emotions were clearly his weakness.

"Different intentions?" he echoed, his voice cracking slightly. "What do you mean?"

"Yeah, you know," I said, trying not to laugh at his obvious discomfort. "Like... love. How do you know when you're falling in love with someone?"

His hands fumbled slightly as he set the cotton swab down and reached for the syringe. "Uh, that's... a big question."

I nodded, waiting for him to continue.

He glanced up at me briefly, then quickly looked away, his blush deepening. "I guess," he began hesitantly, "it's when... they start showing up in your thoughts all the time. Like, you can't help but think about them. Even when you're busy or doing something completely unrelated."

His voice was soft, almost as if he were afraid someone else might overhear.

"Okay," I said, encouraging him. "What else?"

Frank cleared his throat, focusing intently on finding the vein in my arm, though I suspected it was more about avoiding my gaze. "It's, uh, when you care about their happiness more than your own. Like... if they're smiling, it doesn't really matter how your day's been—you feel lighter just seeing them happy."

I studied his face as he spoke, noticing how his lips twitched into a small smile as if the very idea made him happy.

"And," he continued, his voice growing softer, "it's when the things that normally don't matter... suddenly do. Like, you start paying attention to the little things they like or the way they laugh. It all feels... important."

I felt my chest tighten slightly, his words resonating more deeply than I expected. "That's... sweet," I admitted. "But how do you know it's love and not just... I don't know, a crush?"

Frank hesitated, his hands stilling as he finished the blood draw. He placed the vial carefully into its holder before finally meeting my gaze. His eyes, shy but sincere, held a quiet kind of wisdom.

"I think you know it's love," he said, his voice barely above a whisper, "when being around them feels like home. Like... no matter what's going on, they make you feel safe. And you'd do anything to protect that feeling, even if it scares you."

For a moment, the room was silent, his words hanging in the air between us.

"That's beautiful," I said softly, my heart swelling with an emotion I couldn't quite name.

Frank's blush deepened, and he quickly busied himself cleaning up the supplies. "I don't know about that," he mumbled. "It's just... what I think."

As he stood to leave, I reached out and touched his arm lightly. "Thank you, Frank. Really."

He looked at me, his eyes widening slightly in surprise before softening into a shy smile. "Anytime," he said, his voice quiet but steady.

When he finished and left the room, I leaned back against the pillows, my mind spinning. His words replayed in my head, stirring something deep inside me.

Was that how I felt about Liam? Or was it something different, something I hadn't fully understood yet?

Frank's timid honesty had left me with more questions than answers, but for the first time, I didn't mind. Maybe love wasn't about knowing—it was about feeling. And for now, I was okay with that.

The only thing left to understand was why Liam acted so differently towards me.

CHAPTER 21

$\mathcal{N}$ervousness

MONDAY WAS A RAINY DAY. The whole morning was cloudy, preventing me from going anywhere to experiment with the camera, so I started to watch videos on how to use the device correctly until my time to sleep came.

When I woke up at night, it was still raining.

Weeks ago, the weather was just background noise to me. I didn't care much whether the sun was shining or the rain was pouring. My world was confined within these four walls, and what happened beyond them didn't matter.

But now, everything has changed. My perspective has shifted completely. Suddenly, I found myself caring about things I had never given a second thought to before. The weather, once insignificant, was now relevant to my mood and plans.

Hellen entered the room and found me staring at the window. "You seem disappointed, dear," she remarked. "Did the rain dampen your spirits?"

"I was hoping to do something today, but it seems the rain will keep me from it," I admitted, my face still fixed on the outside. There was absolutely no one in the parking lot or the green area, and small water spaces were forming where there was no drainage nearby.

She started working on our nightly routine and watched the camera on the nightstand. "Don't worry, little one, tomorrow will be another day. It won't rain forever."

"Of course," I said in a low voice. The rain might not be here forever, but not every night was a Monday. The camera was the least of my concerns; what weighed on my mind was Liam's absence.

I hadn't seen him since our hug on Saturday, and now that I was feeling much better, I wanted a chance to talk to him. But beyond everything we could speak about, I wanted to know if he was going to touch me or hug me again, or if our magical moment was just because I was very sick.

He didn't use the door anymore, which made me think he didn't want to be seen by anyone. It was dangerous and impractical to use the metal stairs in the rain, so it was evident he wasn't coming.

My disappointment must have been evident because Hellen decided to stay with me during dinner. Something she never did. When I finished, she cleaned everything and said, "Get ready, let's take photos of the girls at the station."

I looked at her, confused. "What do you mean?"

"You're sad because you can't take photos outside, right? Well, let's get out of this room and take photos of the girls at the reception. It might not be what you had in mind, but it's a chance for you to practice."

Her suggestion caught me off guard, and I couldn't help but smile. It was incredible how everyone made a constant effort to make me feel better now, which made me wonder if it was always like this. I hadn't noticed it until now because I was too focused on being miserable all the time, and it made me a little sad to think of all the things I could have accomplished before if it weren't for my mindset.

I glanced out the window one last time. The rain was still very heavy. He wasn't coming, so it was better to focus my night on something else.

I got up from the couch, put on my sandals, and took the camera. "Let's go then."

Hellen and I made our way down to the reception area, where a group of nurses was talking and laughing.

"Hey, everyone," Hellen announced as we approached the group. "Today's your lucky day. Jasmine will do some charity work with you and take some photos."

I got a little nervous. This was my first time actually using the camera, so I knew it wouldn't produce anything incredible or professional. Still, the enthusiasm of the girls around me helped ease my nerves. The nurses were just happy to do something different to get entertained tonight, so we took action.

I took photos as if they were for ID cards, photos of the nurses smiling, photos of Anna and Ronnie posing as if they were for magazine covers, and photos as if the guys were working. Frank, who was there by chance as it was his day off from college, didn't like the photos, but he cooperated just "for the cause." The nurses wanted different themes, so I could "practice all possible forms of photography," which led to some pretty different and amazing results.

Two hours later, the camera ran out of battery.

It was incredible how being around the right people sparked my creativity. And how even if it's raining outside, you can still do something fun inside.

I came back to my room with a smile on my face, thinking about all the edits I would do with the pictures I'd just taken, when I saw him. Liam was seated in the window, completely soaked, reading one of my books.

As I closed the door behind me, he raised his gaze to me and smiled. "Hi, Mine."

"What are you doing here? It's raining a lot." I said, scanning the room for something to dry him off, but he stood up and took my left wrist gently, making me stop to look at him.

"You forgot to leave me a drawing, and I need something to do for this week..." he trailed off, studying my expression for a moment before continuing, "Also, I wanted to make sure you were okay. I didn't come on Sunday, so I didn't know how you might be feeling today."

When he finished talking, I realized something: It didn't matter what I did during the day; seeing him had become the best part of it.

Liam and I stood facing each other, a palpable tension between us. Our eyes darted everywhere but to each other's gaze as if we were both afraid of what we might find there. I noticed his Adam's apple bobbing nervously as my eyes lingered on him.

Was he feeling as nervous as I was?

It was as if we no longer knew how to act around each other or even what to say—like he knew he'd crossed a line and needed to confirm that we were fine.

He released my wrist slowly, but his fingers continued brushing mine slightly.

I wondered if, in a different situation, I might have closed the gap between us, taken his hand, or brushed his cheek.

I might have found the courage to express my feelings or ask him about his intentions if I weren't sick?

I know that, at that moment, I couldn't bring myself to do any of those things. Not because I was afraid of rejection, but because I was scared of driving him away. I didn't want him to feel uncomfortable in my presence and decide to never return.

The whole world had changed around me, and I couldn't bear to go back to the loneliness I was used to before he came into my life. I craved his presence, his understanding, and his subtle touch more than I could ever express. Finally, I broke the silence between us. "I feel much better now."

He lifted his eyes to me and whispered, "I could see it."

The way he answered made me sigh. I had no doubt that I was starting to have feelings for this boy.

I didn't know what he was playing now, but I knew I had to stop him before things went too far. At the end of the day, I knew what I was feeling was impossible for a million reasons, and giving free rein to my feelings was only going to get me hurt.

"Look." I put my camera in front of him. "My parents bought me a camera. I'd love to show it to you along with all the photos I took today, but it ran out of battery."

"Don't worry. Next time, we can plan a date so you can show me all the things you've learned."

A date.

That sentence hung in the air. It wasn't just any guy inviting me to get ice cream; the fact that it was Liam who had said those words made it more than just a suggestion to me.

But there was something in his eyes I couldn't place.

These last words carried a weight impossible to ignore. There was something off about Liam. He felt different. He had a sad, worried expression and a somber look, like the time I saw him in the parking lot looking up at the sky. I felt he wasn't here to know if I was really okay, but because he needed someone.

I moved nervously to the table where my drawings were, hoping to divert his attention from whatever was happening in his mind. "I've made some drawings before the chemo; maybe we can go through them together and decide what to do this week."

"Jasmine," he said, like a demand. There was urgency in his words. "I have to tell you something."

Now, it was clear. He wasn't here just to check on me. But I didn't know why he was acting like that. Maybe it was just relief to see me well, or maybe it was something deeper, something he was struggling to articulate.

I left the papers on the table and looked at him. He was still in the same spot but shaking a little, his damp clothes clinging to him uncomfortably.

"My God, Liam, you're too wet and shivering from the cold. You could catch a cold like this." I moved to where he was and touched his forehead. To my surprise, he was cold— very cold.

"I'm fine, I promise," he insisted, his voice tight. "About Saturday…"

"Liam," I cut him off before he could say anything else. There was something that had been bothering me since the weekend, and I wanted to make it clear. "I'm the one who needs to apologize for what I said."

"What are you talking about?"

"The promise," I responded. "I know I told you I'd be more positive and that I'd live, but now that I've had the time to think about it more clearly, I think it was a mistake to agree. There are a lot of things that are out of my control, so even if I have all the desire in the world, I don't want you to have hope."

I felt a lump forming in my throat. I'd made the promise in a moment of vulnerability when I didn't even know if I would wake up the other day, and I just didn't want to disappoint him. But now that I was feeling better and had time to think about everything, I felt like it was a selfish thing to say, even if it was to make him happy at that moment.

"Let's sit, mine," he interrupted gently, taking my hand and leading me to our usual spot by the window, one in front of the other, as always. "Pay total attention to what I will tell you now; this is probably the most important thing you'll learn from me."

I took a deep breath and nodded. I knew he wouldn't accept my answer without refuting me in some way, so I was ready to debate whatever he wanted to tell me.

"One of the last self-help books I read was called 'How to Make Good Things Happen to You,'" he began speaking. "I was incredulous at first because we're conditioned to believe that when something happens to us, it means external factors completely influenced it."

"Most of the time, it's like that," I replied. "I can bet almost all of them, honestly."

"Not necessarily. Especially if you learn to control it, that's what I learned in the book. When you decide to let all the good things happen, they eventually will."

"How?" I asked, too skeptical to hide it. The idea seemed too idealistic. If this really works, then bad things simply won't exist in the world.

"With your mind and actions. But they have to be in total coordination for it to work. Let's see an example: what was the last good thing that happened to you?"

I didn't have to think much about it. "My parents gave me the camera I wanted. When I received it on Sunday, I thought that the universe was in my favor since I started acting positively, but the reality is that they probably had bought it before I made the promise to you on Saturday, so it has nothing to do with it."

"This is partially correct," he responded. "For that good thing to happen to you, you had to want a camera first and express your desire. Without your parents knowing that you wanted to be a photographer, and without you wanting to have a camera first, that good thing wouldn't have happened to you."

"Of course, if we look at life that way, then my life would be full of positive things," I said ironically.

"Exactly."

"But that can go both ways," I complained. "For example, it was raining all day, and I couldn't go out to take the photos I wanted and test the camera. The rain has nothing to do with any negative or positive thoughts I had."

"But what you did, even with the rain, does." He responded. It was like he had an answer for everything I had against his theory. "When I entered your room hours ago, you weren't here, meaning that you found a workaround that resulted in something positive for you."

I thought about how much fun I'd had with the nurses and all the photos I took of them inside. None of that would have been possible if it hadn't been raining. "Maybe you're right with that example, but that doesn't mean my positive thinking could cure me."

"But it can play an important role. If you want to live, your body will try to heal and take advantage of all the treatments you receive. Your brain will work with all its power to make your desire come true." Liam opened the window and extended his hand to the rain. When it was wet enough, he rubbed it over my cheek, making me smile. "So even if it's raining, it will find a workaround."

"So my promise won't magically cure me, but all the things my body will do with that mindset from now on," I realized.

"See how smart you are? I knew you'd understand it right away."

I still had doubts, but it didn't cost me anything to try. After all, being an optimist was less miserable than the condition I'd been in all these months.

However, there was something that still bothered me—the way he was treating me.

"Can I ask you a question?" I could feel the tension in my chest as I waited for his reaction.

He looked at me like he was going to regret letting me do it. However, he agreed anyway. "Sure, as many as you want."

"Why are you fighting so much for me?"

He stayed quiet for some minutes and then said, "I don't understand."

"You're fighting more than me to keep me alive. You're helping me physically and mentally, and it doesn't matter what I tell you; you don't give up." I met his gaze, my heart pounding frantically against my ribs. "You may be an excellent nurse, but not even Hellen would waste a day off to spend it with me."

He opened his mouth to answer me, but before he could say something, an alarm started sounding in the building. The loud noise in the hallways cut through the tension between us, forcing us both to jump from where we were.

"What's going on?" I gasped, the panic rising in my chest.

Liam's gaze darted from me to the source of the sound. "I don't know, maybe it's a fire alarm," he responded, his voice with a different kind of urgency now.

I started to hear a group of footsteps, almost running down the entire hallway. It was clear—we needed to evacuate.

I moved towards the door, but as I reached for the handle, a horrifying realization slammed into me. Liam hadn't followed. I looked back and saw him in the same place.

"What are you waiting for? Let's go."

"I'll go out the window; see you around."

The window? No. That wasn't happening. Adrenaline began to flood my body, lending me a strength I didn't know I possessed. I went back to where he was, ignoring what he just said. Then I took his hand.

"Please, Liam, it's an emergency; no one will mind," I pleaded, hoping reason would break through whatever mental block he was experiencing. But his expression remained unreadable.

"They will," he countered, his voice barely a whisper. "Stop worrying about me and leave. I'll be okay."

My heart hammered faster and faster. Did he think this was some kind of game? Before I could argue further, he surprised me with a brief, yet surprisingly tender, hug. Then, with a final glance in my direction, he turned towards the window.

Panic clawed at my throat. I couldn't let him do this. But the urgency of the situation was undeniable. People were already evacuating, and every second I wasted increased the danger I could face.

I tore my gaze away from Liam and sprinted towards the door. Whatever Liam was hiding, it was clearly serious enough to risk getting caught. A part of me yearned to stay and fight for him, to drag him out of there kicking and screaming if necessary. But the other, more rational part knew I had to get myself to safety first.

So I opened the door and left.

Please, Liam, be alright.

Luckily for us, the heavy rain had stopped, and only small drops were falling from the sky. We'd been evacuated to the parking lot because of a gas leak in the kitchen, and the medical staff began moving some patients to other buildings. The frantic energy of the evacuation slowly subsided into a tense calm.

As I waited for instructions, my gaze darted through the crowd, searching for Liam. But he was nowhere.

Had he managed to leave the building without problems?

I glanced at my room. My window was slightly open, but

there was no sign of him. Whatever he did was pretty quick. He was probably assigned a few patients before I came down, and that's why he wasn't here anymore.

"Hello, miss," a nurse approached me, taking me out of my thoughts. "Are you alright? Can you walk by yourself?"

"Sure, I'm fine," I answered, but my gaze was still on the group.

"Glad to hear that; follow me."

As I walked, I tried to put positive thoughts in my mind.

At least I'm not injured. At least it stopped raining heavily. I'm safe. I'm alive; everything will be fine.

The more I tried to convince myself, the less I believed in my words. But I'd promised to be positive, and that's what I would do.

Following the nurse's lead, we entered the building closest to the one I stayed in. Inside, a large room had been converted into a temporary holding area. Dozens of patients, some in wheelchairs, others huddled in blankets, filled the space— some of them trying to rest, others conversing. Different nurses entered throughout the rest of the night, monitoring our vital signs and checking if we needed anything.

Five hours later, someone entered to tell us that it was safe to return to our rooms and that nurses would be there soon to help us walk.

I never thought I'd be so happy to return to those four walls that were driving me crazy for so long. I needed to know that he'd escaped safely.

When I finally arrived, I took a deep breath and started scanning the place.

There was no one there.

And my drawings folder was on the bed—as if someone had taken one.

Journal entry 7

August 18, 2024

On Saturday, she told me I was her angel, and I couldn't say anything back. I was speechless. If only she knew the truth—the monstrous reality of who I was pretending to be—those words would never have come out of her mouth.

All Sunday, the weight of that moment pressed down on me. How could I have dared to play the hero's role when, in truth, I was fueled by the most selfish desires?

I couldn't continue this lie. The more time passed, the more I risked her hating me. For this reason, I decided to be honest.

I went to the hospital on Monday, scared but ready to tell her the truth, even if that ruined everything we'd built until now, because it was worse to be doing what I was doing, knowing that it was all a lie.

I was going to tell her that I didn't believe in my words, that I wasn't who she thought I was, and that I was an impostor.

But everything worked against me as if the entire universe was composed to make me come to my senses.

It started to rain so hard that it was almost impossible to climb the emergency stairs without slipping. The wind was so strong that I could barely see what was in front of me. But I didn't give up there. I waited patiently for an opportunity and climbed as slowly and confidently as possible. When I finally reached her room, she wasn't there.

My heart was racing, and I had to look for something to entertain myself while she appeared. But I couldn't concentrate, and everything I'd planned to tell her disappeared from my mind. The only thing I could think of at that moment was whether she was okay.

Had something happened to her, and the nurses taken her to the emergency room? Had the treatment been complicated, and was she in intensive care?

I felt it was my fault; I hadn't taken

care of her properly, and that's why she was gone.

I knew staying in the room was risky in case she entered again with someone else, but I didn't care; I had to make sure she was okay, so I stayed.

She returned hours later with a smile on her face, making all my worries fade away. But when I had her in front of me, the words didn't come out.

She needed me to give her more hope, so I lied again. How could I confess now when her eyes needed support, and I was all she had?

The worst part of the night was the question that I didn't have the courage to answer because, as if all the rain wasn't enough, the emergency alarm of the building began to sound, forcing us to separate.

Too many people were in the parking lot, so I couldn't go down the emergency stairs as if nothing had happened. So I had to go up and stay on the roof until it was safe to come down.

It was a foolish move. Everything I did that night was reckless and nonsensical, so I decided to take a few days to think about my next move.

I think I'm losing my mind.

157

CHAPTER 22
Excitement

I DIDN'T HEAR from Liam all week. I tried to convince myself that he could have simply been busy, or maybe he had a vacation. But deep down, I was worried.

I couldn't shake the image of him standing alone in that room while the alarm rang. I never saw him leave the building, not even through the window. He wasn't there when I returned to my room, but I didn't know how he'd managed to get out.

He should have come on Thursday, but he didn't show up that night either, which made my anxiety increase a little more. Maybe my impulsive questions the other night had scared him off, and he realized we'd gone too far. Or perhaps he thought I was going down the wrong path, and I'd misinterpreted his good intentions, so he decided not to keep risking his job.

If that were the case, I know the best thing he could do would be to get away from me. But I wanted to be selfish for the first time in a long time. I didn't want people to get away from me anymore; it didn't matter what consequences they could face for that decision.

The bad thing is that it was too late. He hadn't returned,

and I couldn't justify myself sufficiently the last time we saw each other. Since there was no way to take back my words, I decided to focus my energies on more productive things, like practicing with the camera and learning more about this new hobby.

My parents came on Sunday as usual with the things I'd asked for. My mother was so excited about the clothes she bought that we spent a long time trying on dresses, skirts, and blouses that she brought me.

Then I sat down at the computer to show them the photos I'd taken during the week.

With the time I'd had free this week and my spirits regained, I'd also been practicing a little editing. So my photos looked more and more professional, which made me feel proud of myself.

Plus, I no longer had only the photos I took on the day it rained. Hellen and I went out one morning and took photos of some plants and places that didn't look like part of the hospital, so I put together a mini portfolio I felt comfortable showing.

My parents were proud and happy. My father said that if he'd known in advance that I would be so productive, he would have bought me the camera sooner. A comment that made me laugh because the camera hadn't been what had revived my spirits, but my little secret friend.

One of the things that had me most boosted this week was that in two and a half weeks, I was going to have my last chemo. Seventeen more days and then the surgery, and all of this would be over. For the first time in a long time, I counted the days I had left to start living again, and I didn't feel like it was just another extra day in my life.

∼

The next day was beautiful. The sunlight flooded my room with incessant rays that made me squint. There wasn't a single cloud in the sky, the trees looked greener than ever, and the birds were singing.

I sat in the window to watch the sunrise. I took the opportunity to draw some mountains with an atmosphere similar to the one I was seeing. From here, I no longer saw just a grey parking lot but all the things that lay beyond my limited vision.

Hellen found me at the window putting the finishing touches on my drawing and said, "Breakfast is served, your Majesty."

I rolled my eyes and looked at her with a fake smile she noted right away. "If I weren't in such a good mood today, I would have found a way to throw you out of the window."

"Little Jasmine is in a good mood; what a strange change of scenery. What did I do to deserve such a piece of great news?" Hellen's lips had a big, sarcastic smile as she teased me.

The reality is that there was nothing meaningful for my mood. Liam's absence was still a gaping hole in my world. My parents were talkative, as always, and I was in the same place.

"Someone told me that if I was positive and optimistic, the universe would conspire to make good things happen, and I want to try that theory," I said, more to myself than to Hellen.

"I love it! You know what? I'll help you with your theory. Finish that breakfast fast; we should take a walk to take advantage of the day."

I found myself returning her smile, a genuine one this time. "That's an order, boss."

I ran to the couch and started eating, then we walked side by side to the exit, with the camera in my hands.

I don't know what I expected to find outside, but it was a much calmer day than usual. We walked aimlessly for a while, and I had to sit down a couple of times to catch my breath since I still didn't have enough energy or strength.

On one of our breaks, we sat next to one of the benches where some nurses I didn't recognize—probably from building 1—were gossiping.

I wasn't particularly interested in their conversation until one sentence caught my attention. "This has been a tough week," one nurse sighed. "I think I'll do the same as the new guy and take a few days off."

"Definitely," the other replied. "The best thing he could have done was take that vacation; after the chaos of the other night, I would have done it too."

I don't know if they're talking about Liam, but it makes sense that it's him. A new nurse, a chaotic night. They belong to a building I don't know, and they're talking about an employee who decided to take a break after a hard week.

I started smiling out of nowhere, which made Hellen look at me strangely. "Everything alright?"

"Absolutely perfect," I said, ignoring her concern. "Actually, I think I've had enough excitement for one day. Let's head back to the room."

"Let's go then," she replied, a little confused.

We both stood up and started our way back. This time, we walked faster, as if my energy had suddenly recovered, because I felt there was hope. I'd gotten an answer to where Liam could be that made sense. Even if the girls didn't mention his name, I sensed they were talking about him. There was no other reason why he could have abandoned me from one moment to the next.

"Hellen?" I said before entering my building.

"What?"

"I don't need you to go to building one anymore to verify that Liam exists."

The nurse just smiled. Deep down, she knew that I was the one who had to resolve my own doubts.

When I returned to the room, the first thing I noticed was a paper that I didn't recognize on my bed, so I hurried to the corner to take a better look at it.

As I got closer, I could see what it was—the drawing I lost the day of the gas leak, with a note attached that I read out loud:

"I owe you an answer; see you tonight on the roof."

The cool night air wrapped around me as I opened the window to climb the stairs. It was still very early to feel autumn's cold, but the breeze was already beginning to cool in the evenings.

When I reached the roof, Liam was already there, setting up a telescope. His dark hair was blowing slightly in the wind, his eyes shone in the dim light of the night, and his immersed face made him look flawless.

Seeing him there, so absorbed in what he was doing, made my heart skip a beat. I'd missed him more than I'd allowed myself to admit.

I spent a few seconds just admiring him. Part of me thought I'd never see him again, so I was totally relieved to see him as full of life and energy as always.

He must have sensed my presence because his head snapped up, and a small smile appeared on his face when he positioned his eyes on me. He moved his hands, gesturing for me to come closer. "There you are," he said naturally, as if he hadn't disappeared for a whole week. "Come, I have to show you something."

His casual tone almost made me laugh. Typical Liam, acting as if everything was perfectly normal. But that was how he was, and maybe it was better this way. No heavy explanations or apologies. At the end of the day, we didn't owe each other anything.

I approached where he was and started looking curiously at the object in front of me. "So we'll see the stars tonight."

"The drawing I borrowed was a camping area on the outskirts of the city, so I took advantage of the fact that the night was so clear to bring up the main reason why people camp," he replied, proud of his idea. "To see the wonders of the sky."

"It's yours?" I said, pointing at the telescope. I'd never seen one in person, and although I'd never been interested in stars, the way Liam talked about the world made me curious about even the most banal things in life.

"No, I borrowed it from a friend," he said. "Come, take a look."

Liam adjusted the telescope and peered through it for a moment, then stepped back and motioned for me to take his place. "Look, this one is Vega," he said, pointing to a bright star in the sky. "It's the start of the Summer Triangle."

I leaned in, positioning my eye against the lens, and saw Vega twinkling brightly. It was stunning, like a diamond set against the velvety blackness of space.

Suddenly, I felt a warm presence behind me. Liam's hand brushed against my lower back, making me lose concentration momentarily. "And on the side is Deneb," Liam continued, his voice soft and full of awe this time. "It's another part of the Summer Triangle. It's also part of the constellation Cygnus, the Swan."

I shifted the telescope slightly, finding Deneb as he described it. The stars seemed so much closer, their light more intense than I'd ever seen with the naked eye. I glanced up at Liam, impressed by his knowledge and the way he made the dark sky come alive.

"And which one is the big one over there?" I asked, pointing to a particularly bright object.

Liam grinned, clearly enjoying my curiosity. "This is actually a planet. It's Jupiter," he said. "You can see it from a telescope, and if the conditions are right, you might even catch a glimpse of its moons."

It was mesmerizing. I felt a deep sense of connection to the universe as if the vast expanse of space wasn't so distant after all.

"Wow, this is incredible," I whispered, still peering through the telescope. "Thank you for showing me all this."

Liam smiled, his eyes reflecting the same wonder I felt. "I'm glad you like it. Sometimes, looking at the stars helps put things in perspective, you know? Makes everything down here seem a little less overwhelming."

My body reacted to his words. I felt like he was no longer talking about the stars. But I stayed quiet, waiting for him to continue.

"Why am I fighting so much for you? At first, I wasn't sure," he finally confessed. "I entered your room, and the mess caught my attention. It was like a magnet, pulling me in and forcing me to take action."

He was answering my question from the other night.

Suddenly, I no longer wanted to know what he was trying to say. I'd asked him that question because I couldn't make sense of how hard he was trying to make me feel something. But right now, I felt like words were unnecessary. And deep down, I was afraid to know the answer.

I turned to look at him, discovering that he was so close that our breaths danced together. His eyes searched mine with an intensity that made me lose balance. I took a step back, but the wall was right there, keeping me from going too far.

"Then you woke up and tried to push me away, but your eyes achieved the opposite effect to what your words suggested. It was as if I couldn't hear you because all my senses were focused on your gaze."

The vulnerability in his voice was palpable, and it resonated with something deep inside me. His nearness was electrifying, and I couldn't escape even if I wanted to. His words wrapped around me, forcing me to confront the feelings I'd tried so hard to bury.

"Liam," I whispered, my voice barely audible. "I…"

"Don't say anything yet," he said softly but firmly. "I haven't finished."

He stepped even closer. "I approached you out of pure selfishness. I wanted to prove to myself that I could enter your world and break it. Everyone was talking about how impossible it was to be able to talk to you, and I wanted to be the one to change you." He put his hand on my waist so firmly that I whined. "But in the process of trying to change you, I failed in every possible way someone could fail a mission."

My mind raced, trying to process the depth of his words. "But you didn't fail, I changed."

"The problem is that you also changed me, Mine. And that wasn't part of the plan." He paused as if trying to process his next words. "I thought I was helping you, but in reality, I helped myself, and now I don't know what to do."

I had a million doubts. I didn't understand how I'd helped him or where he wanted to go with this speech. I thought about all the things he'd told me so far until I remembered one specific phrase he'd said to me during one of our first encounters.

Maybe I'm trying to save myself by saving you.

"How?" I asked. "How did I help you?"

"I had no hope either, but all I want to do now is make you happy. Make you feel life is worth it. Make you see that the world is beautiful, even if I don't believe it myself. I didn't care about bars, libraries, or mountains. Now I find myself stealing your drawings, going to places I never imagined I would go, so I have a new adventure to talk to you about."

There was something different in the way Liam looked at me. I was used to fading into the background or being seen as the poor, sick girl who "had a life ahead." However, Liam saw me as an enigma, something he had to solve. "I never thought I could have that kind of power."

"Never let anyone, not even yourself, make you feel you can't make everything around you better."

"I'll keep it in mind," I said, distracting my gaze to the sky so that he wouldn't notice how nervous and red I was because of his words.

Something inside me connected in a way I couldn't explain with this boy. I wanted to be a better person just for him. I wanted to do impossible things just so he would be proud that I could do it. I wanted to be different.

"Jasmine?" He paused as if waiting for me to look at him again. When I did, I realized that he was completely serious, his breathing was faster, and his hand on my waist was no longer so firm.

"Yes?"

With a voice barely above a whisper, he asked, "Can I kiss you?"

I knew this was one of the worst decisions in the world. That I shouldn't let him get any closer, that I shouldn't let our lips touch. But there was nothing in the world that I would love more at that moment. So, for the first time in my life, I decided not to think about the consequences of the future and let my heart decide what was best for me at that moment.

"Yes," I whispered.

Liam closed the distance between us, his hands gently cupping my face as he leaned in. Our lips met, softly at first, then with more intensity as the world around us seemed to fade away. At that moment, under the vast night sky, surrounded by stars that I now knew the names of, I felt a connection that went beyond words, beyond doubts, and beyond fears.

He lowered one of the hands that were on my face to my waist and pressed me against his body. The firmness with which he held me felt like he never wanted to let me go, but I was delighted to be a prisoner of his arms.

I'd never felt like this. It was as if I was already missing a moment that was still happening. I tried to memorize every breath, caress, and movement of his lips because I knew I wouldn't be the same person after this moment. This first kiss was the confirmation that I'd never lived properly and that everything that had happened in my life before was precisely to get where I was now.

My mind stopped thinking about pain, the future, the past, or even where I was standing. All I could feel and see was Liam. I knew this boy gave me millions of emotions without even touching me, but feeling his lips was a totally different experience.

I felt alive.

We broke the kiss between laughs while we put our foreheads together. Both of his hands went up to cup my cheeks again. Mine were around his neck, rubbing his hair gently.

"Sweet Mine," he murmured, his breath warm against my lips, his eyes fixed on mine. "Do you want to escape with me?"

CHAPTER 23

Luck

IN THE PAST HOURS, my emotions had been a whirlwind, pulling me through a dizzying spiral of highs and lows. It felt like I was stuck on a roller coaster, teetering between happiness and fear with every passing moment. I'd never felt this way before, like I was standing on the edge of something incredible and terrifying all at once.

"Escape with you?" The words barely left my mouth. I was still breathless from that first kiss we'd shared. The idea seemed surreal, and yet, here he was, offering it so casually. "Where to? How?"

My mind raced. What Liam was suggesting was insane—something impossible in my condition, given where we were. But instead of rejecting the idea outright, I found myself wanting to hear more. I needed to know what was going on in his head, even though part of me knew how reckless it all sounded.

At this moment, Liam could ask me to bring him the moon, and even though I knew it was impossible, I would find myself thinking of ways to make it happen. That's what his presence did to me. I wasn't focused on my illness or the consequences if things went wrong. I just wanted to feel alive again.

He stayed quiet for a while, his eyes searching mine like he was trying to figure out the right words to convince me. I could see the weight of the silence, like he was planning every possible response in his head.

"I don't want to continue living your dreams for you. I want you to be the one living them, experiencing them yourself." He took my hands, gently intertwining his fingers with mine and bringing them close to his chest. His heartbeat was steady, grounding me. "I've been watching your room long enough to know that no one comes in after 9:00 p.m.; we can sneak away and complete the things on your list that don't take much effort."

"But what if we get caught?" I asked, my voice trembling slightly.

Liam's grip on my hands tightened, and he looked into my eyes with a determination that made me feel safe despite the risk. "We'll be careful," he said softly. "We'll take it one step at a time. I just want to give you a taste of the freedom you deserve, even if it's just for a little while."

He sounded desperate, like convincing me was his only goal, and saying yes was the only thing that kept him alive. His words made me believe that maybe this could work.

However, even if we could escape every night successfully, my poor health condition was still there, so I added, "But what if something happens to my health when I'm outside?"

"I'm a nurse, and I've been with you in every stage of your illness for the past month; I know how to treat everything that could happen to you."

It was like he had a response to every question I had. But I was full of doubts. What Liam was offering me was extremely crazy. I was in the hospital for a reason. My parents brought me here because they wanted me to be as well as possible so that I could heal without any complications. That's why I was monitored 24/7.

Yet, at the same time, something about Liam's plan made sense in my head.

But what if I don't survive even if I stay locked here? The possibility was still there even if I was more optimistic about my future.

I needed to feel that my life was worth living, and if these were my last moments alive, I knew I didn't want to spend them in a hospital room but rather doing the things I wanted to do.

And I was tired of being locked up.

The more I thought about it, the clearer the answer became. I preferred to live a short life full of happy moments worth living than an eternity of confinement.

I looked at Liam and nodded. "When do we start?"

"Right now, if you feel you have the energy, I have something in mind."

My body filled with nervousness again, but I tried to banish those thoughts from my mind quickly.

Stop overthinking. This is what you want.

"Let me change my clothes then."

"I'll wait for you in the park," he responded, and we started walking to the stairs.

Back in my room, I tried to change from my pajamas into one of the clothes my mom brought me on Sunday as fast as possible. Since I had no context for where we were going and it was too late for anything fancy or out of the ordinary, I decided to put on some jeans, sneakers, and a hoodie.

Then, I went to the bathroom mirror to put on my hat and brush the little hair that came out of the sides. I hated that they were so short that I felt uncomfortable going out without something on my head, but I had no other option.

Looking in the mirror, I noticed that I looked thinner and paler than usual. The chemotherapy had taken away the little weight I'd achieved until then. However, I felt more beautiful than ever. I had an inexplicable smile and a spirit that no one would be able to shake, no matter what news they gave me right now.

When I left the bathroom, I took my camera and put a note on the bed, just in case someone entered when I wasn't there.

"I went for a walk for a while."

And then, I jumped up the stairs.

When I reached the park, Liam was there, leaning against a tree with a smile on his face. He extended his hand towards me to take it. "Ready?"

I took his hand. "Ready."

We walked to an old blue car in the parking lot. I looked at it for a few seconds, feeling a little shy about doing something. Every step I took felt forbidden, different. For many people, this was a normal action. For me, it was a new experience that I wasn't supposed to be having tonight.

Liam must have noted my indecision and decided to open the passenger seat for me. When I was inside, he gave me a little smile that made me feel less tense.

When he got into the driver's side and closed the door, he didn't turn on the vehicle right away. He looked at me with the same intensity as before, as if I were the only light in all the darkness around him, as if, with a simple touch, I could make all his pain go away forever.

So I bowed my head towards him, removed all the hair from his face, and we kissed again as if the correct functioning of the world depended on this moment.

This time was better than the last. I felt more confident. I knew what to do. My hands rested on the back of his neck as I stroked his hair. Liam's hands were on my cheek as he took all the breath I had left. Everything felt so right, as if we were always meant for each other.

When our eyes opened, I felt like I could finish this night right now and would feel satisfied. But I knew he wouldn't let me return to my room, so I asked, "Where are we going?"

"I thought we could start with something simple," he said, looking at me out of the corner of his eye. "Don't worry, Mine, I know you'll like it."

He started the car and started driving. On the way, I looked at the city like it was the first time I saw it—full of lights, dreams, and life, even at night.

I tried to memorize every second that passed.

Tonight was just the beginning. I would start enjoying life from now on.

Twenty minutes later, we parked at a coffee shop that I recognized instantly. It was the place that Donna had recommended to me, the one with the delicious cookies I still think about. Cookies paradise.

"How did you know this was on my *to dream list*?" I asked, surprised by his selection.

I remembered that the night I was going to show him the list, he left before Anna found us together, so I didn't have the proper time to show it.

"You gave me one of the cookies in a bag with the restaurant's name on it and mentioned how much you liked them. Figured it'd be a good first stop. I'm quite observant when I want."

I blushed. Liam was so good at everything, so effortlessly thoughtful. His attention to detail was both impressive and overwhelming in the best way possible.

"You're full of surprises," I said, smiling at him.

"Just wait until you try their hot chocolate," he replied with a wink. "There you'll also feel that I'm full of good ideas."

We entered the cozy coffee shop. The aroma of freshly brewed coffee filled the air, and soft jazz music played in the background. It was quiet, with only a few people at the tables, lost in their own conversations.

We found a small table by the window and ordered some cookies and chocolate.

Liam reached across the table and took my hand, his thumb gently stroking my knuckles. "How are you feeling?"

"Better," I lied. By the time I got to the cafeteria, I was feeling a little exhausted. This was due to the adrenaline of escaping and having to go up and down so many steps of the building where I was. But I didn't want to let the sickness ruin the night. It was the first time in a while that I felt like a normal person. "I feel like I can breathe for the first time in a while. This was a good idea."

The waitress brought our drinks and a plate of cookies, and I couldn't help but smile when I saw them. I took my camera to capture the moments of the steam rising from the hot chocolate, the warm glow of the table lamp, and the bustling city life visible through the window. Then Liam and I clinked our mugs together in a silent toast, savoring the sweetness of our second dinner of the night.

For a while, we just sat there, enjoying each other's company. We talked about everything and nothing, our conversations flowing easily. The world outside seemed to fade away, leaving just the two of us in this little bubble of happiness.

The way he looked at me made me feel like I could be loved despite everything. And I couldn't stop thinking about how lucky I was that he came into my life.

By the end of the night, I had a clear goal. Eat everything I could, accept every medication and doctor's recommendation, and, if possible, improve my cardiovascular endurance. From now on, I needed to be in my best condition to enjoy these moments with Liam.

I wanted to be as healthy and strong as I could be so we could have more nights like this.

Journal entry 8

August 26, 2024

I don't remember the last time I felt so good. Full of goals and a clear objective. Who wants to win heaven when I've had the doors of paradise in front of me?

This week away helped me realize what I really needed. I no longer chase stars because there are better wonders on Earth. I was so consumed with saving someone, with being some kind of hero, that I wasted my time.

And I don't want to waste the few moments I have left with Jasmine. I want her to be the happiest she's ever been in her entire life. Let there be nothing else that she wants to do because thanks to me, she was able to fulfill all her dreams. Let her feel like she doesn't need anything else, because I gave her every-thing she ever wanted.

Who would want to live longer if they've already achieved everything they've ever desired?

Here's the thing. It scares me a little. This all-consuming focus on Jasmine's happiness... is it healthy? Is it love or something else entirely? Maybe it's a way to fill the void this whole situation has created inside me.

But the reality now is that I don't care about the mission anymore. Who I am, the morality of it all—it's all faded into the back-ground. I deserve happiness, too, dammit. And all I want is to see her smile and know it's because of me. To take her anywhere her heart desires because I'm the only one who truly understands her. To feel the warmth of her lips because I was the only one who was able to unlock her heart.

And she is all mine. Maybe not in the possessive way it sounds, but mine in the sense that we have this connection, this bond. We understand each other in a way no one else can.

There's a hard truth staring me in the face. I have to show Jasmine the beauty of an authentic new type of life, even if it means letting go of the fantasy we've built together. It's going to be a tough road, but maybe, just maybe, there's a chance for real happiness on the other side.

I don't want to think about the consequences of my actions. Not when I feel so good breaking every rule. When the time comes, I'll accept the punishment, but in the meantime, I'm very clear about what I want to do.

CHAPTER 24

Anticipation

"I CAN'T BELIEVE the last chemotherapy is tomorrow," I said, trying to distract myself from the pain.

Hellen was taking a blood sample to send to the laboratory and finishing a general inspection of my whole body.

"Why not? It's literally every three weeks," she responded as if it weren't that obvious. "Like clockwork."

The truth was that the last few weeks had become something completely different from what I was used to. I hadn't realized how fast the last few days had passed. It felt like it was yesterday when Liam gave me a hug for the first time in my bedroom when I thought I was going to die. When I began to feel what it was like to be alive again. When I decided to fight to be healthy.

Yesterday, Liam and I had our first adventure together, and I thought I'd have more time to go places before lasting five days without even being able to move again.

"I know, I know," I sighed. "I mean, these last few weeks went by extremely quickly. I guess I thought I could do more things before losing my strength again."

"Well, now you know the days go by quickly if you're not

a miserable bitch." She responded, looking me in the eyes to see if I had any negative reaction. When she realized I didn't care about her comment (because she'd always been sarcastic around me), she continued. "Anyway, you did more things these three weeks than you've done in the past three months combined. Don't sell yourself short. I don't know what you're complaining about."

I rolled my eyes, but I couldn't help but laugh at her sarcasm. "I knooooow, but I want to do more things. I feel like time is running out."

Hellen immediately stopped what she was doing when she heard my words and looked at me, worried.

"Hey," she said, her voice more gentle. "Who says there isn't more time? The surgery is your gateway to freedom, remember? No more being stuck in this place. You should be excited."

And she was right. Now that I no longer think these are my last days of life, I realize that the faster this whole process happens, the better it will be.

But part of me couldn't stop thinking about what my life would be like after leaving. So many things have changed since I came here. I felt like a completely different person than the one who discovered I had kidney cancer a few months ago.

Knowing I was going to get out of here also meant planning an entire life.

Will Liam visit me at my house? How will I tell my parents that we met? What would I do to develop my photography career?

"Life was easier when I didn't have to think about actually living," I confessed, the words tumbling out before I could stop them. They weren't meant for Hellen's ears; they were more of a quiet murmur to myself.

Hellen was just about to leave, but when she heard that comment, she turned back. "But it wasn't worth living that way. Remember how happy you are now, how alive you feel. Don't let fear steal that away from you."

I lay down on the bed, staring at the ceiling. How did she always know what to say to oppose my ideas and make me change my mind?

∾

I wouldn't have expected Liam tonight. Tuesdays were always his off days. But things were different now.

He wasn't just the friendly nurse who popped in to check my vitals and chat for a few minutes. He wasn't just another face on the hospital staff rotation. And I, well, I certainly wasn't just another patient on their list anymore.

A nervous flutter danced in my stomach as the clock ticked past eight. Without thinking, I found myself drawn to the closet, subconsciously searching for the perfect outfit. I knew he was coming, so I wanted to be ready in case the chance to escape was there.

After dinner, I went into the bathroom to get ready. I put on a white skirt, a red hoodie, and sneakers so I wouldn't look overdressed. When I was completely satisfied with how I looked, I came out of the bathroom, and there he was, as cute as always, seated in his spot at the window, waiting for me.

Even though I'd been waiting for him all day, I jumped a little from the scare. I wasn't expecting him to be there so soon. "I'll never get used to finding you at the window so randomly."

Tonight, he had his hair up as if he'd also made an effort to look good. I was happy to believe that he also took care of himself to look handsome to me. He wore jeans and a hoodie, so I assumed he wasn't going to work and he was here just for me. I couldn't help but smile at that thought.

He started walking towards me. Every step took my breath

away a little more. "The good thing is that you don't have to get used to it because this time here is ephemeral," he told me, grabbing me by the waist when he was close enough. "The bad thing is that I know you'll miss it."

His touch was electric, a sensation I was quickly learning to crave, a connection that transcended the sterile walls of this room. "You're probably right. I'll miss it," I admitted, looking into his eyes. "But I'll have so many other things to look forward to."

He smiled and kissed me softly on the lips, making me feel like I was in the clouds. It felt surreal, like a dream I didn't want to wake up from or like a scene from a movie where the world around you fades away, and all that's left is the person in front of you. Liam's existence had become a beacon of hope and joy in my monotonous days.

"Are you ready for our adventure tonight?" he whispered, still between my lips.

"As soon as you let me go," I replied, clinging tighter to his neck like I didn't want to let him go.

"Looks like we'll never be ready to leave then."

He surprised me by wrapping his strong arms around my waist and lifting me off the ground. A startled yelp escaped my lips before we were both twirling in a circle.

Liam knew how to make me laugh even if I didn't want to. I clung tighter to his neck without taking my eyes from his face. The way he looked at me back, like he was in love, was something I'll always keep in my heart.

Liam finally let me go and started walking to the window. "Let's go before it gets too late for your surprise."

"Where are we going?" I asked, following him.

"If I tell you, it will stop being a surprise, Mine."

∼

Going in a vehicle with Liam was a whole experience. As soon as we entered his car, he took my hand and never let it go. Not even when he had to turn, which I considered very uncomfortable, but he didn't seem to care. At every red light, he'd lean over to kiss me, touch my ribs with his finger to tickle me, or rub my shoulder.

We acted as if we hadn't seen each other in months, with all the love we were giving to each other. It felt like he missed me as much as I missed him, and I was glad for that. Everything seemed normal and natural between us, like we'd done this forever. I loved how we no longer pretended to be distant for each other's sake.

The best part was when one of his favorite songs came on the radio, and he turned it up and started singing it very loudly, as if he were at a concert.

I'd never met anyone so full of life, wanting to do things he loved regardless of everything else. I promised myself I would work on myself so that one day I would be like him.

When we parked in front of the Public Library, my face lit up like I was a little girl in front of an ice cream truck. It was so big I knew I wouldn't have time to go to every hall, and I immediately thought about what books I would love to choose.

"We have," Liam stopped to see his watch and then continued, "half an hour before they close to choose at least three books. Do you remember what I taught you when I came here for the first time?"

"That you have no criteria or personality when choosing a book?" I responded with a smile.

He looked at me indignantly, as if I'd offended him, but knowing I was joking.

"Close, but no. I told you that sometimes it's more about the experience than knowing what to expect. So don't overthink much and choose as randomly as possible."

"Well, it's a challenge; the person who chooses the best book based on the cover alone wins."

"And how do I know you're not reading the synopses of every book you see?"

"Because we don't have time for that; come on, it's getting late."

I couldn't describe how excited I was to be doing something new, I knew I would like. I was so used to my routine that I forgot what living felt like. It was like my life had a new meaning, and I didn't even think I was sick anymore, even if I was constantly feeling back pain. Every moment felt precious, and I wanted to savor it all.

Liam unbuckled his belt and opened the door. "I love a competitive girl; we have to choose three books; 29 minutes left."

When we entered the library, I was petrified by its beauty. The architecture was beautiful, full of golden columns and windows that looked like something out of an old fantasy book. The place was full of books everywhere. I didn't know where to start wandering.

Liam, however, seemed to have a plan. He marched confidently down a random aisle as if he knew exactly what he would look for, leaving me to make my own choice. So I decided not to think about it too much and chose the one in front of me.

As I walked through the rows of books, the smell of aged paper and leather bindings filled the air. I ran my fingers along the spines of the books, feeling the textures and imagining what stories each one could have.

After a while, lost in the aisles, I began to pick up books that I couldn't stop looking at over and over again. Even though they could be bad stories, I was satisfied with what I'd found. I knew it was my heart that picked them instead of my mind.

After having the books in my hands, I took the camera out of my bag and started taking some photos of the place. I wanted to capture every happy moment I had so I could see them whenever I felt sad.

I glanced back to find Liam focused on his own search at the end of the hallway where I was. Since I already had three books and amazing pictures, I decided to go where he was.

"Need any help finding something?" I asked.

He looked at me with a half smile. "It depends," he said, running his right hand from my shoulder to the tips of my fingers. "How could you help me?"

I darted a nervous glance around, making sure no one was watching our little exchange. Then, I focused on his gaze again.

"Well," I finally admitted with a small grin, "maybe not with the actual book search. But I can help you realize that you're overthinking something that should be simple." I gestured toward the stack of books I'd already picked out. "See? I've already got my three."

He let out a laugh, a genuine, deep laugh that made him cover his face with one hand. "Jasmine," he said, still chuckling, "I hope one day you realize how proud I am of you."

I could feel my cheeks heating up instantly. His words meant everything to me. I wanted to tell him that I couldn't have come this far without him, that he'd given me the strength I hadn't even known I had. But another part of me wanted him to see my own resilience, too.

"What can I say? I'm the best," I finally answered, trying to keep the mood light even though the compliment had made me feel vulnerable.

"That you are," he agreed, his smile widening. He leaned down to kiss my forehead softly, sending a rush of warmth through me. "But seriously, you amaze me. Every single day."

For a moment, time seemed to stand still. We were

surrounded by countless stories, yet I felt like we were crafting our own right there, page by page, moment by moment. His belief in me felt like the ink on those pages, and my determination was the paper. Together, we were creating something beautiful, something unpredictable.

"Alright, let's see what you've got," he said, reaching for the books in my hands. He looked at the covers, nodding approvingly. "Solid choices. Now, let me grab my last one, and we'll call it a night."

I watched him as he quickly selected a book, his decisiveness returning. With our selections in hand, we made our way to the front desk.

I felt like the books we chose were the less important part of the night, but how we'd been making everything seem like an adventure, and I felt lucky to be a part of it.

"This isn't the way to the hospital," I said, watching Liam drive down unfamiliar streets. Although we hadn't done any extreme activities, I was already feeling a little tired. After all, I was battling cancer.

He squeezed my hand a little tighter as if he wanted to ensure I wouldn't slip out of my seat. "I know. I want to make one last stop tonight."

I smiled. I didn't imagine how much fun I was going to have on my last day before my last chemotherapy. The last few times I'd received chemo had been days full of anxiety, expecting to feel worse and worse. This day, I didn't even have time to think that I had to rest a little so I could be awake the whole morning tomorrow.

It was as if Liam's presence took away all my worries, and the only thing that mattered right now was him and me. I wanted to enjoy every minute as if they were the last ones. I didn't know when the next time would be, and for some reason, I felt like this feeling of peace would be temporary.

So I decided to make an effort to be able to enjoy the few hours I had left with energy.

My gaze drifted back to the road. The city buildings I was familiar with were no longer visible. But I was calm. Liam could be driving to the end of the world, and I felt safe by his side.

We drove for a long time until we reached a lonely, dark street that led to a dock with a river that connected to the sea. He turned off the engine and looked at me with a smile that made my heart skip a beat.

"Come on," he said, getting out of the car and coming around to open my door.

I stepped out, and we walked to a bridge where we could see the boats, yachts, and large ships parked there. By this time of night, most of the boats were already there, giving us the opportunity to appreciate them up close. Their masts swayed gently with the movement of the sea. The air was cool, and the soft sounds of the night surrounded us.

I stood on the edge of the bridge to admire them all, imagining what they would look like inside and what it would feel like to go to sea on one of them.

After a few moments of comfortable silence, Liam spoke, his voice warm against my ear. "I know I can't offer you a fancy yacht like Dr. Butler," he said, wrapping his arms around me from behind, "but at least I can bring you to see them."

It took me to another place on my to-do list. But how did he know about my conversation with my doctor?

Liam definitely paid too much attention to my words—or maybe he'd spied on my list when I wasn't around. Either way, I didn't mind. He was doing all of this for one simple reason: he wanted to see me happy.

A soft laugh escaped my lips. There it was again—Liam, somehow knowing exactly what I wanted, fulfilling a wish I hadn't even realized I'd spoken aloud. Maybe he had peeked at my list. Maybe he'd heard the story from other nurses. Whatever the reason, my heart felt complete. He was doing this for me, to see me smile.

So I decided to focus on something better, like where I could go on one of those big ships. I imagined myself traveling along the coast, or perhaps to a nearby island. The mere thought made me feel happy, as if there were moments where dreaming was enough.

"I don't need you to have one. I think this whole gesture was perfect."

He smiled, satisfied with my response. "Well, tell me then, where did you imagine you were sailing?"

I blinked, caught off guard. "How did you know I was thinking about that?"

"Because I've spent enough time with you to know how your mind works."

I turned to face him, my hands instinctively reaching up to cradle his neck. "You think you know me?"

He met my gaze with confidence. "I like to think I do."

Before I could reply, he started mentioning everything he knew about me.

"You like waking up at 8:00 p.m., so you see the least amount of people possible," he began, his voice dropping to a low murmur. "You avoid them because you're scared of the pain they'll feel if you're gone. You don't want people to get used to your presence and then lose you. But the truth is, you're the one terrified—terrified of hope and the disappointment that follows if you don't get what you expect."

His words hit me harder than I expected, exposing the vulnerability I tried so hard to hide. But there was no judgment in his eyes, only understanding. It was as if he could see through all the layers I'd built around myself.

"You thought I was annoying until you realized you couldn't fight me anymore, and it was easier to just go along with me."

A laugh bubbled up from my chest, the memory of our early interactions still fresh in my mind.

"You love short movies and books with predictable endings," he added, a knowing smile gracing his lips. "Because you crave certainty, a world where the unknown doesn't sneak up on you and knock you down."

Then, his voice softened, his eyes searching mine. "And photos? You love capturing moments because, for the first time, you feel like you're truly good at something. Something that no one can take away from you."

I felt my breath catch in my throat. Liam saw me—not just the surface-level me, the girl fighting an illness, but all of me. My fears, my quirks, my little obsessions. And, for the first time, I felt truly understood.

I felt a sense of completeness I hadn't known I craved.

"You're missing something," I replied, feeling like I owed him one last fact about me.

He raised an eyebrow, confused by what I might say to him.

"The main reason I stay up all night is not simply because I can be free by myself at that time. The truth is that one of my biggest fears is dying alone, and I don't want to be in a position where I couldn't ask for help. I hate early mornings because I always feel like I will die at that time. So I always try to stay as awake as possible so I can call someone in time."

"Jasmine," he whispered, his following silence making me turn to him. "I'll make sure you never feel alone on the nights you feel down."

Leaning in, Liam closed the small distance between us, his

lips brushing against mine in a tender kiss. For that brief moment, it was just the two of us sharing a connection that felt timeless and profound.

When we pulled away, we stayed looking into each other's eyes, the soft glow from the distant boats painting a warm reflection in Liam's eyes. Then, a raindrop fell on my cheek. I looked up and saw the sky darkening with clouds. "Liam, it's starting to rain."

He tilted his head back, a playful grin erupting on his face. "Looks like our adventure just got a little more interesting, wouldn't you say?"

I looked at him with a serious expression this time. "I can't afford to get sick, much less today. The last chemo is tomorrow and..."

"And I'm a nurse," he cut me off gently, placing a finger on my lips. "And I know exactly what to give you so you won't catch a cold. Stop living based on your fears. Stop letting that feeling dictate every move, Jasmine."

His words hit deeper than I cared to admit. Every decision I made was steeped in worry—about my health, my future, what could go wrong. I lived so cautiously that I had forgotten what it felt like to really live. And in that moment, I realized he was right. If I kept letting fear guide my steps, I'd never really experience life.

Within moments, the rain began to pour down in earnest. Instead of running for cover, Liam took my hands, and we started dancing right there on the dock. We laughed, spinning and twirling as the rain soaked us through. His hands were warm on my waist, and I could feel the heat of his body through the cold rain.

"I can't believe we're doing this," I gasped, breathless from laughter, trying to catch my breath between twirls.

"Why not? Sometimes you just have to live the moment," he replied, his eyes shining with joy.

We danced until we were thoroughly drenched, the rain mixing with our laughter.

Finally, we made our way back to the car, dripping wet and utterly exhilarated.

"This night was incredible," I said, my heart still racing.

"It was," he agreed, leaning over to kiss me gently. "I wanted to give you a night you'd never forget."

"You did," I whispered, my fingers tracing the outline of his jaw. "Thank you, Liam."

He smiled, his eyes full of warmth and love. "Anything for you, Mine. Always."

When I entered the room through the window, I felt a presence that made me look everywhere. As my eyes adjusted to the darkness, I noticed Hellen standing in the hallway next to the bathroom with her arms crossed.

"Jesus, Hellen, you scared me."

She, however, had a face of disapproval. "Are you going crazy?" She began to speak, her tone showing how upset she was. "I've been here waiting for hours. Where were you so late? And why are you so wet? You're ruining everything we've been fighting for these months with your irrational actions."

"I just went for a walk, and it started to rain. No big deal." I tried to sound as calm and normal as possible so she wouldn't ask any more questions, but she didn't look convinced. "Everything will be fine. It's just water."

Hellen's skeptical gaze swept over me, making me feel like a little girl. "Everything will be fine? Jasmine, everything is not fine, and you know it." She gestured toward my wet clothes, making me realize the mistake I'd just made. "Tomorrow's your last chemo session, and you're doing everything but stay healthy. I came by to give you your pretreatment meds and had to wait here for you. It's getting late."

I stayed silent while Hellen looked for some towels and pajamas so I could change out of my wet clothes. She was right; I'd acted recklessly. But I wouldn't change the night I had for anything.

When I was totally dry, I sat on the bed. Hellen handed me the pills, and I began to drink them one by one.

"And why did you come in through the window? Do you know how dangerous it is for you to go up there? They're emergency stairs, not a way to escape at your convenience."

"I was trying to avoid confrontations with people like you." The words, with a hint of bitterness, slipped from my lips.

She looked at me in disbelief, as if she were the one who had made the mistake.

"I'm tired, and I have anxiety. I just thought a little fresh air would help me. I'm sorry that I made you worried," I added in an attempt that my feelings would make her soften her anger.

"You were with him, weren't you?" She asked like she knew the answer.

I paused. There was no point in denying it. But I didn't want to cause Liam any problems. So I didn't say anything.

Hellen realized that I wasn't going to speak, so she continued. "Jasmine, I understand that you're trying to live your life and find moments of happiness, but you need to be careful. You can't risk your health like this for someone you don't know."

I sighed, feeling the weight of her words. It could have been worse. My parents could have been the ones waiting for me. I should be more careful next time.

"Sure," I finally answered. "I understand."

The nurse sat down beside me, her voice gentler now.

"You have to balance those moments with the reality of your situation. Tomorrow's chemo is important, and you need to be ready for it. Promise me you'll be more careful."

I was disappointed to have spent an incredible night where I forgot all my problems, to a scenario in which I was constantly reminded of how bad I was and how I couldn't live until this process ended.

What if it never ends? Should I be miserable my whole life because I'm sick?

I didn't say these words to Hellen because I knew that arguing with her was pointless. No matter how much I tell others I'm tired of being locked up, no one has ever done anything for me. Liam might be a bad influence, but he was giving more meaning to my life than the rest of the people around me ever did.

"I promise," I finally said quietly. "I'll be more careful." It was useless to fight with her. Especially because I knew she wouldn't understand my reasons. And there's nothing she could say that would keep me locked in here anyway.

Hellen gave me a small smile. "Good. Now, get some rest. Tomorrow's a big day."

As I settled into bed, my thoughts drifted back to the whole night I'd just spent. Was I really irresponsible, or was everyone around me exaggerating my condition? Was Liam really someone I should be careful of, like Hellen said?

After a few minutes, I realized something. Liam could know every part of me the way he did.

But I still didn't know anything about him.

Hellen was right.

I was between fulfilling my dreams or falling into darkness.

CHAPTER 25
Distrust

THE CHEMOTHERAPY WENT AS SMOOTHLY as it should have. As always, on the first day, I only felt drained, but by the end of the second day, the symptoms were so severe that I could barely stand on my own.

Just like last time, Hellen was in charge of being with me in the mornings, my mother spent the afternoons with me, and then at night, when everyone thought I was going to rest and I wouldn't need anyone else, Liam showed up.

His job was to ensure my vital signs were stable, help me go to the bathroom if needed, and read me one of the books we'd chosen from the library with the excuse that "I was too tired to do it on my own."

I loved how he'd chosen to go to the library the other night because he knew I couldn't do anything else in these five days I would be in bed. It was like he'd planned for us to have an activity to do regardless.

So, whenever I was awake, Liam would take a book and try to act as excitedly as possible, reading in the most dramatic voice ever to cheer me up. He'd get so into it, pausing mid-sentence to explain some plot twist or brag about the author's brilliance.

I mostly just listened. I didn't have the strength to do anything else. But I enjoyed every moment I spent there, even if I didn't do anything.

On the third night, I couldn't sleep. I had so much nausea and dizziness that I couldn't even lie down. He was by my side, about to start reading today's chapter.

"Today, I don't want you to read to me," I whispered.

He looked at me, disappointed, placing the book on the nightstand. "You're not liking the story, right? I knew that I shouldn't have chosen a book by Yana Freid. Let me take another book. We still have that mystery novel untouched, or maybe a classic love story would be more your—"

"No, wait," I cut him off gently, reaching out to take his hand in mine. "The problem is not the story. Tonight, I just want to hear about you."

His brow furrowed in surprise. "About me?"

"Yes, I feel you know me so well, but I know practically nothing about you. I want to get to know you."

After he told me all those beautiful things about me the other night on the pier and how Hellen was worried I was being influenced by someone that no one knew, I couldn't stop thinking he was a stranger.

Liam was becoming not only an important person in my life but also someone who gave me the strength I needed whenever I was down, yet he was still an enigma.

Even if I didn't care who he really was, I wanted to be able to feel like I knew him as much as he knew me.

"Well," he began, scratching the back of his neck sheepishly, "there's not much to tell, honestly. I'm just a regular guy."

There was a flicker of something in his eyes, a fleeting sadness that I couldn't quite place. It was as if he wanted to avoid having to answer because the truth about him was not pleasant.

"You're not boring, Liam," I said, squeezing his hand. "Please, tell me something about your life. Anything."

I just wanted Hellen to be wrong. I wanted to know that Liam was a good person and that there was nothing to worry about. But the more I tried to think about Liam, the more unknown he was.

He hesitated, his gaze drifting out the window momentarily before returning to meet mine. "Alright," he sighed, a hint of a smile playing on his lips. "But only because you asked so nicely."

I smiled encouragingly, waiting for him to begin.

"I grew up in a small town not far from here," he started. "It was one of those places where everyone knows everyone. My parents are pretty strict, but they're good people. My dad's a mechanic, and my mom's a teacher. They're both very dedicated to their work, and I guess that's where I got my inspiration to do something I loved and put everything into it."

"Did you always know you wanted to be a doctor?" I asked. I wanted to understand every detail of his life.

He made a significant pause as if he was trying to think when his passion started. "Not really," he finally confessed, "but I felt my goal in life was to save people. Becoming a doctor felt like the most tangible way to achieve that."

"Why?" I asked. I knew doctors always had specific reasons for pursuing their profession. The path isn't easy, so there must always be something deeper that drives them to continue. I wanted to know what it was that drove Liam so much. This wasn't just idle curiosity. This was a chance to truly understand the man who held my heart, his motivations, and his core.

"Why what?"

"Why do you want to save people?"

Liam leaned back in his chair, like he needed an impulse to answer that question. "I told you that answer a while ago," he responded. "Maybe saving others is a way to save myself."

There was another great silence. Each response I received from Liam seemed to peel back one layer only to reveal another, more complex one beneath. It was as if he didn't want me to know what was really going through his mind on purpose.

But I couldn't figure out why.

Picking up the book that was resting on the nightstand, Liam began reading again. "In today's chapter, we'll finally find out what happened to the fairy who fell into the cave."

I remained silent. That was his way of telling me the conversation about him was over. And I still felt like I didn't know anything about him.

CHAPTER 26

Despair

"So, Dr. Butler, what's the verdict?" Dad's hand landed heavily on my shoulder, a gesture meant to comfort but somehow feeling like an anchor. My mother squeezed my left hand next to me.

Today was the day the doctor would decide the course of my medical treatment. I'd already completed four pre-operative chemotherapy sessions successfully, and all day long, the nurses and technicians were doing blood tests, ultrasounds, and different types of studies to find out how my body had received the treatment.

Depending on how the results came out, the doctor would decide whether I could have surgery or not.

"Well, Mr. and Mrs. Russell, the blood tests show Jasmine's holding steady. Hemoglobin and platelets are good, considering the chemo's impact," he started talking.

I nodded. But my expression remained unchanged. I wasn't prepared for anything he would say from now on.

"The treatment seems to be working. We've managed to shrink the tumor significantly. That's fantastic news."

The doctor cleared his throat, setting my file down on the

table to focus on us. "Given the positive response to chemo, we're happy to report we can focus solely on removing the affected kidney. The rest appears healthy and clear." He placed a sonogram image in front of Dad. "Here's the latest scan, showing the localized area of concern."

He paused to let my father examine the ultrasound. He and Mom began to watch it in silence. My gaze remained fixed on the doctor.

"So, what does that mean for surgery?" Dad asked, impatient.

"The sooner we remove the tumor, the less chance of complications," Dr. Butler continued, his voice taking on a more clinical tone. "Which is why we recommend scheduling the surgery for Saturday, September 7th."

Five days. Twelve days earlier than I'd planned.

The words echoed in the silence of the room. Suddenly, I felt like the office was turning black and white, as if the end were too close yet extremely far away. "In five days?" I finally asked, but I already knew the answer. It was more of a way to try to process the information.

The doctor nodded. "That's right, Jasmine, it's the best way to get better."

My father put on an instant smile, though he seemed extremely nervous. "That's excellent news," he said, looking at me.

Mom chimed in, her voice thick with emotion. "Yes, honey, it's almost over. Just a little more, and you'll be cancer-free."

"Sure," I said, still unable to believe it. In five days, I'll be cancer-free. I'll finally be out of this hospital.

I looked at my parents, their faces filled with hope and love. I knew I had to be strong for them and for myself, but I was a little terrified. I was no longer so focused on dying, and this was the most complicated part of the process.

～

When night fell, and I was finally alone, I went up to the roof to watch the stars and breathe some fresh air. The autumn air hit me like a wave, making me think that, eventually, coming up here would be impossible due to the cold.

But I wouldn't need that information anymore.

I had too many feelings fighting in my head. Relief, fear, and hope were all there trying to be the main one, but I still couldn't figure out how I really wanted to feel. It still seemed unreal how quickly these months had passed. At first, the time in this place seemed eternal. Now, I didn't even have time to process what was happening.

"I knew I was going to find you here." Liam came in through the front door and sat next to me.

"Hey," I replied, my voice shaky. I didn't look back until he was close enough that I couldn't ignore him.

His hair looked lighter than ever under the moonlight. Even with the shadows of exhaustion under his eyes, he had a glow that made him look like he was from another planet. There was something about him that always made me feel safe, like everything would be okay as long as he was around.

"So, what were you thinking?" he asked, his voice gentle and curious.

I turned my head again to the sky, unable to meet his gaze for too long. "I got the news today. The doctor said the chemo worked. The tumor shrank enough that they can do the surgery in five days. They think I'll be cancer-free after. I won't even need more chemo."

For a moment, there was something in his eyes—relief, perhaps, but there was something else too, a fleeting glimpse of something darker, a shadow that flitted across his eyes before vanishing as quickly as it appeared. He looked away, staring out at the horizon, his jaw tight.

"That's... that's amazing news, Jasmine. You should be thrilled," he said, but his voice sounded hollow, as if he wanted to say the opposite of what he meant.

"Why do you sound like that?" I asked, feeling a knot of worry tighten in my chest. "Aren't you happy for me?"

He turned back to me. The usual warmth I always found in his eyes had been replaced by a swirling vortex of doubt. "Of course, I'm happy for you. It's just... It's just that there are a lot of things from your list that we still need to do; we haven't gone to a bar, or that place Ronnie recommended to see the stars, or even..."

"Liam, what are you talking about?" I interrupted him. "We can still do those things when I get better. It will even be more pleasing because I'll be able to do more things; now I'm limited."

I didn't understand why Liam felt like our time was running out if he was the one who had convinced me that my life was just beginning. I was the negative person who didn't know whether I would have a future tomorrow. However, he was acting as if he wasn't the one who'd given me back all the desire to fight.

"I'm not so sure about that, Mine," he lamented.

"Why not?" He wasn't acting like the Liam that I was used to.

What was he hiding behind those clouded eyes?

Maybe he never thought I would recover, and he only wanted my last days to be as painless as possible. Just thinking about that made my stomach twist.

"You never thought I would get better, did you?" I accused him, looking at his eyes to see if there was some honesty in his expression.

He looked at me, offended. "What are you talking about? Of course, I did. I still do."

"Then why don't you look happy? Are you not so sure I'll get out of the surgery room?"

Every question hurt more than the previous one. Something inside me didn't want to know the truth that his limited words hid. But at the same time, I wanted to feel that he wasn't as bad as I felt.

After a moment of silence, he finally confessed. "Because you won't need me anymore."

My breath hitched. That couldn't be it, could it? The very notion felt absurd.

He was the center of my universe; all I could see, all I could feel. Every inch of my body reacts just by thinking about him. And he knew it. Or that's what I thought from the way he kissed me. Those kisses felt like he was sure there was no one else in this world with whom I wanted to spend my days.

I took his hand. "I'll always need you. Maybe not for the same things, but you're part of my life now."

He shook his head, a sad smile tugging at his lips. "Things will change, Jasmine. You'll go back to your life, and I'll... I'll just be another memory of this place. Maybe even a blurry face."

Nothing he was saying made any sense. I just couldn't understand why he was thinking that way. "No, Liam," I insisted, my voice stronger than I felt. "You're not just a memory. You're the reason I've made it this far. I need you in my life, healthy or not."

I wanted to tell him everything he meant to me. I wanted to tell him I'd never felt that way with anyone else. But part of me thought that nothing I could say right now would change his mind. So I didn't say anything.

"I want to believe that," he whispered. "But it scares me. It scares me to think that once you leave here, I'll lose you."

He moved towards me to hold my face in his hands. Then he placed a delicate kiss on my forehead.

"You won't lose me," I promised, squeezing his hand. "I won't let that happen."

"It's easier to get rid of broken toys than keep them."

"But I'm broken too," I admitted, taking his face with my hands too.

He shook his head slowly, putting on a small smile as he stared into my eyes. "Not anymore, my love."

Journal entry 9

September 2, 2024

I'm surprised at how ironic life is.

I've spent all these years looking for a way to make my time on earth meaningful to someone, to make an individual feel that they've changed because of me, and to give purpose to a person's life.

And just when I achieved it, I feel an emptiness inside me. This has been the only time when I wanted to fail.

Because I did the thing I never thought I would do in this process, I started to love.

This feeling is a messy, unpredictable thing. It throws all your carefully constructed plans into disarray because suddenly, your own happiness becomes intertwined with another's.

And this destroyed all my plans. I no longer want the things I used to want. I no longer know if the meaning of my life is to save someone.

The selfish part of me, the part that craved purpose, now craves something far more terrifying—an eternity with her.

The only thing I want right now is to drag the love of my life to the hell where I belong, where we could be together forever.

Because the simple fact of knowing that she'll have a good, long life while I'm not is eating me up inside. I don't want her to get over me, to meet someone else, or to be happy without me.

She is mine and always will be, no matter what I must do to achieve it.

And I know I'm a monster for thinking that way, and I don't know what I should do now, but one thing I'm sure of is that it's not too late.

I know I have to make a choice, and no matter what I do, it will change both of our lives forever.

CHAPTER 27

Happiness

THE FOLLOWING day was full of happiness and positivity among everyone who had contact with me. The news that I was going to have surgery had spread everywhere, causing people to congratulate me and talk about my plans.

Hellen insisted I stay out of the room while I was awake. We spent the morning strolling through the common areas, and now, as night fell, we found ourselves in a waiting room, surrounded by nurses on their break. It was as if everyone was determined to make the most of the time I had left in this place.

"Your first stop after you're out of here," Donna declared, her voice thick with mock offense, "is Cookies Paradise. Hot chocolate on the side is mandatory. Don't even think about arguing with me, Jasmine!"

I just smiled and nodded.

Neither she nor anyone at the nurses' station could know that I'd already been there thanks to Liam the other night. For everyone, I'd never left this hospital in the last few months.

"Absolutely not," Hellen chimed in. "She should have a

party and celebrate with some friends. Maybe a beach trip? Some fresh sea air would do her wonders."

Across from me, Ronnie stood up. "My idea of camping was always the best one ever, right, Jasmine?"

I laughed, shaking my head. "Honestly, you all have such great ideas. I'm sure I'll try them all eventually."

Frank opened his mouth to speak for the first time, his tone playful but with an underlying seriousness. "Let's not get too ahead of ourselves. We need to focus on getting you through surgery first."

"Of course," I replied. "One step at a time."

Anna nudged me gently. "But after that, the world will be your canvas, right?"

"Absolutely," I agreed, feeling a warmth spread through me at the thought. "There's so much I want to do."

As the conversations continued, I glanced around the room, taking in the familiar faces that had become so much more than just medical staff. They were friends, supporters, and part of this unexpected journey that changed overnight.

It's a shame that I hadn't been able to enjoy moments like these from the beginning, I thought.

This process would've been easier if I'd known that I had their full support. Or if I'd simply let others guide me instead of blocking all interaction.

Later that night, after everyone had gone back to their duties, I found myself alone with Hellen. She was cleaning up some paperwork, but I could see the concern in her eyes.

"You're handling all of this remarkably well," she said softly, not looking up from her papers.

I shrugged, trying to downplay the mixed emotions I had. "I have to. What other choice do I have?"

She set the papers down and walked over, placing a hand on my shoulder. "You're stronger than you know, Jasmine.

And no matter what happens, you have a lot of people here who care about you."

She didn't know how much those words meant to me, especially after my strange encounter with Liam last night. Hellen knew what to say even when she didn't know what was going on in my life.

Part of me still wanted to defend Liam's reaction.

Maybe he thinks I won't want to hear from him once I get out of this hospital.

But even if that was the case, it was selfish of him to feel like I had to be stuck here because of him.

He must've been happy even if he was never going to see me because that meant I would have a life.

"Thank you, Hellen," I said. "I couldn't have made it this far without you."

She gave me a reassuring smile. "And don't you forget it. Now, go to your room—I'm tired of you already."

I chuckled, a genuine laugh that surprised even me. "Someday," I teased, "you'll miss me so much you'll wish you'd never said that."

"I hope that day when I can miss you comes."

And I smiled because I knew that deep down, those words meant that she didn't want to see me sick ever again.

I went back to the room, planning what series or book I'd try to finish by Friday, when a voice from the couch exclaimed, "Finally! Hasn't anyone told all those employees that you're just mine?"

CHAPTER 28
Compassion

"Thank goodness you weren't popular when I met you, or you would never have paid attention to me," Liam said from the couch without moving a single finger.

I knew he was waiting for me to come to him. But I still felt weird about our last conversation on the roof the other night.

When the person who you thought would be the happiest for you is the one who makes you feel the worst about your achievements, there's a bit of disappointment that makes you not see them the same way.

It wasn't like the feelings were gone. Liam was still the most ridiculously good-looking guy I'd ever met, and my mind reacted the same way to his presence. He was also the person who'd pulled me out of the hole I was living in, making me see life completely differently.

However, something inside me felt different. I was upset with him for not feeling happy for me, but at the same time, I felt like I shouldn't have the right to feel that way because he had valid points. Besides, he'd been a great support all this time. But that was the problem with disappointments—they made you forget 95% of the positive things because of a single mistake.

"What are you doing here?" I asked, my tone sharper than I intended.

He looked at me, confused. Being in that room had been the most common thing he'd done in the last few weeks. However, I didn't expect him here anymore.

"I wanted to see you. I couldn't just keep living my life knowing you'd be alone in your last days here."

I crossed my arms, trying to keep my distance. "I'm not alone, Liam. The nurses and staff have been with me the whole day. I'm fine if this is what worries you."

He raised an eyebrow in disbelief. I was also surprised to hear myself say those words. The Jasmine of months ago would've been just as confused by what I just said. But I decided not to react to his expression so he would know I was completely serious.

"That's good. I'm happy for that." He sighed and leaned forward, resting his elbows on his knees. "But you know I have to be here too. It's important for me to see you well. Or don't you want me here anymore?"

I wanted to believe him, to let go of the hurt from our last conversation, but it wasn't that simple. "It's just... what you said on the roof. It's hard to forget that."

Liam ran a hand through his hair, looking genuinely distressed. "I know, Jasmine. I'm sorry. I was selfish and scared. The thought of losing you, of you moving on without me... it messed with my head."

This time, I wasn't in the mood to fight. I sat up in the bed and looked at him. "I get it. You told me that already. I just wanted you to be happy that everything would be over in one way or another."

He stood up, approaching the bed cautiously as if he were

waiting for me to react somehow. "I'm happy for you, more than you'll ever know."

"So?" I said.

"So I want to compensate you for hurting you," he replied. "I want to show you that your happiness and well-being are so important to me that you'll never again have any doubts to the contrary. I want to make you feel so good that nobody could ever make you feel down ever again, because you already know what it means to be appreciated."

My whole body reacted to those words. I didn't want to sound excited by his words, but my curiosity won that battle. "How?"

"Let's go on one last adventure before the surgery. Just you and me. Let's make your last day here unforgettable."

"When?"

"Friday night." He extended his hand for me to take.

I looked at it for a few seconds, then I took it.

Instead of just holding my hand, he pulled me toward him with an intensity I hadn't expected. His lips met mine in a kiss that was different from all the others we'd shared before.

There was an unexpected urgency now—like he was desperate to let me know we belonged to each other. His hands found my waist, gripping me firmly as he lifted me onto the table behind us.

I gasped softly against his lips, but any protest I might've had melted away as he leaned into me, his kisses deepening until all the words I wanted to say disappeared from my mind.

We kissed until neither of us had breath left, and even then, he lingered, his forehead pressed to mine, his warm breath fanning over my lips.

When I tried to stand up, needing a moment to process everything, he pulled me back, wrapping me in a hug so tight it felt like he never wanted to let go.

In that instant, a thousand unspoken words found their

voice. Maybe he was right. Maybe his fear had twisted his words on the rooftop, turning them into a reflection of his own anxieties.

So, I promised myself I'd find a way to let him know he'd always be in my heart.

CHAPTER 29
Enthusiasm

I NEVER THOUGHT I'd wish for one day to arrive as much as I wanted Friday to come. I waited, and waited, and waited, until it finally happened.

As the hours ticked by, my palms grew clammy, and my heart raced. I couldn't pinpoint exactly why I felt this way— Liam and I had gone out before. But tonight felt different; it carried a weight I couldn't fully grasp.

Maybe it was the feeling that the surgery was approaching, making every moment seem more precious and limited. Or perhaps it was the still unresolved tension between Liam, me, and all the unspoken words and hurt feelings.

Whatever it was, the incoming night seemed electric, charged with a nervous energy that terrified and excited me at the same time.

That morning, Donna was cleaning my room as she always did on Friday morning. On a good day, I'd chat with her, asking about her children or the latest drama with her neighbors. Her stories often filled the silence, making the hours pass a little quicker. But today was different. My attention darted between the clock and the window, counting down the hours, the minutes, the seconds. My foot tapped against the floor as if trying to keep up with the rhythm of my racing thoughts.

Donna noticed, of course. She paused mid-swipe, her hands clutching a spray bottle and cloth. "You're jittery today, Jasmine," she said, raising an eyebrow. "More so than usual."

I let out a nervous laugh, brushing it off. "Just... waiting for something."

Donna's lips curled into a knowing smile as she set down her cleaning supplies and pulled up a chair. "Waiting, huh? Well, that's a skill in itself."

I frowned. "How is waiting a skill? It's just... sitting here and doing nothing while time tortures you."

She chuckled, shaking her head. "That's where you're wrong, sweetie. Patience isn't about doing nothing. It's about learning to find peace while you wait. Because when you do, the reward feels so much sweeter."

I looked at her skeptically. "And how exactly am I supposed to do that?"

Donna leaned back in her chair, crossing her arms. "Let me tell you a story. When my youngest, Ben, was little, he wanted a bike more than anything. But money was tight, and I couldn't just buy it for him outright. So, I made him save for it. Every week, he'd do little chores—helping me with laundry, tidying up, even washing the neighbor's car—and put away whatever he earned in a jar."

She smiled, her eyes distant as she recalled the memory. "At first, he was impatient, asking me every day if he'd saved enough. But as the weeks went by, he started to enjoy the process. He'd count his money proudly, imagining the bike he'd buy. And when the day finally came, and he had enough to get that bike, the joy on his face... it was worth every bit of waiting."

"So, you're saying that I should enjoy the waiting?" The thought itself sounded absurd.

"I'm saying you should trust that the best things are worth the wait. Instead of focusing on what hasn't come yet, look around. Find something in the now that makes you happy. Because once the moment you're waiting for comes, it'll be gone before you know it."

I glanced at the clock again, then at the window, but this time, her words softened the edge of my impatience.

Donna stood, picking up her cleaning supplies. "You've got a big day ahead, Jasmine. Don't let the waiting steal your joy. You'll get there soon enough."

As she left the room, I took a deep breath, her story replaying in my mind. I looked around—all my stuff now organized on the table and in the corner, the sunlight streaming through the window, the faint scent of lavender from Donna's cleaning spray.

Maybe Donna's right, and the best thing I can do is to find something to spend my time on.

When the floor looked completely dry, I stood up and took my tablet. At least by drawing, I could daydream while expressing my imagination.

Liam was supposed to pick me up at 8:00 p.m., so by 7:20 p.m., I was walking from one spot to another in my room, unable to sit still. Drawing had helped the hours pass more quickly, but as the time approached, my mind became more and more blocked, making it impossible for me to focus.

I changed my outfit twice, finally settling on a simple blue dress, a jacket, and sneakers that felt both casual and special. I wanted to look nice but not like I was trying too hard.

My hair was already forming brown curls on my forehead, so for the first time in months, I decided to leave them free, combing it back so they wouldn't interfere with my vision.

215

When I looked at the mirror, I almost didn't recognize the person in the reflection. For the first time in a long time, I felt myself. Not just because the sickness was almost over, but because I was more satisfied with my life.

I wasn't going to have to wear that stupid hat anymore.

I no longer felt sorry for myself. I no longer felt like a dying person. I was just a person.

By the time the clock hit 7:50 p.m., I was waiting by the window, watching for any sign of his car. Each minute seemed to stretch on forever.

Would we talk about the future? Would he open up more about himself?

At 8:00 p.m., I saw his car pull up. My heart did a little flip, and I grabbed my little backpack, taking one last deep breath before heading downstairs. I didn't even wait for him to come for me. The less time we wasted, the more we could enjoy the night.

The cool evening air hit my face as I stepped outside, calming me a bit.

Let's go, Jasmine, one more time.

Liam got out of the car, and the sight of him made me smile instantly. Thankfully, he looked almost as nervous as I felt, which was oddly comforting because I thought I was going to pass out at any minute.

"Hey," he said as soon as I was close. "You look amazing."

"Thanks," I replied, feeling a blush creep up my cheeks. "You too."

He opened the car door for me, and once we were both settled in, he took my hand. "How are you feeling?"

"Fine." Even if I were falling apart, that would be my answer. This time, I wasn't going to let cancer ruin my night. I would do everything possible to be happy because I could control today, but I wasn't so sure about tomorrow.

Liam stood still for a few minutes, studying me. After

making sure I was telling the truth, he put his seatbelt back on. "Perfect, let's go then."

"Tonight, we'll go to multiple places. Can you guess the first one?" Liam said while driving.

I took the list out of my bag and started rereading it. Some things were already marked as ready, but many were still pending. I knew we wouldn't be able to do everything before the surgery, so I assumed the ones we were doing tonight were the most important.

"Are we going to go bowling, maybe?" I guessed, hoping to start with something fun and light-hearted.

"No, but close," he said with a grin. "We're going to an abandoned theme park."

An abandoned park was not on my list. Either Liam misread my notes, or he was going to improvise. "Why an abandoned one? There's a new one that's very popular and open two hours from here."

"Because I want to show you the beauties you can find in lost causes, too. We can go to a normal park on any other day."

For some reason, I loved that last sentence. Liam was making plans with me for the future. This night was the end of something, but it also felt like the beginning of a new Jasmine. And Liam was finally accepting it.

When we arrived at the park, I was surprised to see that some lamps still illuminated the streets. But apart from that, everything looked awful. The concrete of the paths was broken, there was grass and trees everywhere, and everything seemed very dirty.

"Do you come here often?" I asked him as I scanned the place. In another scenario, this place would be terrifying, but I felt safe and at peace. I knew there was nothing to fear here, especially if I was with Liam.

"Since I returned to the city, yes. I can hardly sleep, so I thought this would be a good place to spend some time when I'm not at the hospital."

We started walking, and I started imagining how wonderful this place must have been when it was operating.

"I used to come here when I was a kid," Liam said softly, his eyes scanning the familiar yet changed landscape. "It was always so full of life and excitement."

"I could see," I responded. "This place must have been the happiness of many children at some point."

"But not anymore," he lamented.

He must have had a good time here from the weight of his words, so I decided not to say anything, as there was nothing positive to point out at the moment.

We walked for a while, looking at the broken machines, games that had never been turned on again, and grass that was there from the abandonment of the place.

"We arrived," Liam said, smiling, pointing me to some-thing in front of us. "This is where I wanted to bring you."

My eyes widened in shock. In front of me was an old carousel that looked like it didn't belong there. Contrary to everything around it, that machine was in good condition. Yes, it was old and needed some paint, but it looked good.

"How is this possible?" I asked. There was no way that carousel could have stayed that way for so long.

I took my camera out of my bag and took a picture of it. The contrast with everything around it looked beautiful in its own way. I was thrilled to be able to capture this feeling on camera. It was as if the photographs spoke for me.

"I fixed it," he replied proudly. "Let's test it out."

We approached one of the horses, and Liam helped me get on. Then, he went back to the control center to turn it on.

Incredibly, it worked, and seconds later, I was spinning around while listening to a happy song.

Liam sat on the metal horse next to mine, and we both began to enjoy the ride. I felt like I was in an oasis in a desert. As if among all the bad things, I could still find a small space of peace.

The lights at the entrance and the path now made sense. Liam must have been coming here occasionally to fix the place up.

When it was over, we sat on a bench near the exit. "Why did you decide to fix it?"

"I knew I wasn't going to be able to fix the whole park at once, so I focused on my favorite game of all," he replied. "I just wanted to prove to myself that everything can be fixed, no matter how terrible its condition, if you put the necessary attention and care into it."

For some reason, that last sentence made me feel sad. I felt like Liam was constantly forcing himself to fix all the lost causes. Like it was his obligation to make everything feel better. But at the same time, I was happy he was sharing a little of his personality and the burden he carried. This was his way of showing me who he was.

I thought about the hospital, and how there are so many damaged things; maybe one person couldn't handle everything. But there are enough people so that everyone can focus their time on each one.

"You know," I said, "Even if you couldn't fix everything, the grass around here shows us that there could be another new beginning. We can't keep the world turning by ourselves, but the world shows us that it can take care of the broken parts and be reborn from nothing, too."

He put his gaze on me, surprised by my words, but didn't say anything.

His silence made me feel like maybe that wasn't the lesson

he was hoping I would learn here. But I wanted him to see my perspective on the place, too. I wanted him to know that he shouldn't carry so much weight on his shoulders. That he might be good at many things, but that didn't mean he had to be responsible for all of them.

After several seconds, he broke the silence, ignoring everything I just said. "Ready for the next place?"

"Of course I am," I replied, jumping from the bench. "There's a list we must complete tonight."

❧

The second place we arrived at was a museum. But it wasn't the art showroom that was on my list. To my surprise, it was a science museum. "This specific place has a meaning, too?"

I knew Liam loved science in some way. That's why he was a doctor. However, my interests were always more on the creative side than in the scientific realm. I don't know why Liam thought it was a good idea to bring me here—I never gave him any indication of being that interested beyond the night he showed me the stars.

"Everything we'll do tonight has a meaning, Mine," he answered confidently, like he was expecting this question at some point in the night.

I nodded silently as we started walking to the entrance. Even though the museum was closed, the lock was deliberately opened. It was as if someone had left it that way on purpose.

As we passed through that door, Liam motioned for me to move quietly and carefully to the back of the building, where a window had also been left open.

We climbed through the window and found ourselves in a dimly lit hallway, the glow of the exit signs casting eerie shadows on the walls. But Liam knew exactly where to walk, as if he'd been here a hundred times.

He led me to a large exhibit room filled with interactive displays and scientific wonders. The room had an other-worldly feel, with models of planets hanging from the ceiling and glowing panels explaining various scientific phenomena.

He stopped in front of a large glass case containing a replica of the solar system. The planets were meticulously crafted, each one rotating slowly on its axis.

"Humans believe they know everything about life and the earth," Liam began, his voice soft but firm. "But the reality is that we don't know even 5%."

I began to see each of the planets while listening to Liam. All of them were in their place, functioning in the same way around the sun. It was incredible to see how big the universe was compared to the Earth.

I tried to analyze what he'd just said: how sometimes it seems like we know everything, but the solar system is probably just a small part of something much bigger.

"What do you think we're missing?" I asked him.

I didn't know much about the world's advances, but I did know that we were very developed in terms of science and technology. For example, thanks to the knowledge of multiple people, I can fight cancer and be alive today.

"The most important part of everything. Death."

My heart jumped. Death was one of the things that scared me the most, especially now that I was so close to it. I was terrified of not being able to live life, of not doing the thousands of things I dreamed of, and of not having experiences that many people had already had, and I had not. The only thing I knew about death was that I didn't want to feel like I was close to it anymore.

"What do you mean? What should we know about death?"

"We're not scared of death. We're scared not to know what

happens after," he responded. "If we knew there was something more, we wouldn't be so scared to experience it."

"And do you think there is something more?"

"I'm certain of it," he answered without hesitation.

"Why?" I started to think about what Liam wanted me to learn about this place. Maybe that, despite what happens tomorrow, I shouldn't be scared. However, being positive about either option was difficult, especially after living the way I was now.

"Come here; I'll explain why I'm so sure in my favorite place in the museum."

I followed him down a narrow hallway to a dark, seemingly empty room. When we were inside, he quietly locked the door behind us and turned something on.

Suddenly, lights began to appear around the room, flickering like distant stars and planets. The darkness transformed into a breathtakingly vivid representation of the cosmos. The walls and ceiling came alive with swirling galaxies, twinkling stars, and vibrant nebulae. It felt as if we were floating in space, suspended in the vastness of the universe.

The planets moved slowly in their orbits, casting soft glows that illuminated our faces. The Milky Way stretched across the ceiling, its countless stars shimmering like diamonds on velvet. A comet streaked across the room, leaving a trail of sparkling light in its wake.

I stood in awe, my breath taken away by the beauty and immensity of the scene. The room seemed to expand, making me feel both small and infinitely connected to the cosmos.

Liam stepped closer, his hand finding mine in the dim light. "This is my favorite place," he whispered, his voice full of emotion. "Whenever I feel lost or overwhelmed, I come here to remember how vast and beautiful the universe is. It always gives me a different perspective, reminds me that we're part of something much bigger than ourselves."

I squeezed his hand. I felt like I was finally getting to know him, and every place we were going was part of who he was.

"We're such a small part of the universe that I find it hard to believe that life is just what we know," he continued. "I firmly know there's something beyond this life because we're very limited beings in a large and eternal universe, and I know that humans can't know everything."

"I've always feared death because I feel that when I die, I'll simply cease to exist," I responded. "I think your perspective is a more positive way of seeing things, although I still don't know what would be a better alternative to living."

I felt like the way he explained death to me was a way of making me feel like I shouldn't worry. But as much as I wanted to think that I was going to be okay with any outcome tomorrow, I wanted to live.

He smiled, his eyes reflecting the starry glow around us. A shower of stars began to fall everywhere, making us both look at the ceiling and what was around us. He began to talk while we watched the show. "I wanted you to see this because, to me, you're like a star. Bright, resilient, and full of wonder. No matter what happens, you'll always shine."

I started looking at him, no longer interested in anything that was happening around me. He was the only thing I wanted to focus on right now.

He turned to me, his eyes reflecting the glow of the planets. "You've become a part of my universe. Just like these planets, each moment we've shared orbits around us, creating something beautiful and meaningful."

I was touched by his words, feeling a deep connection to him that I knew I'd never experience with anyone else.

I put my hands around his neck, and then we kissed slowly. The kiss felt as magical and infinite as the space surrounding us, where the two of us were the center of the universe, orbiting each other in a dance of love and light.

We spent the next hour exploring the exhibits, laughing, and learning together. Liam explained the science behind the displays with enthusiasm, making even the most complex concepts seem fascinating. I found myself captivated, not just by the exhibits but by the passion in his eyes as he spoke.

I took out my camera and photographed my favorite places in the museum that I wanted to remember, especially the dark room, where the only things visible through the lens were the stars illuminating the place.

Liam made even the least exciting thing fascinating. He had the power to make whatever he said incredible.

And I knew I never wanted to be away from it.

CHAPTER 30
Love

IT WAS 1:00 a.m. Liam was driving to our third and final spot of the night while I was trying to rest with the passenger seat down. By this point, I was exhausted. I had walked a lot, and every muscle in my body ached softly as a result.

I was never sleepy at this time. However, at this moment, I had a deep desire to close my eyes, even for a few minutes. I started thinking that maybe everything I was feeling was thanks to my illness, letting me know that it had reached its limit.

The engine's hum and the car's gentle vibrations began to lull me into a light doze. Liam's hand found mine again, his thumb tracing soothing circles on the back of my hand.

The night had been magical, and despite my exhaustion, a part of me desperately wanted to stay awake to savor every moment. But my eyelids were heavy, and the pull of sleep was irresistible.

"Almost there," Liam murmured, noticing I was quieter than expected.

I nodded, too tired to respond. The last thing I saw before

sleep claimed me was the silhouette of Liam, focused on the road, a small smile playing on his lips.

When I woke up, the car was no longer moving. We were parked in a secluded spot, surrounded by trees and the distant sound of waves crashing against the shore. Liam gently squeezed my hand to wake me fully.

"I'm so sorry," I mumbled, my voice thick with sleep. "I don't know why I fell asleep. Did we lose a lot of time?"

"Don't worry, I just parked. How are you feeling?" His voice sounded worried, as if it had been a bad idea to have forced myself so much.

"I'm fine, don't worry," I lied, forcing a smile. "The trip relaxed me too much, that's all." The truth was, exhaustion gnawed at the edges of my consciousness, and despite having slept, I now had a slight headache.

However, I wasn't going to let the illness ruin my last night, so I took a deep breath and pressed the passenger seat button that had me pinned down.

As I sat up fully, the world outside the car window came into focus. My breath hitched in my throat, and I suddenly stopped thinking about how bad I felt.

We were in front of a beach.

My happiness was inexplicable, and I instantly smiled when I realized what being here meant for us.

My drawing of Liam on the beach was the reason we started talking. Knowing that this was one of the places that represented meaning in his life felt incredibly good, as if I had made Liam change somehow.

I represented a special part of his heart.

We stepped out of the car, the cool night air instantly refreshing me. Liam led me down a narrow path that opened up to the beach. The moonlight reflected off the water, creating a shimmering pathway across the ocean's surface.

"I saved the best for last," Liam said in my ears, wrapping his arm around my shoulders.

"I wonder why," I responded without taking the smile off my face.

We walked along the shore, the sand cool beneath our feet. The world felt calm and peaceful, the only sounds being the gentle lapping of the waves and our footsteps. We weren't talking, but the existing silence didn't feel awkward. It was as if we both needed this quiet space, this shared serenity before the night drew to a close.

I pulled out my camera, drawn to capture the moment's beauty. The camera clicked softly as I snapped photos of our footprints in the sand, of the moon casting a silvery sheen on the water's surface, and of the wispy clouds scudding across the star-dusted canvas of the night sky.

At one point, Liam took the camera from me, his touch lingering a beat too long before he pointed the camera at me. I instinctively raised a hand to shield my face, a self-conscious reflex born from months of feeling out of place in my own skin. But Liam was quicker, snapping the photo before I could fully react.

In the photo, I had an inexplicable smile; I'd never seen myself so happy before. In that instant, I knew this picture would become one of my most treasured possessions.

We stopped at a large rock, smooth and worn by the relentless caress of the waves, and sat down, side by side.

"So, why are we here?" I asked, eager to know what he had to say.

He took a deep breath, his gaze meeting mine with an intensity that made me feel shy. "June 19, 2019," he said. "That was the day my life changed."

"Five years ago," I replied, the pieces slowly starting to click into place. "That was the day you decided to become a doctor?"

"Not exactly, but it was a start," he said, his eyes distant as if reliving that pivotal moment. "It took me four years to get to where I am today, but that day was the turning point."

"So what happened that made you change in that year?"

He hesitated for a moment, but then he opened his mouth again, the words feeling heavy. "I opened my eyes that morning and knew my life had to change immediately. I was lost," he explained. "Until then, I felt like I'd done nothing in my life. And it was like I ruined everything up to that point. I wasted too much time focusing on too many unimportant things."

I wasn't fully understanding what he was trying to tell me. "Were you in a bad place? Did you do something illegal?"

"I was sick, Jasmine," Liam said gently. "And depressed. That day was the day I realized I wasted too much time lost in sadness."

I felt like my heart stopped. Liam had been sick. That's why he decided to become a doctor: he wanted to save people the way someone had saved him. That's why he chose to save me and never gave up. He had been as depressed as I was. He knew what it felt like to be in the same position as I was.

A lot of thoughts started running through my mind. I felt a little guilty about the way I had treated him when we met. I wouldn't have been so cruel if I had known from the beginning.

"Why hadn't you told me before? I would've been less harsh on you, or maybe I would've felt you understood me better."

"I didn't want you to see me as a poor, sick patient. You know that feeling perfectly."

I stayed silent for a few minutes. He was right. The worst thing I have felt in these months while being sick is being treated just like an ill person.

Part of me wanted to know everything—what kind of

illness he had had, how long he was locked up, what had made him change his mind about his sadness, and how he had dealt with his recovery. However, I knew from personal experience that forcing him to talk about his disease was not the best thing to do right now, mainly because this night was a time to forget about the bad things.

"So after that day, you decided to make a change."

"Yes," he continued his story. "I didn't know exactly how my life was going to change. But a year later, I discovered that what I had to do was save people."

Now everything clicked into place.

I understood perfectly why he never gave up on me; Liam saw himself in me. He always knew he could fix me because he had gone through the same thing I was going through now.

"Though I haven't had much luck saving people so far," he confessed. "I feel like I'm more of the angel of death."

"That's why the beach is important," I realized.

"Yes, because that day I saw your drawing, I felt that I was making an impact on someone, even if at first it was a negative one. When I was here on the beach that day, I realized you were the person I was always destined to save."

His story made everything make sense, especially the way he had been so persistent and dedicated. It was more than just a desire to help; it was deeply personal for him.

"You did save me, Liam," I said softly. "Not just physically, but you gave me hope and made me believe in the future. You were my rock through all of this."

He smiled, but there was a trace of sadness in his eyes. "I just want you to be happy, Jasmine. That's all I've ever wanted."

I sighed. "I am. Especially because now I feel like I finally know you."

He laughed hard. "As I told you before, I'm a pretty boring boy."

"That's not true," I laughed. "I want to know everything about you. I hope one day I can."

We sat in silence for a while, just enjoying each other's company. The night was perfect, the kind of night you wish could last forever.

And for a moment, it felt like that as if this moment wasn't going to end. I started wondering whether all this was real or just the kind of feeling you get when life is over.

Was I really going to have surgery tomorrow, and everything would end, or was this going to be my last night?

Why did everything suddenly feel like it was in slow motion?

"Okay, let's start with my most important fact about me." Liam interrupted my thoughts, making me go back to the present. "I want to tell you something, but promise me you won't answer until we see each other again."

"I promise," I said nervously, feeling a knot tighten in my stomach.

Liam took a deep breath, and his eyes searched mine with an intensity that took my breath away. Then, with a voice hoarse, he whispered three simple words that echoed in the quiet night:

"I love you."

CHAPTER 31
Fatigue

LIAM SAID HE LOVED ME, and I knew I didn't have to wait another day to tell him my answer. I loved him back very deeply, with all the strength I didn't know I owned.

There hasn't been a moment when I haven't thought about Liam since the first time I saw him. He was woven into the fabric of my days—in my dreams, in the mundane tasks I performed, in the decisions I made, in the very core of my being.

He'd shown me a world painted in brighter hues, a world where even if tomorrow wasn't guaranteed, today held the potential for joy. He'd rekindled a flicker of hope within me, a fight I hadn't known I possessed. There weren't enough words, no grand declarations, to express the depth of my feelings for him.

But he didn't want an answer. He wanted to ensure I would fight a little more to have the strength to respond.

And that was what I was going to do.

I will wake up tomorrow, not just for myself, but for the chance to see the love in his eyes mirrored back in mine.

Taking a deep breath, I met his gaze. "Well, it's your decision," I finally responded, my voice stronger than I expected. "If I die, you'll regret every day for not knowing my answer."

He smiled evilly. "Who knows, maybe I'll follow you to hell just to know your response."

With my left hand, I pushed him lightly on his arm, pretending to be offended. "It's obvious that I'm going to heaven. I'm the purest person you've ever met."

"Sure, sure, little angel. So where are you supposed to be right now?" He looked at me like he was challenging me to answer, and I was enjoying every little thing about it.

"This doesn't count," I countered, approaching his face and giving him a light kiss on his lips. "Technically, you kidnapped me."

"That's what you'll say if you get caught?" He teased, grabbing me by the waist to prevent me from going back to where I was.

The action took me by surprise. No matter how tough I was trying to appear, Liam always found a way to make my legs feel weak with his actions.

"Maybe," I whispered to his lips. "I have a whole story prepared."

"You know what? I don't even want to know," he said, kissing me on the cheeks. Then, he glanced at his watch. "We still have a couple of hours before you need to be in your room. Is there anything you'd like to do before we head back?"

I couldn't think of anything else I wanted to do today, even knowing that tomorrow was uncertain. Liam had made this night exactly how I imagined it would be, and I wouldn't change a thing that had happened so far.

Even though we hadn't accomplished anything on my list, I had gotten to know a side of Liam that I never thought I'd be able to understand. So I was satisfied with the happiness that everything I'd done today had brought me.

"Not really," I finally said, my voice soft. "This night has been... more than perfect."

He looked at me disappointed, as if he didn't want the night to end as much as I did. "Well, do you want to swim then?"

The suggestion startled a laugh out of me. "Are you joking? We could die."

He laughed so loud that it made me blush. "My sweet Mine, if you die tomorrow, I'm sure what you would regret most is not swimming with me tonight."

And as if he knew he didn't have to tell me anything else because I was already convinced, he stood up and helped me to my feet, too. When we were both standing, and he made sure I was okay, we jumped off the rock into the sea.

I didn't care that my body felt weaker than ever, that the September cold was already making the nights unbearable, that the water had been so cold that it made my lungs gasp for air for a moment. The only thing that mattered was being in Liam's arms.

The water was shockingly cold, sending a jolt through my body. But the initial sting quickly faded as I surfaced, laughing and gasping for breath. Liam's arms encircled me, pulling me close. The moonlight reflected off the water, creating a magical, shimmering dance around us.

In my mind, we were the only two people in the world at that moment.

"You're crazy," I laughed, shivering slightly but feeling more alive than I had in months.

"Crazy for you," he replied, his voice low and tender. He held me tighter, and we began to sway in the water. It was an impromptu dance, our movements slow and fluid, guided by the rhythm of the waves.

We moved together; our bodies pressed close, the water around us like a silken embrace. Liam's hand found its way to the small of my back, guiding me gently while his other hand held mine securely. I rested my head against his chest, listening to the steady beat of his heart. It was a sound I never wanted to forget.

He tilted my chin up, our eyes locking in a moment of perfect understanding. His lips met mine, and the world seemed to dance around us. The kiss was slow, deep, and filled with all the unspoken words we couldn't say. It was a promise, a plea, and a declaration all at once.

Time lost all meaning as we danced and kissed under the moonlit sky. The cold water was a distant memory, replaced by the warmth of Liam's touch and the fire of our connection. I felt safe, loved, and profoundly at peace.

But as the minutes passed, I began to feel a creeping fatigue. It started as a dull ache in my limbs, then like a heavy weight in my chest. I tried to ignore it, to focus on the joy of being with Liam, but it grew harder with each passing moment.

"Liam," I murmured, my voice weak. "I think... I need to rest."

He pulled back with concern, "Jasmine? Are you okay?"

"I don't know," I admitted, feeling a strange lightheadedness. My vision blurred, the stars above us turning into smudges of light. "I'm so tired."

Panic flashed in Liam's eyes as he held me tighter. "Stay with me, Mine. Stay with me."

I tried to respond, to reassure him, but my body felt like it was made of lead. Everything around me started to fade, the world going dark at the edges. The last thing I saw was Liam's terrified face, his voice a distant echo in my ears.

"Jasmine! Jasmine, wake up! Please!"

And then, there was nothing but darkness.

CHAPTER 32

Relief

SOME MOMENTS in life create a line between who you were and who you become.

You don't recognize them immediately. They arrive quietly, like a whisper.

But as time passes, the weight of those moments grows heavier, undeniable.

They shape you, break you, rebuild you.

And one day, you see it clearly: you are not the same person.

Some people are reborn in the aftermath of tragedy. Some through survival, others through loss.

I was born again when I realized that even though I felt like I was going to die, I could still enjoy what was left of my life. And I didn't regret each of the moments in which I was happy.

Every moment mattered. Even locked in a room.

Every laugh, every touch, every fleeting second of happiness was a gift.

And when I looked back, I didn't regret anything.

I cherished the courage it took to find joy in the face of everything.

Because, in the end, happiness isn't about how long it lasts — it's about having the bravery to feel it, even when it feels like the world is ending.

CHAPTER 33

Faith

I woke up in my hospital bed, the cold plastic tube of an oxygen machine pressed against my face. My body ached, and my head throbbed with a dull, persistent pain. I tried to move, but every muscle protested.

I wondered how Liam managed to bring me back here, but my memories were nonexistent.

In the distance, I could hear Hellen's voice raised in anger. "Who authorized giving her oxygen? What exactly happened last night?"

A voice answered, "According to her record, one of the nurses found her on the floor of the shower while she was short of breath and had to give her first aid to revive her."

I recognized the voice as Butler's.

"Why was she in the shower that late? None of this makes sense," Hellen responded, frustration evident in her tone. "We have to wait for her to be stable for the operation. She can't go to surgery in those conditions."

"We can't wait another day, and her collapse is a big indicator for that," Butler insisted. "The surgery is now, whether you like it or not."

I moved slightly, drawing their attention. They both approached the bed, concern etched on their faces.

"How are you, little one?" Hellen asked softly.

"Where's Liam?" I barely managed to whisper.

They exchanged puzzled glances, clearly unsure of who I was referring to.

"Your parents are in the waiting room," Hellen answered.

The doctor stepped forward, his expression serious. "Last night, you had a collapse. We assume it was the cancer fighting against your body. That's why we want to remove the kidney as quickly as possible. We're going to move you to the surgery room soon. The nurses will come to check your vitals, and then we'll proceed."

I nodded weakly, too exhausted to argue. My thoughts were a whirlwind of fear and confusion, but one thing was clear: I had to live.

This couldn't be the end.

The nurses arrived shortly after, checking my vitals and preparing me for surgery. My parents entered the room after I was able to breathe on my own, and my mom's face was clearly concerned about the lack of information about what happened last night. Hellen also stayed by my side; she doubted the doctor's decision, but I tried to make her feel that everything was okay.

"You're strong, Jasmine," she said softly. "If you believe you can do it, then you will."

As I was wheeled towards the operating room, I clung to those words. I focused on the image of Liam's face in my mind. The memories of everything that happened last night were still vivid in my mind, and I tried to relive every moment as they prepared me.

Even though I wasn't at my best, I didn't feel scared. I would fight. I would face whatever came next. Because if I survived, I had a future waiting for me.

The bright lights of the operating room greeted me as the doors swung open. I felt a rush of cold air and the sterile smell of antiseptic. The anesthesiologist leaned over me, his voice calm and soothing. "I'll give you something to help you sleep now, Jasmine. Just relax and count backward from ten."

I nodded, my vision already beginning to blur. "Ten, nine, eight..."

Darkness enveloped me, and I let it take me, knowing that when I woke up, I'd be one step closer to a new me.

CHAPTER 34
Nostalgia

IT'S BEEN three months and a few weeks since I had surgery. Thankfully, everything had gone well.

The physical transformation was undeniable. I've been gaining back a little weight, my hair is longer, and overall, I've had more energy. I felt prettier, more confident, and like a person my age.

A month after my operation, Dr. Butler gave us the excellent news that I wouldn't need more chemotherapy because all the malignant cells were gone in the procedure, so I was officially cancer-free.

That was the best news my family could receive after fighting so much this year, and everything got better and better every day from then on.

My parents encouraged me to paint more by setting aside an area in the patio gazebo for it. They bought me weekly books, so I always had something good to read, and they looked for photography schools, so when I was ready, I would have all the best options.

With each passing day, I felt more alive, and little by little,

I began to make plans for my future when I got well enough to start making things.

When December arrived, I decided to move my painting space to the house's living room. The cold was making me not want to go out. The once-vibrant garden now lay dormant under a thin layer of frost, and the sky seemed perpetually gray, making me nostalgic for some reason.

Everything was going excellently, except for one thing. I hadn't seen Liam again after my blackout at the beach.

I replayed the events of that night in my mind countless times.

The memory of his touch, his words, and the love that had filled every moment haunted me. Despite the joy of being cancer-free, there was an emptiness I couldn't ignore. I had expected to see him again, to share in my recovery and celebrate that I was alive together. But he had vanished without a trace.

Every day, I hoped for a call, a message, anything to let me know he was alright. I reached out to Hellen to see if she'd seen him in the halls, to Anna to see if she could look for him in building number one, and to the other nurses to see if they knew him, but no one seemed to know who he was.

It was as if he'd disappeared into thin air.

I thought he would find a way to go to my house to see how I was doing, but he never made the slightest effort to contact me again. Realizing he wasn't coming when I was recovering in the first weeks was a bitter pill to swallow. I felt betrayed, although we never promised each other anything when I left the hospital.

Part of me thought that maybe his mission was over the moment I entered the operating room. Maybe his goal from the beginning was for me to want to live and to make sure I had hope that everything would be okay. So once he made sure I survived, he walked away from me once and for all.

And if that was the case, I knew I had to be strong and move on. But it broke my heart to think I was just another number in his personal goal.

It didn't make sense at all.

He loved me. I knew it not only because he told me directly that night on the beach but also because I felt it. I remembered the fear in his eyes before I fainted, and I knew that he didn't want anything to happen to me.

But also saying that he loved me could have been his last way of making sure my mind and body would fight just a little bit harder. Knowing that was a possibility made every beautiful memory I had of him seem smaller, so I tried to avoid that scenario as much as I could.

So why hadn't he come back to me?

The uncertainty was a heavy burden to bear. I missed Liam, his laughter, his touch, the way he made me feel seen and understood. And as the days turned into weeks, the longing for answers grew stronger, a persistent ache that refused to be silenced.

One day, I woke up and realized something: He always looked for me even when I wanted him away. Now it was my turn.

When I entered the hospital, I felt my heart sink. I was locked up here for months, and although there were beautiful moments that I would never want to forget here, it was a period of my life that I preferred not to think about again.

In my right hand, I clutched a folder of drawings I hoped to show Liam. In my left hand, I held gifts for some of the nurses. As I walked and met them, I gave them something and chatted a little. When Donna saw me, she hugged me so tightly I thought it would leave me breathless.

I was happy to see how everyone was genuinely delighted to see me, and even if I wanted to stay a little longer with each person, I came with a mission. I decided to go to Building One, the only building I had never visited. That was where the last Liam who worked here was.

Even though I had been re-envisioning the moment we would see each other again over and over again in my head, I was now feeling a little nervous. He always had that effect on me. Like, no matter how much trust we had, I would always feel shy around him.

I knew I'd never be completely ready to face it, so I decided to just do it anyway without thinking about it too much.

When I entered the emergency room and asked for him, the secretary pointed out a tall man I had never seen before. He was not the person I sought.

Liam was never the nurse from building number one.

I thanked the girl and walked out without trying to look too disappointed, but dissatisfaction was fully taking over my body. Liam was lost again. But this time, I had no idea where to start looking.

I walked through every hallway in the hospital where I thought he might be, from the parking lot to see if his car was there, to the roof, hoping he was sitting there staring at the sky like he was when he was there with me. But I got no results. He was nowhere to be found.

After a pointless search, I went to the cafeteria, disappointed about my wasted time. I was frustrated.

Months ago, it seemed easy to find him everywhere I went, as if he indirectly followed me around. Now, it seemed like the opposite, as if he didn't want to be found.

I opened the folder to look at some of the drawings I had made of Liam and whispered, "Where are you, mystery boy? And why don't you want to be found?"

A voice behind me broke my trance. "You have an exceptional talent for drawing realistic faces; it almost feels like I'm seeing that boy again."

I turned around to see Dr. Butler standing there. He was the only person I never asked about Liam, but it was logical that he was one of those who knew him. He was an old man who had worked here practically all his life.

"Do you know him?" I asked, hopeful I would finally get an answer.

"Of course, I knew him," Dr. Butler replied, a warming smile on his face. "He was one of my more difficult patients, and I deal with a lot of challenging people here. Like you, for example," he added, making me laugh.

Patient?

All this time, I had been looking in the wrong place. Dr. Butler's words made everything fall into place.

He wasn't a nurse. He was a patient.

Suddenly, everything made sense. The way he had appeared out of nowhere, his deep understanding of what I was going through, and his own struggles, he had hinted at. Liam had even given me the answer that night on the beach. He was sick.

But I didn't know he was still ill. He told me the story as if it had happened years ago. Maybe he didn't want to tell me so I wouldn't get worried before my surgery, or maybe he got sick again.

I needed some answers, so I looked at the doctor again and asked him, "Do you know where he is now?"

Dr. Butler seemed confused at first, but his expression softened when he felt my stillness. He remained silent for a few minutes, searching for the right words, and then he said, "Jasmine, that boy is dead."

CHAPTER 35
Sanity

I FELT like my heart stopped.

"There must be a mistake," I replied.

I realized my voice was shaking after saying those words.

"I may not remember his name, but I remember the face of every patient I've ever seen who doesn't make it. It's been about five years since that event," he replied. "It's the downside of being a doctor who gets so involved in the lives of patients."

Everything around me seemed to be in slow motion. I started to see everything gray. As if the colors that the world once had no longer existed.

My gaze was focused forward, but I couldn't see anything. My mind had thousands of thoughts simultaneously, but I couldn't concentrate.

The words "he is dead" echoed in a deafening silence. Five years ago, he was gone. My Liam, the one who'd been my constant companion these past months, didn't exist.

That didn't make sense. I was with him three months ago. He was by my side during my last months in this hospital. He couldn't be dead.

If he were dead, who was the person who was with me all this time?

"Are you okay, Miss Russell?" Dr. Butler asked after noticing my silence.

"No... I mean, yes," I hesitated. "Are you sure he's dead?"

Something inside me still couldn't believe what the doctor had just confessed to me. I wished with all my strength that he had been wrong. That he didn't really talk about Liam because the alternative was terrifying.

There was no way Liam wasn't alive.

"Of course I am. He passed away after fighting cancer several years ago. I was the one who issued his death certificate."

Panic surged through me.

My world began to collapse. My head was spinning. I couldn't understand what the doctor was telling me. Liam couldn't be dead. I had seen him a few months ago.

Or not?

"That doesn't make sense," I replied, unable to believe his words. "He was... I..." I stopped. I didn't even know what to say.

It was as if everything I had believed until now was not true. I began to question everything that had happened over the past months. But nothing was logical. It was like I couldn't trust my mind.

Dr. Butler's gaze held a mixture of concern and confusion. "I'm sorry, Jasmine. I had no idea you knew him." There was a silence between us, as if we both knew there were no words to fill this void. "I must go," he finally said, his voice gentle. "It's always a pleasure to see you doing so well."

I tried to say something, but I couldn't. I just watched from my seat how he walked away after telling me the worst news I could receive.

The weight of this revelation was unbearable. I was alone,

adrift in a world that made no sense. As the door closed behind the doctor, I was left alone to confront the terrifying truth: I had lost not only Liam but also the fragile remnants of my sanity.

I felt like I was going crazy. If Liam wasn't real, who had I drawn then? Who was the person who was with me all this time, who gave me hope? Who gave me my first kiss? Who told me they loved me on the beach? Who was the person who haunted my dreams every night?

I slumped back into my chair, my hands trembling as I picked up the scattered drawings. The images of Liam seemed to blur together, and I couldn't tell if the tears in my eyes were making them look that way or if my mind was playing tricks on me.

Why hadn't anyone else seen him? Why did everyone act as if he had never existed?

Could it be that he was a figment of my imagination? But how could something so real, so vivid, be just in my head?

The memories of our time together felt tangible. His touch, his voice, the way he made me laugh, even when I felt like crying. These were not things I could have conjured up on my own.

I left the hospital in a daze, barely noticing the cold December air biting my skin. My thoughts were consumed with trying to make sense of the impossible.

Who was Liam?

What was Liam?

I began to walk senselessly through the streets. It was as if something was guiding me somewhere, but at the same time, I didn't know where I was going. The familiar streets seemed foreign, each step feeling heavier than the last.

Several minutes later, I stopped in front of Cookies Paradise, the coffee and cookie shop where Liam and I had escaped the first night.

I hesitated for a few minutes about whether to enter. The thought that I would never be there with Liam again made every part of my body shudder.

I didn't even know if I was here that night anymore. My mind was fighting internally with what I felt was real and the doctor's words.

I looked inside the cafeteria, and everything looked the same as when I was here with Liam.

Why did I remember this place so clearly if I had imagined all that?

I had never been to this place before Liam brought me.

Someone came out of the place, and I smelled hot coffee and freshly baked cookies that seemed quite familiar. So, I gathered all the strength I had left and entered the store.

There were many more people today than the last time I was here—or that I imagined having been here; I wasn't so sure what was real anymore.

After scanning the place, I sat down at a table alone in the corner and started looking at the menu. Everything was exactly as I remembered. *There was no way I could have imagined this place so vividly.*

A few moments later, a waitress came to take my order. When I looked up, I could recognize her. "Hey, I know you," I said. "You were the same girl who took our orders the last time I was here."

She looked at me strangely, like trying to remember. "Well, a lot of people come here every day; I can't remember exactly all the faces that come here, but I hope I've been a good waitress."

I nodded disappointedly. Part of me wanted her to recognize me, to tell me that she remembered that I was here four months ago with a guy. But she was right, it was impossible, my visit here was very random and brief.

"I want a hot chocolate and the Christmas special, please."

After ordering and eating dinner, I felt a little calmer. I still couldn't understand exactly what had happened, but I was sure of one thing: I hadn't imagined all this. This place was exactly the same. I remembered the taste of cookies and chocolate. I was here with Liam.

I needed to find a logical explanation.

～

Determined to find proof of Liam's existence, I went back home and straight to the attic. I needed to find everything I had from my hospital room—books, drawings, and any objects that connected me to Liam. Anything that could confirm he had been real.

When I entered the house, all the lights were off, and the door to my parents' room was closed. That was perfect because that way, they couldn't question what I was going to do. I knew that if one of them saw me climbing into old things, they would stop me right away because they didn't want me to think about the past.

I spent hours sorting through boxes, feeling a mixture of frustration and hope. Finally, I came across a box with my name on it. My heart raced as I opened it, revealing the contents from my time in the hospital.

There it was: all the books I had read, the drawings I had made, and the small gifts that Liam had given me. I carefully picked up each item, examining it for any clues. My hands trembled as I found the little bottle with sand from the beach —the one Liam had given me on the night that everything changed between us.

I pressed the bottle to my heart, tears welling up in my eyes. "I didn't imagine anything," I whispered to myself. The physical evidence was undeniable. Liam had been real, and he had been with me. Now, I needed to find out how all this had happened.

I took a deep breath, feeling a little better. There had to be an explanation, and I was going to find it. I gathered all the items and went to my room. Then, I sat down with them, trying to piece together the puzzle.

But nothing came to my mind.

Hours later, still blocked and unsure where to continue my investigation, I decided to take the camera to review all the photos I had taken at the hospital. This was an activity that I had decided not to do since I had surgery, because I did not want to relive any moment I had there.

And yet, now, I was prepared for whatever I would find there.

There were the photos I had taken in the park, photos with the nurses on the day it was raining, and photos I had taken of my parents. Little by little, I began to remember each of those moments, and even though it had been the darkest stage of my life, I felt a little nostalgic when I saw all those images.

However, I never took a photo of Liam.

Even though he had been an important reason I started photography, at that time, I felt embarrassed to take photos of him. Now, I greatly regret not being bold.

But then, I started looking at the photos of the activities I did with Liam. Even if he wasn't in the pictures, there were things I did with him: the coffee date, the rooftop with the telescope, the library, one by one, all the images of our adventures were there.

Could I have done all those things alone? Of course not. I didn't have the strength or the resources for it.

I continued flipping through the photos, each one reinforcing my belief that Liam had been real. There was no way I could have done all those things alone, not in the state I was in. Liam had been there with me, helping me, guiding me.

I stared at the photo of the rooftop with the telescope, remembering how Liam had set everything up for me, how he had pointed out the constellations and shared their stories. I remembered the warmth of his presence, the way he made me feel safe and cared for. The memory was too vivid, too real to be a figment of my imagination.

Finally, I got to the photos of our last day together. The abandoned park was a real place, and I didn't know about it until Liam took me there. The science museum, a place I never considered because I was a creative person, and finally, the beach.

The photo of me smiling with one hand, trying to cover my face without success, was there. Someone must have taken the photo because both of my hands were clearly visible in the image. I hadn't gone to the beach alone. Liam was with me.

Everything was real, and this was the proof I was searching for. I didn't imagine those things. Liam existed.

Tired of all the things I did today, I finally gave up with the camera in my hands.

Tomorrow, I will keep searching for you. I will not give up until I find you.

I needed answers, but the only person who could give them to me was someone who shouldn't exist. Someone who was supposed to be gone.

CHAPTER 36
Frustration

THE NEXT DAY, I returned to the hospital.

I found Hellen in the halls, her expression a little surprised and confused that I was there again.

"If I'd known that even if you healed, I'd have to see you every day, I would've looked for another method to get rid of you," she said, smiling.

"Glad to see you again, too, Hellen." I paused. "I need a favor from you."

She looked me up and down while crossing her arms. "Why do I feel like what you're going to ask me is illegal?"

"Because depending on your morals, it may be," I confessed. "I need information about a person who died five years ago in this hospital."

"Definitely illegal." She started walking away. "I can't help you with that."

I knew she'd say no the first time I asked her. But I wasn't going to give up that easily. I knew I had to convince her to make her understand the urgency of my situation, so I started following her. "Please, Hellen, it's important. I'll tell you the whole story if you agree to help me."

She stopped and looked at me. "You don't have friends to hang out with instead of bothering me while I'm at work, Jasmine?"

I couldn't help but smile. "You know I don't."

"I know, and you know why? Because you were here 24/7. I just want to remind you how miserable you'll be if you don't get out of here."

She started walking again, this time faster. But I took her by the wrist. "I won't leave if you don't help me."

"Well, why don't you bother your little nurse boyfriend instead of me? What was his name?"

"Because he's the person I need the information about. He's dead, Hellen."

Hellen looked at me in shock. "When? Oh my God, I'm so sorry, Jasmine."

"That's the worst part, Hellen. He died five years ago."

There was a big silence between us—as if she needed to process those words in the same way I had when Dr. Butler told me. "There's no way. I saw all the small gifts, the day you returned wet from the rain, and how your mood changed from one moment to another. You couldn't have done all that alone."

"Exactly," I said, my voice urgent. "That's why I need to investigate his death. I don't understand what happened."

Hellen's expression softened as she realized the seriousness of my request. She motioned for us to sit down, and I told her the whole story. She opened her mouth in surprise many times, her eyes widening with each impactful detail.

When I finished, she stood up abruptly without another word.

"Where are you going?" I asked, startled.

"Well, to find Liam, of course. Hurry up, we don't have time, and I might change my mind," she replied, already walking toward the records room.

We didn't find anything in the files. It was like Liam didn't want to be found, and my frustration was palpable.

Hellen was at the computer while I checked the folders organized by year on the shelves. However, there was no record of Liam anywhere.

I had a lot of questions.

Why was he never honest with me? Why did he choose me among so many people who needed help? Why did he decide to kiss me if he knew we weren't going to be able to be together?

The emotional turmoil felt overwhelming.

"Do you know how old he was, at least?" Hellen asked.

"Not really. Liam was very reserved with the information he gave me."

And now I understand why. He didn't want to be found. He didn't want me to research him and find out that he wasn't a real person until it was the right time.

But now he'd left me with nothing—unprepared and heartbroken. I didn't want to give up, but I knew Hellen needed to get back to work, and she'd already done too much today, letting me in and helping me look for him.

"Maybe if you ask Dr. Butler for more information about him, we could have more clues about where to look."

"It's too risky. I don't want anyone else to know what I'm doing. He already thinks I'm a little crazy. And I don't think he remembers much about those times anyway." I left the folder I was holding on the counter and went to the door. "But I'll find a way to look for more information about him, and then I'll return."

Hellen also stood up and hugged me. "I'll be here if you need anything, okay?"

I placed my gaze on her one last time before leaving and saw how helpless her face looked for not being able to do more. I knew I was being selfish for making her help me with this mission, but I needed to find Liam, and this was the only way. "Okay, thank you," were the only words I could manage to respond.

Before leaving the hospital, I decided to go to the rooftop one last time. I needed some fresh air, and that place had been one of the few in the hospital where I'd ever felt alive and at peace.

As I walked up the stairs, my palms began to sweat slightly, memories flooding back of all the things I'd experienced there: my first dance, the first time I fell in love, and my first kiss.

Why do I feel so nervous when there's nothing here?

It wasn't like Liam's soul was wandering around on the ceiling or anything. Still, something inside me felt anxious to be there.

I opened the door and stepped out onto the rooftop. The cold air hit me, and as I walked toward the edge, I suddenly stopped.

There, in the same spot as always, was the telescope—untouched and intact. It was another undeniable proof that Liam had existed.

For a few seconds, I stared at it, my mind racing with thoughts. *How has it remained here all this time? And why hasn't anyone moved it?* I felt a strange feeling—it was like relief mixed with anxiety.

After a moment of hesitation, I walked over to the telescope, my heart pounding in my chest. I bent down to examine it more closely, running my fingers over the cold metal. It was just as I remembered; touching it made my skin feel chill.

I stood there for what felt like an eternity, lost in thought. I needed to find the owner to give it back to him, but more than that, I needed to see him so he could explain to me how he'd met Liam and how I could find him.

If Liam's belongings were still here, untouched, then

perhaps there was a chance that other pieces of the puzzle remained hidden out there.

I took the telescope as carefully as possible, closed the tripod that held it, and ran down the exit. I didn't know who this object belonged to, but I had a clear idea of where to start.

I just hoped I was right.

CHAPTER 37
Panic

IF SOMEONE HAD TOLD me two months ago that I'd be coming to the science museum twice this year, I probably would've laughed in their face.

This was the last place I wanted to go back to without Liam. But logic prevailed over grief, and I knew it was necessary if I wanted to solve this enigma.

My plan was to find the person who'd left the door open the night Liam and I snuck out to see the museum. Liam had mentioned a friend who owed him a favor, and I hoped this individual was connected to the telescope as well. The identity of this person was a mystery, but I clung to the hope they would reach out when they saw me with something that was theirs.

I walked in through the front door this time, taking in the details I'd missed the night I was here with Liam when we'd entered from the back. The museum was alive with the hum of visitors, children pointing excitedly at exhibits, and the soft, informative tones of the tour guides. The current environment was a stark contrast to the quiet, almost magical atmosphere of that night.

Despite the melancholy, I found myself captivated by the wonders of science on display that I hadn't seen the last time I was here. The place was truly fascinating, and I was grateful to have the opportunity to appreciate it, even if it wasn't what I normally sought out. The exhibits were filled with the wonders of science—astronomy, biology, physics—all laid out in a way that made them seem both accessible and awe-inspiring. It was easy to see why Liam had loved it here.

As I wandered through the halls, my mind kept drifting back to that night. The way Liam had explained the stars to me, his voice filled with passion and knowledge, the way his eyes had lit up when he'd talked about the universe. It had been one of the most memorable nights of my life, and now, I was trying to piece together the mystery of who he really was.

I stopped in front of the astronomy exhibit, the one that had fascinated Liam the most. There was a large, interactive display of the solar system, with planets orbiting a glowing sun. I remembered how Liam had shown me this, how he'd pointed out the tiny details that most people would overlook.

"It's amazing how everything works so perfectly, right?" A voice interrupted my reverie, startling me out of my thoughts. I turned to find a young man observing the exhibit. "Did you know that life wouldn't have been viable if the Earth had been a little more to the right or left? We're here because everything is perfectly placed."

I looked him up and down. He wore the same clothes as the other guides there, so I assumed he might be Liam's friend who owned the telescope.

The sudden approach caught me off guard, but I had to keep the conversation going to find out what he wanted or if he was the person I was looking for. "No, I didn't know that," I replied.

He smiled, the kind of smile that made you feel like he was letting you in on a secret. "Yeah, it's pretty incredible when you think about it. The universe is full of these little details that make life possible. Did you know that if the moon were just a bit closer to the Earth, the tides would be so extreme they'd flood the continents?"

"Wow, that's really interesting," I responded, trying to keep my tone light. I was a little nervous by the way he was speaking, but I assumed he knew who I was. Otherwise, he wouldn't be trying to strike up a conversation with me.

He extended his hand. "I'm John, by the way."

I shook his hand, feeling a little more at ease. "Jasmine."

"Nice to meet you, Jasmine," he said, his voice friendly. "Have you seen the exhibit on the origin of man? It's one of our best."

I shook my head. "No, I haven't."

"Follow me," he said, motioning for me to walk with him. "I think you'll like it."

We walked through the museum, past various exhibits, until we reached a door that looked like it led to a storage area. He opened it and gestured for me to go in.

"This doesn't look like an exhibit," I said, my unease growing.

"It's just a shortcut," he assured me. "We'll get there faster this way."

Reluctantly, I stepped inside, and before I knew it, the door closed behind me, and the room plunged into darkness. I felt a strong hand grab mine tightly, pulling me further into the darkness. I started to panic, but I tried to breathe as best I could; if he noticed I was scared, he would win, so I had to act as strong as possible to find a way out.

"What are you doing?" I demanded, trying to pull away. The boy turned on a dim light with his phone—I felt like I was in a police interrogation.

His voice, now cold and threatening, answered, "How did

you get that telescope? How did you get past the security of this place?"

I struggled to comprehend what was happening. "What are you talking about?"

"The telescope you have in your possession," he hissed. "It was stolen a few months ago from the constellation room. I want to know how you did it. You left no trace on the cameras. You must know the place very well."

"I didn't steal anything!" I protested, my heart pounding in my chest. "This telescope was a gift from a friend. I don't even know what you're talking about!"

He tightened his grip on my hand, his voice filled with suspicion. "Don't lie to me. There's no way you could've gotten in here without help. Tell me who you're working with."

"I'm not working with anyone!" I cried, feeling a mix of fear and confusion. "Liam gave it to me. He was the one who brought me here!"

"Liam?" John's voice faltered for a moment before hardening again. "Liam who?"

"I don't know his last name; that's why I'm here. I hoped someone who recognized the telescope could answer me."

John let go of my hand, and his expression looked calmer. For some reason, that gave me the confidence to start talking.

"I met a guy named Liam a few months ago while in the hospital. He made me believe he was a nurse."

He stood before me without saying anything at all, which made me a little nervous, but I decided to continue my story. "He brought me that telescope one night to show me the stars and explain things about space. He told me it belonged to a friend, so that's why I brought it here. I thought that friend would give me some clue as to where he might be."

"And why did you think the friend was here?"

I thought for a few moments about telling him the truth

about someone leaving the door open for us to enter the museum that night, but John already believed I'd stolen something from this place. Two crimes would be too much.

"He told me he loved to come here when he was a child with his friend. I assumed I could find something to guide me to him here."

John leaned back against the door and let out a deep sigh. After a few minutes, he replied, "I'm sorry. I don't know who you're looking for. The only thing I can do for you is let you go without any consequences. Put the telescope aside. I'll say it was there all the time."

I didn't know whether to feel frustrated or relieved by John's help. For one part, I'd hoped to find someone who knew Liam here. On the other hand, I knew there was no way anyone other than me would know he still existed.

I thanked John for his generosity and left the museum. I was running out of ideas, but there was still one last place to investigate before giving up.

CHAPTER 38
Surprise

SEEING the abandoned amusement park during the day felt less creepy, but a weird tension still hung in the air. For some reason, I felt a little stressed about being here alone. The rusty rides creaked in the breeze, and I could see more clearly all the weeds growing around the concrete floor.

Everything looked so dirty but so beautiful that I felt a little nostalgic for what this place once was. It was like looking at a ghost of its former self—a place frozen in time yet decaying rapidly.

As I walked to the middle of the place, I couldn't shake the feeling of being watched, though I knew it was just my nerves.

"No one can be here," I told myself over and over again to calm down, but that wasn't changing my mood. "It must be the vibe of this place," I whispered.

The silence was almost deafening, broken only by the occasional creak of metal. It was as if the park was holding its breath, waiting for something to happen.

I wandered aimlessly at first, unsure of what I hoped to find. By this point, I felt this search no longer made sense.

Nothing I was doing seemed to be working, and I felt like I was already at a dead end.

Doubt crept into my mind.

Am I wasting my time? Have I let my grief cloud my judgment?

Yet, a stubborn determination kept me going. I couldn't give up now, not when I felt so close.

My mind and body were clinging to closure. I couldn't just let go of someone who'd been so important in my life as if nothing had happened, especially when I had so many doubts and things to say. I needed to find answers that would bring me peace.

I knew Liam was dead and that perhaps many of my questions would never be answered. But something inside me told me to keep fighting because that was what he'd taught me—to keep trying even if nothing made sense because life can take a lot of turns.

I felt like someone was whispering in my ear to keep going, so I kept walking.

I stopped in front of the carousel, which was just as beautiful and in good condition as I remembered. However, knowing what it meant for this carousel to look like that in such an abandoned place was heartrending.

I could feel my eyes starting to water. Liam was so desperate to fix something that he didn't realize he needed someone to take care of him, too.

I wish I could've noticed the signs and offered to help.

Sometimes, it was so obvious, like when he would stare at the sky when he was alone or when he would wait for me in the room with his somber gaze focused on the horizon. He was screaming for help, but I was so focused on myself that I never saw him.

When we focus only on ourselves and our problems, we

don't realize that there are people around us who may need us, even if we're broken.

I began to wonder for a moment what I would've accomplished if Liam had allowed me to comfort him, even if I needed comforting, too. But there was nothing I could do now.

I closed my eyes and concentrated on our last conversation in front of the waves, how he was trying to tell me that he'd been sick too, but he never confirmed that he didn't make it.

Unless he'd left it implicit.

June 19, 2019. That was the day my life changed.

"Oh my God," I said, too loud, considering I was alone.

June 19. That was the date he died. That's why he'd emphasized that exact date so much. He wanted me to remember it so that I could find him. This was a good sign. Now, I just needed to find out why I couldn't find his name in the records.

I decided to climb onto the carousel one last time, hoping to recapture some of the magic of that night. And maybe remember anything else he'd told me that I hadn't understood at the time.

As I reached the control center to start the ride, something caught my eye. There, connected to the machine, was an employee card.

My hands trembled as I carefully removed it, examining the faded plastic. My breath caught in my throat as I saw who it belonged to. I couldn't believe my eyes. Disbelief washed over me as I stared at the familiar face. It couldn't be real. I had to be imagining things.

There was a picture of Liam when he was younger, maybe 16? And his real name wasn't Liam.

It was William.

William T. Mariot.

Liam had worked here. In the summer. Before the park closed.

I stared at the card, feeling like I was holding the key to a door I wasn't sure I was ready to open, but I knew I had to. This was exactly what I'd been searching for—a tangible connection to Liam—or William—and a clue that might lead me to him one last time.

CHAPTER 39

Quietness

IT WAS TOO late to return to the hospital, and I knew that Hellen wouldn't appreciate me going back there again on the same day. So, I decided to go to the beach to watch the sunset before going home.

I thought I'd be more anxious about what I'd just found, but I felt at peace. I knew I was close to understanding everything, and something inside me knew that this wasn't the end but the beginning of a new life.

I took out my sketchbook and started drawing the sunset, taking my time to capture every detail I saw. In the middle of the sunset, I drew Liam and me in the water. I was wearing the same blue dress from the last time we'd seen each other; however, this time my hair was a little longer, just like it is now. I was behind him, who was wearing a white shirt. He was looking at the ocean in a melancholic way—as if he wanted to say a thousand words that never found a way out of his mouth.

When I finished the drawing, there was almost no natural light left to appreciate it. However, I decided to admire it for a few moments. It was the first time I'd used so many colors in a sketch. It looked so beautiful that I couldn't believe I had done it. It wasn't my usual style of dark tones.

No one was waiting for me yet. I was free to do whatever I wanted. I had all the time in the world because I was alive and would be for a long time. So I just stood there for a while longer until I could barely see what was in front of me—a landscape full of dark blues.

It was incredible how life looked with so many colors when you glanced at it in a positive way. I wanted my life to always feel like this. That even if things don't turn out as expected, there will always be a sunset to admire.

Still seated by the sea, I promised myself that I'd be satisfied with the results of this investigation, no matter the outcome. I knew I'd never have the closure I would like, but at least I knew I'd tried until the end. And that is how life should always be in everything we set out to do.

CHAPTER 40

Enlightenment

I ARRIVED at the hospital the next day as early as I could. I'd barely slept the night before and clearly needed a good dose of caffeine, but it wasn't my priority at the moment.

I brought breakfast to the girls, and we chatted a bit at the nurse station. I honestly wasn't paying attention to the conversation because my mind was away, thinking about everything that had happened and wondering if I could finally find him this time.

As everyone started to move to begin their jobs, Hellen motioned her head at me to follow her. When we entered the archive room and made sure no one was there, she sat in front of the computer and looked at me. "So, did you find anything?"

"Yes, his full name is William Mariot. We can start by looking at what happened on June 19, 2019."

She stared at me for a few minutes, her face slightly shocked. "I wonder how you got all that information."

"I have my resources," I replied with a half smile.

Hellen's fingers flew over the keyboard, and within

seconds, a file popped up on the screen. My heart raced as I leaned in closer, trying to make sense of the words in front of me.

"William T. Mariot," Hellen read aloud, her voice low. "Date of death: June 19, 2019."

I swallowed hard. There it was.

The words hit me like a ton of bricks. It was the confirmation of what I'd already known, but hearing it spoken aloud made it feel more real.

"Cause of death: Respiratory arrest due to colon cancer." She continued, pausing on every sentence to make sure I was hearing. "He battled the disease for a year. It says here he was in room 605."

I froze, my mind reeling as I stared at the screen. Room 605. The same room I'd been in. The same room where I'd spent countless hours fighting for my life. The room where I'd met Liam—no, William. The room where I'd fallen in love with life again.

Hellen looked at me, unsure whether to continue reading. I nodded for her to proceed. "It also says that he was very depressed, especially in his final days. He spent a lot of time alone, refusing visitors, and only occasionally interacted with the staff."

I felt like the ground was slipping out from under me. Liam had been in that room, battling the same kind of darkness that had consumed me.

But how had I seen him? How had I spoken to him? How had I felt him when he'd died years ago?

My mind raced, trying to reconcile the memories I had with the reality of what I was reading.

I knew this was a question I'd never be able to answer, and I should be grateful that at least I'd have some closure on where Liam really was. But that didn't stop me from feeling frustrated with the whole situation.

Hellen, noticing my distress, took my right hand. "Are you okay, Jasmine?"

I shook my head, unable to find the words.

"Sometimes extraordinary things happen in hospitals that no one can explain. Maybe this will be one of them," Hellen continued. "The important thing is that they helped you to be where you are now."

I just kept looking at the screen, reading the same paragraphs over and over again, and looking at the small picture that his file had. He was just like I remembered him, and that gave me some kind of comfort. William Mariot had been more than just a figment of my imagination. His presence, his impact on my life, had been real—even if his existence defied everything I understood about reality.

"Can I ask you one more favor?" I finally managed to say, my voice trembling. "Can you give me a contact number or address?"

Hellen stood up from the computer instantly and shook her head. "This is already beyond what I could do for you. I'd get in trouble if I gave you classified information. I'm sorry, Jasmine."

Before I could say anything else, Hellen walked quickly to the door and left, leaving me alone in front of the computer with Liam's file still open. Once again, Hellen had given me the opportunity to find my peace.

"Thank you for always saving me and being there when I needed you, Hellen," I whispered, though she wasn't in the room anymore to hear me.

I wrote down the address of the house where Liam had lived and the phone number in his file, closed everything, and left the place as quickly as possible before anyone could note I was there.

My work at the hospital was finally over, and I promised myself to always remember everything Hellen had done for me all these months. I knew she wasn't obligated to do any of that, but she'd done it anyway out of love.

CHAPTER 41

Compassion

STANDING in front of the house where Liam had lived his last days, I started to think about how absurd it felt for me to be there.

What would I tell them? That the ghost of their son was with me and comforted me for months?

Yeah, it was definitely a bad idea to be here. It felt crazy, even to me.

Just as I turned to leave, the front door creaked open, and I froze in place. A woman, likely in her late fifties, with kind eyes and a reassuring smile, stood in the doorway.

"Hello, honey," she said, her voice soft and welcoming. "I saw you hesitating whether to knock on the door from the window. Do you need something?"

My heart raced as I tried to find the right words. "Umm, yeah, well, hi, I'm Jasmine," I stammered, feeling more awkward by the second. "I was just passing by, but—"

Before I could finish, the woman interrupted me, her eyes softening even more. "You came to talk about Liam, didn't you? Were you his friend?"

Her question took me by surprise. I hesitated to say something. The truth stuck in my throat. After a few moments, I finally nodded. "Yeah, kind of. We were in the same hospital."

The woman remained silent, her expression unreadable as she processed my words. Then, after what felt like an eternity, she gave a small nod and stepped aside, gesturing for me to enter. "Come in, dear. We can talk inside."

Reluctantly, I followed her into the house, my nerves still on edge. The interior was cozy and warm, filled with the comforting scent of freshly baked cookies. She led me to a small, sunlit living room, where she motioned for me to sit on a floral-patterned sofa.

"Would you like some tea and cookies?" she asked, already heading toward the kitchen.

"That would be nice, thank you," I replied, almost whispering. I wasn't sure what to expect from this conversation, but something told me I needed to hear what this woman had to say.

A few minutes later, she returned with a tray, setting it down on the table before me. She poured me a cup of tea, her hands steady, as if she'd done this countless times before. After settling in across from me, she offered a gentle smile.

"I'm Leah," she said, her voice tinged with a hint of sadness. "Liam didn't have many friends during his time in the hospital. None of his school friends returned after the funeral. It's nice to meet someone who knew him from that period."

I took a sip of the tea, trying to calm the storm of emotions inside me. "It's nice to meet you, too, Leah," I said softly. "Liam was very special to me. I'm sorry that it took me so long to come." I lied. "I was also battling cancer, so I couldn't go out of the hospital, and then it just hurt so much to do something about him."

Leah's smile wavered slightly, and she looked down at her hands, which were folded neatly in her lap. "Losing him was the hardest thing we've ever gone through."

There was a pause, the weight of her words settling between us. I didn't know how to bring up the strange circumstances of my connection with Liam, so I decided to start with something simpler.

"I want to know more about him," I said, choosing my words carefully. "He helped me a lot when I was in the hospital, but I never really got to know much about his life."

Leah's face lit up as if she'd been waiting for this question for years. "Of course," she replied. "I can tell you everything you want."

As we sat there, sipping tea and talking about Liam, I felt a strange connection with Leah, as if the same grief and longing for answers linked us. I still didn't know how to tell her about the unnatural encounters, but for now, it seemed enough to simply share memories of the man who'd touched both of our lives in such profound ways.

Leah showed me pictures of Liam from when he was younger, beaming with pride as she recounted his achievements as a child. She told me about how they'd discovered his illness and the struggles they faced as a family. In return, I shared some of our "adventures" in the hospital—how he would sneak into my room at night just to talk, omitting the fact that these encounters had taken place months ago, not years.

She was quite surprised that it was the same Liam we were talking about since, in his last days, he hadn't even wanted to see his family.

"If only he'd met you earlier," she said sadly.

"I know," I replied, feeling a lump in my throat. "Sometimes, I think the same thing."

I handed her some drawings I'd done of Liam and watched

as her eyes watered at the sight. "My son hated to appear in any pictures when he grew up. I love how you captured every single one of his features so perfectly."

By the time I glanced at the clock, the sun had already set, casting a warm glow over the room. I knew it was time to leave, but neither of us seemed ready to say goodbye.

I stood up to take the first step. "Well, Leah, it was nice meeting you. I'm so glad I finally had the strength to come."

My heart felt full. Something inside me was finally at peace. Liam was a real person—a good guy with dreams, and he was pretty much the same guy I'd met.

Leah stood up as well, her eyes filled with warmth. "The pleasure was mine, Jasmine. Please, come back anytime. I feel like I still have so many things to tell you about Liam. And I'd love for you to meet Liamel, too. I think the two of you would get along well. She's in college now."

Liamel. Liam's little sister. I wondered if she'd be as kind and welcoming as her mother and brother. The thought of getting to know more about Liam through his family filled me with a sense of joy. It was as if, through them, I could keep a part of him alive.

Before I left, a thought crossed my mind. "Leah," I said hesitantly, "could you tell me where Liam rests? I never really got the chance to say goodbye properly, and I think it's something I need to do."

Leah's eyes softened, and she nodded. "Of course, dear. I'll give you the exact location." She took a notebook that was nearby, wrote down the details, and handed me the slip of paper. As I turned to leave, Leah suddenly stopped me.

"Wait, Jasmine," she said with a gentle smile. "I have a gift for you before you go. Please follow me."

Curious, I followed her down a hallway to a room at the back of the house. It was old, with a slightly worn door, but the room inside was surprisingly intact. As soon as I stepped inside, I knew—this had been Liam's room.

Leah carefully moved aside a few boxes, eventually reaching for something on a shelf. She pulled out a small, worn diary and handed it to me. "Liam loved to write his thoughts," she explained, her voice filled with emotion. "Maybe this will help you know him even better."

"Thank you, Leah," I said with a smile on my face. "This is a wonderful gift."

Leah smiled, her eyes shining with tears that she quickly blinked away. "Take care, Jasmine. And remember, you're always welcome here."

∽

Back in my bed, just before closing my eyes, I decided to take a quick look at the diary.

I'd intended to start with the last pages first, eager to glimpse Liam's thoughts during the final days of his life. But as I opened to a random page, something caught my eye—there were entries from this year.

I frowned, wondering if maybe Leah or Liamel had written something in the diary after his passing, perhaps as a way to keep his memory alive. But as I read further, the words didn't seem like something a grieving mother or sister would write.

The handwriting was familiar too—exactly the same as the earlier entries, or the note that I'd read so many times that a certain person had left on my bed some time ago.

"July 22, 2024
This is my first day back in the city where
I grew up. Of course, the first thing I

decided to do was start writing in my journal again. I used to do it years ago as a way to release everything going on in my mind, and right now I think I need it most. I have no one to talk to about those things, and I feel like a stranger in my own house..."

My heart began to race as I reread the whole entry.

"So, I spent the afternoon buried in Jasmine Russell's medical records. From the first cancer diagnosis at 15 to her return at 18, her whole life feels like a tragedy. It wasn't hard to see where her attitude came from."

I flipped through the pages, each one confirming the impossible truth. The handwriting was consistent through-out, unmistakably his. The entries described events and feel-ings that could only belong to Liam—his thoughts, his reflections about me. Specific scenarios that had only happened between the two of us, and even mentions of places he'd taken me.

Here in front of me was the answer I'd desperately needed. It was something impossible to have and more than what I'd ever imagined; however, I was grateful to have it in my possession.

I'd finally found what I was searching for, but the truth was far more complex than I had ever imagined.

Journal entry 10

September 7, 2024

Since I died five years ago, I have been neither in heaven nor hell. I've simply been wandering the earth without any apparent specific purpose. It was as if something still anchored me to the earth, but I couldn't figure out what it was. I never had any unfinished business or anything that made me want to live, so being here had no point.

But something that I knew was that being in this limbo of death was a desperate and lonely experience.

Maybe this was hell, and it was a punishment for having been an insufferable, immature brat in my last moments of life, or perhaps I wasn't worthy of heaven because I'd never done anything significant in my short time on earth.

And now I was trapped here with my thoughts and misery, and I didn't know what to do.

No one could see me, or so I thought at first. So, I spent my time chasing strangers, going to places I'd loved when I was alive, and thinking about all the mistakes I'd made before I died. I could move objects and eat (although it made no difference to my body if I didn't). So I decided to repair old cars and later, the abandoned amusement park where I'd worked when I was alive. I ate food only when I wanted a treat.

Until one night, an old man on a train spoke to me. We were the only two people on that train, and I was shocked when he started talking. I'll never forget what he told me.

"Liam, you should never leave the earth without impacting someone's life. Find a reason to leave a mark."

I didn't know if that man was someone sent by God to guide me, but that's when I realized the power I had in my hands. From then on, every person I wanted to see me could do it, as long as they were on the verge of death or if I was next to someone who could see me previously.

So, after that day, I decided I wanted to save someone the way no one could for me when I was alive.

From that moment on, I spent my days in hospitals learning first aid, then in libraries when everyone else was asleep, poring over medical texts like they were some kind of life-line. I became obsessed with understanding everything, from basic first aid to complex surgical procedures. I shadowed doctors in the operating room and followed nurses during emer-gencies, trying to absorb their knowledge like a sponge.

And then, little by little, more sick patients could see me.

I started interacting with people of all ages in hospitals, but my time with them was always limited, and by the time I could talk to them, it was too late for both of us.

I spent years like this, wandering from one case to the next, looking for anyone I could help. But it never felt right. There was always something missing.

Then, one day, back in the hospital where I'd died, I saw her.

Jasmine.

She was in the same room where I'd once

been, looking as lost and hopeless as I'd felt in my last days. There was something about her, something that drew me to her. Maybe it was the way she stared out the window as if she was trying to find a way to escape her own body. Or maybe it was the fact that, like me, she seemed ready to give up on life.

I started watching her, following her through the hospital. She reminded me so much of myself—angry and scared but also stubbornly holding on to something, even if she didn't know what it was.

I knew, at that moment, that she was the one I had to save.

I decided to do whatever it took to make her see that life was worth living, even if I couldn't live it myself. But I never thought that in the process, I would fall in love with life too.

And not only with life but with Jasmine.

She taught me the beauty of the simple things. It started with the small moments—like the pure joy on her face the first time I took her to the rooftop. She'd been so excited with the wind in her face and her eyes wide as she took in the view. It was a moment that made her feel alive again, and in turn, it made me feel something I hadn't felt in years.

There was also the night we sneaked out to eat cookies. It was such a small thing, something most people would take for granted, but it was like an adventure for Jasmine. I remember the way she smiled, the way her eyes lit up as if those cookies were the most precious thing in the world. And in that moment, I realized they were. They represented a life she was slowly starting to appreciate again, a life she was beginning to love.

And in those moments, I found myself loving life too. Not just because of the experiences, but because of the way Jasmine experienced them. She was teaching me, without even knowing it, how to see the beauty in the mundane and how to find happiness in the smallest things. Little by little, I started to feel like I needed to be with her forever. But deep down, I knew that was impossible.

I knew my time was limited. I wasn't meant to stay; I was meant to help her find her way back to life. But the more I fell for her, the more I didn't want to leave. I wanted to be there for every rooftop adventure, every late-night library tour. I wanted to be with her and share in those moments, even if I couldn't fully participate in them.

Then, one day, everything changed.

I realized that Jasmine couldn't always see me anymore, even if I tried with all my power. There were moments when I would be in her room, watching over her, and she wouldn't even know I was there. At first, I thought it was just her being distracted, but it started happening more often. She would look right through me as if I didn't exist.

And that's when it hit me—my mission was being completed.

She was starting to live again without needing me to guide her. She was healing, finding her own reasons to keep going. I should've felt proud and happy that I'd made an impact and that I was finally doing what I was meant to do. But instead, it terrified me.

Jasmine had become my reason for existing. She was my connection to the world, my anchor. The fact that she could no longer see me meant I was losing that connection. It meant that soon, I would no longer have a reason to stay on earth. The thought of leaving her, of never seeing her again, filled me with a kind of fear I hadn't felt even when I was dying.

I had found love in a place where I thought love was impossible, and now, I would lose it. And I didn't know how to say goodbye.

I knew I'd fallen in love quickly, but I'd been unable to stop myself once I realized she had noticed me. It was impossible to stop when her happiness was the destination.

For that reason, I decided to do one last selfish thing. I couldn't bear the thought of losing Jasmine, of being alone again. So I made a choice—a terrible, self-interested choice. I decided to kidnap her on her last night and never bring her back. If Jasmine hadn't had the surgery, it would have been just a matter of time before her body collapsed. And if she died, that meant we could be together forever in this void, in this limbo where I'd been trapped for so long.

I convinced myself that it was the only way, that it was what we both needed. I knew she wanted to be with me as much as I wanted to be with her.

The night started like any other. I took her to my favorite places, hoping that she would realize who I really was, that she would see what I saw in this world, and learn to love the things I had come to love in my loneliness. I wanted her to see the beauty in the silence, in the way the world seemed to pause just for us.

But Jasmine, with her tenderness and innocence, only saw the beautiful things in each place. She wasn't seeing what I wanted her to see—she was seeing life, even in the places that were meant to be a reflection of my world. When we walked on the beach, the moonlight casting silver reflections on the waves, I knew Jasmine was reaching her limit. She was tired, her body weak from the strain of the day. But I was desperate. I needed her to know that she was the best thing in my life, the one thing that made this limbo bearable.

So I confessed my love to her, telling her how I felt, something I'd been too afraid to say, hoping she would understand my reasons when everything was over.

But when she collapsed in the water, I felt an overwhelming sense of dread. My desperation to keep her close turned into sheer terror at the thought of losing her—truly losing her.

At that moment, I realized the madness of what I was doing. Jasmine wasn't meant to stay here with me. She was meant to live, to experience everything this world had to offer, even if it meant I had to let her go. I couldn't continue this selfish plan, not if it meant condemning her to the same fate I had suffered. She deserved so much more than that.

So I made one last act of love, knowing it

would hurt me forever and knowing all my decisions would haunt her for the rest of her life. I took her back to the hospital, back to where she still had a chance to live. I laid her in the shower, my heart breaking as I watched her breathe with difficulty, knowing that this would be the last time I would see her in this way. I whispered goodbye, telling her that she had to live, that she had to find happiness, even if it wasn't with me.

And then, I left.

I gave her one last chance to live, knowing that I had to let her go if I truly loved her.

CHAPTER 42
Resentment

WHEN I FINISHED READING the journal, a part of me left my body with Liam's last words.

The realization hit me like a physical blow—the person who'd made me feel alive again, who'd guided me out of my own darkness, was no longer part of this world. And worse yet, there was a point where he'd wanted to drag me to where he was.

The connection we'd had, the bond that had formed between us, was something extraordinary, something that defied explanation. And now, it was over.

Reading those letters felt like the confirmation I needed, all the answers I'd sought. But now that I had them, along with everything Liam had felt and thought, I didn't feel any better. In fact, the pain seemed to come in waves, crashing over me again and again, each time with more force, now amplified by the context of his words. I couldn't remember the last time I'd cried this much, the tears flowing freely as if they'd been held back for years.

Liam was definitely gone. There was no longer any doubt, no lingering hope that he might still be out there, somewhere.

His journal had laid everything bare—his love, his desperation, his final act of letting go. And now, I knew I had to do the same.

I clutched the journal to my chest, feeling its weight as if it were Liam himself. I didn't know how I would move forward from this, how I was supposed to carry on knowing what I now knew. But one thing was certain: Liam had given me a second chance at life, and I owed it to him to make the most of it, even if it meant facing the world without him.

But it was something I wasn't ready to do just yet. I wanted to be able to feel this pain, to grieve for a departure I never thought I would have.

The following days weren't better. I felt like I was living my life on automatic. Eat, watch TV, draw aimlessly, go to sleep. My parents must have sensed that something was wrong, but they left me alone, probably assuming I was dealing with some post-cancer struggle. I was grateful for the solitude. I was also thankful that I'd taken this year to fully heal without any professional or social commitment because I don't know how I would've faced the world with this pain.

Part of me was angry because of how selfish he was. How could he be so inconsiderate? How could Liam make me fall in love with him, knowing that it would all end, knowing that he would leave me with nothing but memories and a heart full of unspoken words? It was as if he believed his departure wouldn't matter, as if I could just move on without a second thought.

But what hurt the most was that he hadn't let me say goodbye. He'd taken that from me, too, as if I wouldn't understand that we were nearing the end. It was as if he'd decided for both of us that I didn't need closure and that the love and connection we'd shared could just be severed without any acknowledgment.

Every time I thought about it, the pain twisted deeper into

my chest. I wanted to scream at him, to tell him how unfair it was, how he'd left me in this limbo of unresolved feelings. But there was no one to yell at, no one to answer for the hurt I was drowning in.

And the worst part was that part of me didn't even want to feel better. The truth is that sometimes we don't want to heal because pain is the connection to what we've lost. And this feeling was the only thing that remained of Liam.

"Mom, Dad, I think I need help."

My parents were sitting at the table having breakfast like every day. When I mentioned these words, they both stopped what they were doing and looked at each other.

I'd woken up that morning with a weight so heavy on my chest that it was hard to breathe. My thoughts had become relentless, a constant barrage that wouldn't even allow me a moment of peace, not even in sleep. I knew I couldn't go on like this.

"It's an excellent decision," my father replied. "Do you have someone in mind? A psychologist? Any other doctor? A friend?"

"A psychologist would be fine. I think one session would be good for me, at least to start and put my thoughts in order."

They nodded, and I could see the relief in their eyes, even though they tried to hide it. They'd been waiting for me to reach out about what was happening to me. And now that I had, they were ready to support me in any way they could.

I knew deep down that the last thing Liam would've wanted was for me to be in this state, especially now that I was healthy. He'd spent so much time trying to show me the beauty in life, to make me see that it was worth living, that it felt unfair to be in this state.

But even though I knew this, I couldn't shake the sadness that clung to me like a shadow.

It was as if my emotions had taken on a life of their own, independent of my logic or reasoning. However, one thing I'd learned over the past few months was that I wasn't defined by what was happening to me but by how I chose to respond to those external events.

So why did I feel so lost? I was alive. I was getting healthier every day. I had a whole life ahead of me, filled with possibilities. Yet, this deep, aching sadness persisted, as if I had lost something irreplaceable, even though I still had so much to live for.

I realized that grief wasn't something that made sense. It didn't follow logic or reason. It was just something that you had to carry until it started to lighten, little by little, with time.

I just needed to learn to live with it, and to do that, I knew I needed someone to guide me in the right direction.

Even when we convince ourselves that we can face our problems alone, the truth is that the burdens become lighter when someone else is there to support us, to listen, and to offer guidance. I didn't want to continue facing each challenge in isolation. I wanted to start relying on others, to allow myself to be vulnerable and seek help when I needed it.

Needing someone isn't a sign of weakness. It's a mark of strength and maturity to recognize that some things are too heavy to carry alone. It is being smart enough to understand that there are things that go beyond what we're capable of doing alone.

By reaching out, I was choosing to heal, to grow, and to embrace the support that could help me become whole again.

CHAPTER 43
Peace

LITTLE BY LITTLE, everything became easier.

The pain became smaller and smaller.

The days passed, and I found myself breathing more effortlessly.

The weight on my chest wasn't as crushing, and the sharp sting of loss had dulled into something softer, something bittersweet.

Not because I was forgetting, but because I was accepting it.

I accepted that I would always love Liam, no matter where he was now.

And that what gave meaning to life was love.

A truth I came to understand through the ache of loss and the joy of memories.

Love in all its forms.

Love that lingers in the smallest gestures, the softest smiles, the quietest moments.

Love we give and the love we're brave enough to receive.

I learned to embrace that love, even when it hurt.

To let it shape me, soften me, strengthen me.

I learned that love isn't diminished by grief; it's amplified.

It's in the laughter we remember, the hands we held, the hearts we touched.

I learned to stop waiting for a grand finale, some perfect conclusion to make it all make sense.

Instead, I found meaning in the in-between.

In the imperfect, messy, beautiful chaos of living.

Grief taught me that life isn't measured by how long we have but by how deeply we feel.

And I chose to feel it all. The joy. The sorrow. The love.

I chose to live in the moments that mattered.

I chose to dream in the darkness.

Because, in the end, those moments are what remain.

CHAPTER 44

Hope

I ARRIVED at the cemetery on a cloudy afternoon. The sky was blanketed with soft, gray clouds that muted the world around me. It was a serene, green place, quiet and full of trees that swayed gently in the breeze. The kind of place where the silence wasn't oppressive but necessary.

As I walked through the gravel paths, past rows of head-stones and memorials, I felt a sense of peace that I hadn't felt in a long time. The therapy helped me see my grief as something that had to happen rather than a punishment.

My fear of death had made it impossible for me to accept that Liam was gone, but the therapist had helped me understand that Liam was probably finally at peace, which made a lot of sense from his letters. This was what he'd been looking for the past few years, and I should be happy that he finally reached it.

Of course, I didn't tell the therapist the whole story.

I simply mentioned that Liam was a patient like me and that we'd talked every day at the hospital until I never saw him again. I told her that he'd lied to me about how serious his health condition was, and that was why it hurt me so much that he was no longer here. I didn't want to end up back in a hospital for a different reason, so I kept the more unbelievable parts to myself.

She'd helped me see that it was normal to hold on to his memory and that I didn't have to force myself to forget him. It was okay to keep him in my heart, as long as I also chose to live my life fully and find a way to honor what he meant to me.

And that's exactly what I wanted to do—to find a way to make Liam's absence less painful while never losing sight of everything he'd done for me. I wanted to honor his memory, not by clinging to the past, but by moving forward in a way that would make him proud. I know now that living my life to the fullest is the best way I can thank him for everything he gave me.

It didn't take long to find Liam's grave. Leah had given me the exact location. As I approached, my heart started racing faster and faster, like I knew he was there, but at the same time, he wasn't.

I didn't know if Liam liked flowers, but I brought him Jasmines. That way, a little part of me would remain here for a while.

His headstone was simple, just like him. It bore his full name, William T. Mariot, and the dates that marked his too-short life. I knelt beside it, feeling the coolness of the earth beneath my knees, and placed my hand on the stone. For a moment, I just stayed there, letting the silence and the stillness wash over me.

"Hi, Liam," I whispered, my voice barely audible. "I'm sorry it took me so long to come here. I guess I wasn't ready to say goodbye."

I took a deep breath, trying to steady myself as the emotions welled up inside me. "I'm so upset with you for so many things that I don't know where to start. On one side, I wish you'd been honest with me, that you'd have warned me that you weren't going to last long by my side, that you'd have confessed to me that you weren't really here. This way, I wouldn't have imagined every future with you."

"But on the other hand, I know that the fact that you didn't tell me anything was what allowed me to imagine a future. I know that if I had known you weren't alive, there would've been no point in me fighting the way I did."

The wind picked up slightly, rustling the leaves above, and I closed my eyes, feeling a lump in my throat. "I'm trying to move on, to live the life you wanted me to live. I even asked for help, like you would've wanted me to. But I can't stop thinking about you, about what we had and what we could've had if things were different. But I know you wouldn't want me to be stuck here in this grief. You'd want me to find my way, to be happy. And I'm going to try, I promise."

I don't know if everything I was saying was meaningful, but saying out loud what I felt in the place where Liam was supposed to rest made me think that somehow he was listening to me, or as if my words might somehow reach him wherever he was.

"But I'll be real with you; I don't want to forget you, Liam. Wanting to forget you would mean that I don't appreciate everything you did for me. It would be like saying your time on earth meant nothing to anyone, that I'm some ungrateful person who, once I got what I wanted, threw you away. And nothing could be further from the truth. I can't stand the idea that we should just let go of people who are no longer with us and move on as if they never mattered. If someone was so important to you in your life, there's no way you can just stop thinking about them from one moment to the next."

"Of course, I want to live my life. I want to fall in love again. I want to do something meaningful here on earth. But I don't want to forget you. Your time here, though brief, was significant. You mattered to me, and I'll carry that with me every day. I promise to make every minute I have left count, to be happy, to live fully—because of you and for you—until one day, we can see each other again."

It felt good to say the things I hadn't been able to say, to finally let go of some of the pain that had been weighing me down. Maybe closure isn't about having all the answers but about accepting that things don't always turn out the way you expect—and that's okay.

Liam would always be a part of me. He'd helped me when I was drowning, showed me the beauty in life when I couldn't see it, and reminded me that there was still so much to live for.

I stayed there for a while longer, just talking to him, letting the words flow out as if he were there beside me, listening. I told him about visiting his mother, how much better I felt after seeing her, and my plans for the future. I mentioned that I was planning to study photography professionally, to pursue something I was passionate about. I promised him that I would look for a job and keep moving forward, always trying to live my life to the fullest.

When I finally stood up, I felt lighter, as if a part of the burden had been lifted from my shoulders. I took a deep breath, feeling the crisp air fill my lungs, and looked up at the sky.

"And one last thing," I said softly, my voice carrying on the breeze, "I love you, too."

Epilogue

ONE YEAR LATER

"That's all for today's class; if you have any questions, don't forget to write them in the forum."

I got up from my seat and started walking toward the parking lot. Today was one of the last classes in the wedding photography program I'd taken this semester, and I was eager to start offering this service on my website.

As soon as I walked out of class, I received a text from my boss:

> Come to the agency as soon as you finish your classes. The clients have already given me the keys to the house we're going to list next week, and I want to have everything ready as soon as possible. This project is a big deal.

Right now, I work at a real estate company, photographing houses. It wasn't exactly my dream job, but it paid the bills and allowed me to save for what I really wanted. Plus, it gave me valuable camera experience for my portfolio. Every time I framed a shot of a house, and my boss complimented it, I was reminded that I was getting closer to where I wanted to be.

My real passion, though, was photographing feelings. There was something powerful about capturing raw emotions in different settings. It was as if I could freeze a moment of truth, a fragment of someone's soul, and keep it alive forever in a single image.

That's why I took this wedding course; this was one of the places where I could see different emotions simultaneously.

However, my favorite place to shoot was the abandoned amusement park. There was something about the contrast between the forgotten rides and the memories they must have held that drew me back again and again, and my clients loved it.

After some research, I'd found out who owned the property and managed to get a permit to go there whenever I wanted. No more sneaking in or worrying about trespassing. It was like the park was mine, a private canvas where I could let my creativity run free.

It felt right, being there. Like I was connecting with the ghosts of the past, capturing not just the echoes of joy but also the whispers of loss, the shadows of dreams that never came true. And in doing that, I was honoring Liam's memory in the best way I knew how—by living fully and chasing the beauty in every corner of life.

Before I got into my car, I received another text, this time from John.

> Remember that today is Sissy's birthday.
> The restaurant reservation is at 8:00 p.m.

I smiled and replied:

> John, you've reminded me three times this week. I've got it covered, don't worry. Everything will be perfect.

He replied immediately, so I took the opportunity to send him one last message that I knew would make him laugh.

> Are you always this intense?

> Just when someone looks interesting enough.

I put my phone back in my pocket.

John was the guy who'd almost gotten me arrested at the museum when I was trying to return that old telescope.

After a month of working at the agency, he found my portfolio on Instagram and sent me a private message to meet with me. He wanted to apologize for how he'd treated me that day, especially after reading on my social media that I was a cancer survivor and feeling extremely guilty for believing that I could have been at the museum at some point while I was battling my illness in a hospital.

I never told him that I was actually there one night. That will be my little secret forever.

That meeting had turned into an unexpected friendship. John introduced me to his circle, and now I've got people to hang out with on weekends. Hellen, of course, jokes that she's proud of me for finally giving her some space, though she does miss our Monday morning donuts and coffee runs.

John and I have been ticking off items on my list of places to visit before I die—a list I'd shared with him on our second "friend date." He practically begged me to tell him everything about my time in the hospital, and when I did, he made a promise. We'd visit every single place on my list, and once we were done, we'd make a new one. That way, I'd always have something to look forward to, something to live for.

It's funny how life works. Sometimes, the people who end up meaning the most to us come into our lives in the strangest ways. And I was grateful for it.

I've also been visiting Liam's mom regularly. Over time, we've formed a bond that's hard to describe—something like a mix of friendship and shared grief, though not the kind that weighs you down. It's been more about celebrating Liam's life and keeping his memory alive in a way that brings comfort rather than pain.

His sister, Liamel, and I have grown close too. She's just as wonderful as Liam was, with that same spark in her eyes. We've spent hours talking about everything, sharing stories, laughing at his quirks, and finding new ways to honor her brother's memory.

I've shown them how to grieve in a way that's not so heavy, not so heart-wrenching, but hopeful.

We've talked about how Liam is probably at peace now, how he's free from all the pain he went through. And the best way to honor him is to live our lives fully, to be happy because that's what he would've wanted for us. I think they appreciate that perspective, and I love that I can be a part of helping them find some peace, too.

It's strange how much has changed since those days in the hospital. I never imagined that my life would turn out this way, but now I'm happy and more in love with life than ever. And every time something bad happens to me, I remind myself that life isn't what happens to us but how we decide to react to it, so even if we're in a moment of uncertainty and pain, we can always seek happiness and peace in those little rays of light that destiny gives us.

To dream list

~~I want to go to the beach at night~~
~~I want to go to a crowded club, have a~~
~~drink, and dance in the middle of the room~~
~~I want to go to a bookstore and pick out~~
~~books at random.~~
~~I want to eat cookies at Cookie Heaven~~
~~I want to go bowling with friends~~
~~I want to go on a yacht and watch the~~
~~sunset at sea~~
~~I want to go to a lake and have a bonfire~~
~~I want to go to the art museum~~
~~I want to see a movie with friends~~
~~I want to go to a food festival~~
~~I want to go to an amusement park~~
- I want to play go-karts

Acknowledgements

My father was the happiest person in the world. He taught me that no matter how bad things were, you could always find something positive in them and have hope.

The first time he was diagnosed with cancer was in 2002. I was about six years old at the time, and I didn't know anything about what was going on. My father did everything he could to keep such a positive attitude that I never thought anything bad was happening.

After my father successfully recovered, my mother started having strange symptoms. That's when we found out that she also had breast cancer in 2007. Unlike my father, my mother took it extremely hard. She always made lists of things she would like to happen if she died and said goodbye to her family every now and then.

She wanted us to "be prepared" in case anything happened to her.

However, my dad's positivity made the whole process much easier and more bearable. He did everything he could to ensure my mother recovered as well as possible, gave her all the comforts he could, and tried to cheer her up and take her to places she liked every time she finished her treatment.

Every time she had to go to radiotherapy, he would take the long route so she could see the sea. It didn't matter if it was raining or sunny; he always took that path.

He always told her the places and things they would do when she was healed, as a way to make her think that she would have a future.

Thankfully, she also recovered, and we were all together as a family for ten more years until my father's cancer came back more aggressively, and this time, he couldn't survive.

Even in his last days of life, he had hope that he would be saved, and it was incredible to see the strength with which he got up every day to do everyday things as if he were healthy.

As I was in the hospital with him in his last days of life, I could see the sadness of all the patients around us. How the nurses did what they could, but there was no hope anywhere except in my father's room. He was always making lists of things he wanted to do and eat. And even in his last seconds, he never lost faith.

No one could stop him, not even cancer in his final days. He was the strongest man I ever knew, and his will to live will always be in my mind.

This story represents what my family has experienced over the years. It shows how one person can change another's perspective by trying to make them see life differently. It also shows how your mindset can help you deal with problems in completely different ways if you put your mind to it.

The doctors gave my father three months to live after his second cancer—he lived one more year thanks to his strength and positivity.

Jasmine and Liam are a little part of my heart because they represent my parents. And I'm very grateful to all the people who decided to read this story because it is a part of me.

About the author

Desiree Peralta was born and raised in the Dominican Republic. She is a software developer by profession but a writer by passion. When she isn't in front of a computer creating new posts for her blog, she is in a corner reading all the books she can. A hopeless romantic, she gives life and love to all her imaginary characters.

instagram.com/Dessybooks

tiktok.com/@Dessybooks

youtube.com/DessyPeralt

goodreads.com/DessyPeralt